THE RAVEN'S REVENGE

Also by Kevin Sands

The Blackthorn Key
Mark of the Plague
The Assassin's Curse
Call of the Wraith
The Traitor's Blade

THE BLACKTHORN KEY

THE RAVEN'S REVENGE

BOOK 6

KEVIN SANDS

ALADDIN

NEW YORK   LONDON   TORONTO   SYDNEY   NEW DELHI

ALADDIN

An imprint of Simon & Schuster Children's Publishing Division
1230 Avenue of the Americas, New York, New York 10020
First Aladdin hardcover edition January 2023
Text copyright © 2023 by Kevin Sands
Jacket illustration copyright © 2023 by James Fraser
Interior illustrations on pages 65, 169, 194, 267, 306–307, 378
copyright © 2017, 2021, 2023 by Jim Madsen
Cards on pages 205, 271, 333 courtesy of The Cloisters Collection, 1983 (public domain)
Trithemius Polygraphiae on page 315 courtesy of Wikimedia Commons (public domain)
All rights reserved, including the right of reproduction in whole or in part in any form.
ALADDIN and related logo are registered trademarks of Simon & Schuster, Inc.
For information about special discounts for bulk purchases, please contact Simon & Schuster
Special Sales at 1-866-506-1949 or business@simonandschuster.com.
The Simon & Schuster Speakers Bureau can bring authors to your live event. For more
information or to book an event, contact the Simon & Schuster Speakers Bureau at
1-866-248-3049 or visit our website at www.simonspeakers.com.
Series design by Karin Paprocki
Jacket designed by Karin Paprocki
Interior designed by Hilary Zarycky
The text of this book was set in Adobe Garamond Pro.
Manufactured in China 0922 SCP
2 4 6 8 10 9 7 5 3 1
Library of Congress Cataloging-in-Publication Data
Names: Sands, Kevin, author.
Title: The Raven's revenge / Kevin Sands.
Description: First Aladdin hardcover edition. | New York : Aladdin, 2023. |
Series: The blackthorn key ; Book 6 | Audience: Ages 10 to 14. | Summary: Christopher,
Tom, and Sally engage in a dangerous cat and mouse game with the Raven
as Christopher attempts to finally unmask him.
Identifiers: LCCN 2021049634 (print) | LCCN 2021049635 (ebook) | ISBN
9781534484597 (hardcover) | ISBN 9781534484610 (ebook)
Subjects: CYAC: Adventure and adventurers—Fiction. | Secret societies—Fiction. |
Friendship—Fiction. | London––History—17th century—Fiction. | Great Britain—
History—Charles II, 1660-1685—Fiction. | LCGFT: Novels.
Classification: LCC PZ7.1.S26 Rav 2022 (print) | LCC PZ7.1.S26 (ebook) | DDC [Fic]—dc23
LC record available at https://lccn.loc.gov/2021049634
LC ebook record available at https://lccn.loc.gov/2021049635

TUESDAY, APRIL 6, 1666

Through me you pass into the city of woe;
Through me you pass into eternal pain;
Through me among the people lost forever.

CHAPTER

1

I COULDN'T SEE.

The hood that bound my head was canvas, so my only light was what filtered through the weave. I gasped, drawing what air I could through the fabric. It stank of dried blood and stale sweat. I wasn't the first prisoner to wear it.

The cart thundered down the road, bumping on the cobblestones, the wood rattling my bones. I lay in the back, wrists and ankles clamped in chains that jingled with the wagon's rise and fall. My heart thudded, keeping time with each bang and shudder.

This was the third time they'd moved me since I'd been

3

captured. I didn't know where they were taking me. But then I didn't even know why I'd been arrested.

It had happened yesterday, late afternoon—at least I think it was yesterday; I'd lost track of time in the jails. I'd been at Blackthorn with Tom, searching for the few copies of my master's journals we hadn't yet been able to find. I needed to replenish some of the ingredients I kept in the apothecary sash I wore hidden around my waist, so I left Tom hunting through the books upstairs while I went down to the workshop to refill the vials.

A commotion in the alley behind my shop drew me to the door. There was a small crowd two doors down, huddled around the crates behind Mr. Ralston's grocery. I'd made it halfway there when a voice cried out.

"That's him! The boy! He did it!"

Three men were on me in an instant. I recognized the constable, Mr. Pettiworth, but the other two were strangers. They grabbed my arms and lifted me bodily from the ground.

"Hey!" I'd cried, trying to pull away. "What are you—"

Someone cracked me on the head before I could finish. Dazed, I was carried into the streets, brought to our parish's jail, and tossed in a cell. I huddled against the back wall, confused and scared, for only a short time before two new men arrived and hauled me out.

Again I tried to ask what was happening. This time, I got a club to the gut for my trouble. I'd obviously been accused of some crime, so I expected the men to cart me off to the courthouse. I almost welcomed it; at least someone there would tell me why I'd been arrested.

Yet I wasn't taken to the courthouse. Instead, the men threw a hood over my head and carted me to a different jail. There I remained for several hours until I was moved once again. With the hood on, I couldn't tell where. All I knew from the pinpricks of torchlight through the canvas was that it was the middle of the night.

I'd never been arrested before. I didn't know what the procedure was, exactly. But I knew nothing about this was normal. And that scared me more than anything else.

They left the hood on in my new cell. I huddled in the corner until they moved me a third time—and by the daylight now streaming through the fabric, I could tell the whole night had passed since I'd been captured. They dumped me in the back of this cart, and now we were headed somewhere new.

I knew better than to ask where. I just lay there,

breathing the stink through the canvas, until the cart was finally reined to a stop.

Strong hands grabbed me under my shoulders and hauled me out. I wasn't expecting to be let go, so when they released me, I stumbled and fell.

I hit the ground hard. I could tell I was on dirt—little specks of earth and gravel dug into my fingers—but the hood still blinded me as to where I was.

A voice spoke, low and gruff. "Name?"

I heard paper crinkling above me; one of my captors handing over a letter. Then the gruff voice called out.

"Fleming! Packard! One for the cellar!"

Footsteps approached. I was hauled up by my arms again. These were different men from before—one of them smelled worse than the two who'd dropped me here, which was saying something—and they dragged me off without a word. I heard the cart creaking and the clopping of hooves as my old captors rode away.

The light coming through the canvas dimmed, and our footsteps began to echo. We were marching through a tunnel, or a gate. I stumbled as they dragged me and felt the dirt switch to stone under my shoes. Then the light all but vanished. We were inside, going down stairs.

I'd been ordered to the cellar, but it didn't smell like a cellar. It smelled like a sewer. The stink of it overwhelmed everything, even the body odor of the man next to me. I gagged, praying I wouldn't throw up. My hood was still on.

I heard voices cursing from below. Then the shouts suddenly broke into a roar, a dozen men jeering at once. It made me cringe, and I tried to tug away from my new captors.

They didn't like that. The man on my left gripped me harder. The one on my right twisted my arm until he just about popped it from its socket. I cried out, my howls lost in the din.

The two men carried me into the screams. Then they shoved me up against a stone wall. One man held my arms high while the other locked manacles around my wrists. They did the same to my ankles, then tore off the hood and walked away. I blinked, the first time I'd been able to see since yesterday.

A single torch flickered across the room, hanging from a sconce on the wall. I could see steps going up—the steps they'd just dragged me down, the only way out of here. The center of the cellar gave proof to the stench I'd smelled: It *was* an open sewer. Waste and refuse floated in a thin pond of scum, draining from one low grating in the wall to another on the opposite side.

The reek hit me fully now that the hood was off. I couldn't help it anymore. I retched. But my stomach was empty—they hadn't fed me since the constable had hauled me away, not even a drink of water—so nothing came up but thin, sour bile.

"Don't like the smell, eh?" a man said, practically in my ear. "Just wait till they bring the food!"

He cackled at his joke. The man was thin, with a leering smile and a gap between his teeth, which were chipped and rotted black. Like me, he was chained to the wall by manacles, four feet to my left. Next to him was another prisoner, half naked, curled in a ball and moaning. A dozen more men lay about the room, all shackled the same. A few strained to look me over. The rest just stared into the gloom.

A dungeon, I thought. *This isn't a jail. It's a dungeon.*

Why was I here? For that matter . . . "Where am I?" I said.

"You mean you don't know?" The man beside me laughed. "You're at the gates of hell, boy. They brought you to Newgate Prison."

CHAPTER

2

NEWGATE . . . *PRISON?*

Impossible.

Newgate was notorious. The worst of London's criminals were held here, a house of thieves and killers. Full of tiny, cramped cells, with barely enough room to stand and move.

Except I wasn't in a cell. They'd taken me to the dungeon, the rough cellar beneath the jail keeper's house.

This was where they kept prisoners condemned to die.

Panic rose in my chest. "But I haven't even had a trial," I said.

"What's a trial going to do?" the man next to me crowed. "By the time you see the magistrate, it's already over!"

He said it like it was some grand joke. Except he was right. Nearly every trial ended with the same verdict: guilty. After all, if you hadn't done the crime, why would you be in a courtroom?

I yanked desperately at my chains. The iron bit into my wrists, leaving my skin raw and red. "I have to get out of here," I said, frantic. "Help! *Help!*"

The man chained beside me thought I was the funniest person he'd ever met. "Ain't no one going to help you down here, boy."

"But I haven't done anything!"

I didn't think he could have laughed harder, but he did. "Of course you didn't! None of us have! I didn't murder that lady at all. And ol' Butcher John here"—he nudged the moaning body chained next to him—"he didn't kill eight people! Did you, John?"

John groaned, trembling on the stone. He had no shirt or shoes, and his breeches were soaked, whether with sweat or waste from the sewer, I didn't know. There were blotches all over his skin. At first, I thought they were birthmarks, but now I saw they formed a rash. Some of the blotches were bumpy, some flat. I understood now, too, that his trembling wasn't from cold. It was the shaking of a man with high temperature.

I recognized what he had right away. Master Benedict had taught me about it long ago. "That's jail fever," I said breathlessly.

The man next to me nodded. "Well, we're in jail, ain't we?"

"That's deadly!"

This sent him into a new fit of laughter. "The fever ain't going to be what kills you, boy! Ha-ha-ha!"

I couldn't think. I couldn't *think*. "The king will get me out of here," I said mindlessly. "He won't let me die. He'll save me."

"The king! Ha-ha-haaaa! Hey, lads, good news! Merry ol' Charles is coming to visit!"

The rest of the dungeon joined in mocking me. "Tell him I need new stockings!" one of the prisoners shouted, and soon they were all calling for something. I sat against the wall, trying to cover my ears, shaking like a leaf.

The dungeon thundered with their laughter. It was so loud I almost missed the clomp of footsteps on the stairs. It sounded like a troop of armored men.

The jailer, I thought. Coming with guards to shut us up.

But it wasn't the jailer. I saw that when the boots first appeared on the steps. And my heart leaped.

I *knew* those boots.

They were fine, black leather, normally polished so they'd shine, though today they were spattered with mud. The breeches above them were black, too, as was the man's silk shirt and waistcoat. The twin pistols he wore in his belt offered the only splash of color, with their pearl handles and finely engraved steel. A patch covered his left eye, an angry scar running from underneath it to the corner of his lip, twisting his mouth in a permanent half scowl.

This was the King's Warden, Lord Richard Ashcombe, right-hand man to His Majesty, Charles II. Most people found him terrifying. I don't think I'd ever been so happy to see anyone in my life.

He stormed down the stairs. Two of the King's Men followed him, the royal emblem emblazoned on their tabards. The prisoners chained with me quieted, watching with startled curiosity as the jailer scurried behind them, protesting.

"You have no right." The jailer squeezed between the King's Men to argue with Lord Ashcombe. "This is my domain. I have the papers of transfer right here."

He stuck the letter he was holding in Ashcombe's face. Ashcombe plucked it from his fingers and handed it to the nearest King's Man. "Keep this."

The soldier tucked the paper into his belt.

The jailer protested. "That's official business," he said. "You can't confiscate it." He tried to grab it back.

The second King's Man put a hand on the jailer's chest. "You should rethink your choices, mate," the soldier said.

The prisoners loved every bit of this. "Stick 'im with your sword!" one called out.

Lord Ashcombe continued down as if he'd never been interrupted. For the jailer, this was one humiliation too far. "I haven't even been paid for the boy's keep," he said. "I don't care who you are—you're not taking him anywhere." And he grabbed Lord Ashcombe by the arm.

Big mistake.

Lord Ashcombe swung round. At first, I thought he was going to knock the man's hand away. Instead, he swept his arm around the jailer's elbow, pinning it against his chest. Off balance, the jailer stumbled, wheeling to face the King's Warden, almost as if they were dancing.

Then Lord Ashcombe rammed his forehead into the jailer's nose.

The crack echoed in the dungeon. Blood poured from the jailer's broken nose over his lips. Lord Ashcombe released the man, and the jailer crumpled to his knees.

There was no fine swordplay here. That was a brawler's

move, brutal and efficient. And the dungeon thundered with the cheers of every prisoner.

They shouted and called like they were watching a fight at the bear pits. They cheered even harder when the King's Men drew their short swords and stepped forward, ready to finish the fool who'd dared to manhandle their general.

Lord Ashcombe raised a hand to stop them. "If you kill him," he said, "he won't be able to tell us where the key is."

Bleeding quietly, the jailer dug in his pocket and held it up.

CHAPTER

3

THE KING'S MEN UNLOCKED MY manacles.

The prisoners kept cheering as I was released. It was strange; I'd barely been there five minutes, but they already thought of me as one of their own. It lightened their hearts to see a fellow captive go free.

The man beside me was actually jumping up and down—as high as he could, anyway, with irons clapped to his ankles—laughing like a madman. "Tell the king we love him!" he said. "From me and ol' Butcher John both!"

The other captives shouted their own requests, some vulgar, most a plea to let them out, too. Lord Ashcombe ignored them all. He watched silently as his men brought me over, limping.

"Thank you, my lord—" I began.

He cut me off sharply. "Say nothing."

I shut my mouth. Was he angry with me? It was impossible to tell. His gruff manner and that scar on his face meant he always looked as if he was one annoyance away from drawing his pistols and giving everyone a piece of his mind.

The bloodied jailer slunk off, tail between his legs, as the King's Men helped me up the steps and out of the dungeon. The guards on duty all watched, but no one tried to stop us. They'd heard that conversation and wanted no part of it.

We exited the prison into the courtyard, leaving Newgate's stone towers behind. I couldn't describe the relief I felt at seeing the sun again—to say nothing of breathing fresh air. Yet it wasn't until we left the main gate and reached the street that I truly felt free. It was like noticing for the first time that everyone else seemed so . . . well, *normal*. As if being stuck in that prison was a worry that had never crossed their minds.

Just like I'd believed until a few minutes ago. And I *still* didn't know what I'd done wrong.

I wouldn't get any answers soon. Two more of the King's Men waited with the horses. They'd brought my own mount, Blossom, for me to ride. I recognized her right away: her chestnut coat, the white socks on her hind legs, the star on her forehead. But, most of all, her curious, intelligent eyes.

She nickered when she saw me. Tom's midnight-black warhorse, Lightning, was waiting next to her, and my heart leaped again as Tom stepped from behind the horse's hind-quarters. As usual, Tom was wearing the feathered, wide-brimmed, silver-trimmed hat the king had given him last month. He'd taken to dressing more fashionably overall to match it; today he had on an embroidered waistcoat with silver piping.

The worry that lined his face melted away when he saw me. He wrapped me in a bear hug.

"You stink," he said.

I laughed, almost giddy.

Tom put me down and spoke seriously. "I thought they'd killed you. We went looking at the jail, but you weren't—"

"Silence," Lord Ashcombe said.

Tom quieted as quickly as I had. Lord Ashcombe mounted his horse, and Tom swung himself into his own saddle. With time only for a quick hand of comfort on Blossom's neck, I got on, too. She snorted, shaking her head. I guess I really did stink.

My whole body ached so badly I practically flopped over my saddle. Then we were off. Lord Ashcombe set the pace, twisting through the streets, barely giving the traffic time to get out of our way. Even if the King's Warden hadn't told us to keep quiet, there was no chance for Tom and me to talk. I just gripped the reins and prayed I wouldn't fall off.

We rode straight for the Palace of Whitehall, keeping our breakneck speed until we reached the stables. As the grooms stepped forward to take our horses, Lord Ashcombe called a pair of servants over to attend to me.

"Clean him up," he said.

The servants escorted me into the palace, politely avoiding crinkling their noses at my stench. Tom and I had been living here for a month now. When we'd first returned to London, the king had installed us in the parlor of one of his knights, Sir Thomas Killigrew. After we'd foiled the Covenanter plot against His Majesty, we'd been ordered to remain at Whitehall—though Sir Thomas's objections had finally had their effect, and we'd been moved.

Our quarters were now a small room on the second floor that I was pretty sure was a repurposed linen closet. Sally, whom the king had made his ward, was still living at Berkshire House, staying in much nicer quarters on the edge of Saint James's Park. Though frankly, it didn't much matter where we laid our heads, because we'd all been kept busy.

As there wasn't room in our quarters for a tub, the attendants escorted me to the servants' bathing area instead. After a pair of maids filled the tub with buckets of heated water, the men stripped me down, dunked me under, and scrubbed at my skin with a giant sponge. I found the whole thing mortifying. At least the maids were gone.

By the time they finally let me out, my filthy clothes had vanished, replaced by freshly pressed togs brought down from my room—and blissfully, a plate of fruits and pastries. Too starving to be polite, I guzzled down an entire pitcher of water, then stuffed my face as I dressed, trying not to leave sticky smears all over my shirt. When I was done, the attendants returned me to Scotland Yard, near the stables.

Lord Ashcombe was still there, giving orders to the King's Men. Tom waited by the stalls, running a brush through Lightning's coat and rubbing the blaze on his horse's forehead. He hurried over when he saw me.

"Are you all right?" he said.

I nodded, shaking soapy water out of my ear. "I even feel sort of human again."

"How did you end up at Newgate? We looked everywhere for you."

I waited to explain until Lord Ashcombe had dismissed his men and joined us. I told them how the constable had seized me in the alley behind Blackthorn, then how I'd been moved from jail to jail, until they'd finally shackled me in that dungeon. "I still don't know why," I said, confused.

"Likely so we couldn't find you until your trial had already begun," Lord Ashcombe said. He told me that as soon as Tom had discovered I'd been arrested, he'd hurried back to Whitehall to tell Lord Ashcombe, and Lord Walsingham, too: the king's spymaster and, secretly, my new master as well.

"By the time we arrived at the first jail," Ashcombe said, "no one knew where you'd been sent. It took a full day and a pair of Walsingham's agents to track you down."

His mention of the courts chilled me. "Why would I be on trial? For what charge?"

"Murder."

"What?" I stared at them. "I didn't kill anyone!"

"No one here believed you did."

"But . . . why would anyone accuse me of murder?"

"For very good reason," Ashcombe growled. "Come with me."

CHAPTER

LORD ASHCOMBE LED US INTO THE
Wood Yard. He made for the beer buttery, but instead of
going inside, took us down a wide set of stairs into the cellar
underneath.

I shivered, and not just because it was cooler under-
ground. Going down those steps made me remember every
second I'd spent in Newgate. But there were no chains here
to bind me. It was just a storage area for the upstairs, beer
casks stacked all over, with three prep tables in the center.

Two of those tables had something on them, covered
by a heavy cloth. One of the King's Men, standing watch
between them, nodded to Lord Ashcombe, moving aside as

we approached. The light was dim down here, so it wasn't until we got close that I realized what we'd come to see.

There were bodies under those coverings. I could make out the silhouette of their shapes under the linen, the cloth sticking up at the heads and the toes.

I paused. *Murder,* I thought. *I've been accused of murder.* Were these the people I'd supposedly killed?

"They were found in the alley behind your home," Lord Ashcombe said.

He pulled back the first cloth. Underneath was the body of a man approaching his sixties. All his clothes had been removed, showing skin of pallid white. He had a bit of a belly. And there was a stab wound in the center of his ribs.

There was no blood; the man had died hours ago. The wound was clean, with smooth edges. A wide dagger, or a short sword, had been plunged into his chest. From the angle, the strike had gone straight to his heart.

"Do you recognize him?" Lord Ashcombe said.

I'd barely glanced at the man's face; my eyes had been drawn straight to the wound in his ribs. Now I looked more closely. He had a beard, dark, like his hair, and his eyes—

I gasped.

"That's Mr. Sinclair!" I said. It was the beard that had

thrown me off; I'd never seen him with one before. "He owns the confectionery next door to Blackthorn."

"Is there any reason why someone would think you had a grudge against him?"

"No." My heart sank. "He was always kind to me."

Tom was just as dismayed to see the man lying there. When Master Benedict had first taken me in, Mr. Sinclair gave me a free candy every Sunday. After Tom became my friend, Mr. Sinclair had extended his bounty to him, too. *A little Christian charity on the Lord's day,* he'd say, and drop the sweets into our palms with a wink. "He made me smile," I said sadly.

"Did he have any enemies?"

None that I could think of. "He left when the plague broke out. I didn't even know he was back in town."

I looked to Tom. He shook his head; he hadn't seen the man, either.

"Why on Earth would anyone kill him?" I said. "Why would anyone think *I* killed him?"

"Apparently," Lord Ashcombe said, "because he stumbled upon you committing the *other* murder."

He nodded toward the second body. I drew back the cloth to take a look.

And suddenly, I couldn't breathe.

CHAPTER
5

I STARED AT THE CORPSE ON THE TABLE.

This one was a boy. He was older than me, about seventeen or so. He had red hair and a stocky build, with close-set eyes and a sloping brow. Half his face was a mess, the flesh on the left side a writhing, twisted mass. The same was true of his neck, shoulder, and arm.

He'd been burned sometime in the past, but that wasn't what had killed him. There was a small wound above his breastbone. An exit wound, by the way the flesh protruded. I bet that if I'd turned him over, I would have seen the same gash as on Mr. Sinclair, a wide blade entering from the back. Yet even if I hadn't seen the wound, I'd have known he didn't die from the burns. Not just because they were healed.

Because *I* was the one who'd burned him.

"Wat," I whispered.

This was the boy who'd been apprenticed to the Cult of the Archangel. The boy who'd murdered my master.

It was no wonder why anyone thought I'd killed him. If I'd seen him again, I very well might have.

Tom was as stunned as I was. I looked up at Lord Ashcombe, who nodded; he'd recognized Wat, too. But then he wasn't likely to forget—after all, his missing eye and the scar on his face were the boy's handiwork.

"Have you seen him since?" Lord Ashcombe asked quietly.

Tom and I shook our heads. "You told us he'd fled London."

"He had," Ashcombe said. "I don't know where he ended up. But I stopped looking for him when the plague struck. I assumed he'd gone for good."

So had I. It made me think of what Lord Walsingham had told me. *Always question your assumptions, apprentice. Failure to do so leads to complacency. And complacency is often fatal.*

How right he'd been. Here was Wat lying dead on the

slab. I stared at the body, thinking . . . I didn't know what. That Wat had taken away the first man who'd ever cared about me. That the boy deserved what he'd got. That he deserved worse even than this.

"How do people say I killed him?" I said.

"The claim," Lord Ashcombe told us, "is that you found Wat lurking around the back of your shop. You confronted him, and when he turned to run, you chased him and stabbed him in the back. Sinclair supposedly heard the fight and came into the alley. To stop him reporting your crime, you killed him, too."

"I wouldn't have harmed Mr. Sinclair for anything," I protested.

"I know. As for Wat, if you'd seen him, you'd have shot him. You wouldn't have used a knife."

I wasn't sure I liked Lord Ashcombe's cold assessment of how I'd have taken my revenge. Probably because he was right. Still, it was a relief to have him believe me. He could vouch for me at my trial.

As it turned out, he could do much more than that. "We need to ensure there isn't any doubt at all," he said. "We have to show you didn't kill *either* of them. Fortunately, we can prove exactly that."

CHAPTER

6

"HOW?" TOM SAID, SURPRISED.

"Examine the bodies," Lord Ashcombe said.

Tom recoiled, horrified by the thought. I wasn't all that keen on it, either. But my years with Master Benedict had exposed me to the dead plenty of times. His remedies hadn't always saved our patients, much as we might have wished otherwise.

In this case, however, I wasn't sure what I was looking for. If I'd been with Master Benedict, I'd have looked for signs of infection or disease. And indeed, Wat did have a boil on his calf. *A cat scratch that got infected,* I thought. I could still see the claw marks on his skin. I shook my head. Wat had once been an apothecary's apprentice, too. He should have known to get it treated. Made me wonder just what he'd been doing since he'd fled.

But Wat's more immediate problem had obviously been the stab wound in his back. There were the usual scrapes and scratches on his hands, but I didn't think they were defensive marks. His knuckles lacked the bruising that would have come from being in a fight.

With Mr. Sinclair, the knife had entered from the front. I lifted the body enough to see that he, too, had an exit wound. And Mr. Sinclair had no defensive wounds on his hands at all. Just some freshly burned skin, likely caused by hot sugar dripping on his fingers.

"They were killed by the same blade," I said. "A foot long and two inches wide at the base. A long dagger."

Lord Ashcombe nodded. "The wounds tell us the murder weapon. Anything else?"

"No defensive wounds meant they either knew their killer, or he surprised them."

"Yes. And?"

I thought about it. "The blades went straight to the heart. One thrust, no hesitation. The killer knew what he was doing."

"Yes. And?"

I was running out of things to tell him. I studied the corpses again. "When the body dies," I said, "blood settles at the lowest point. The discoloration on these two says that Mr. Sinclair lay on his back, but Wat fell on his side. His left side."

"Does any of that prove you didn't kill them as the witness claimed?"

"No. If I'd chased Wat, I'd have stabbed him from behind, just like that. And if Mr. Sinclair had confronted me, he knew me well; he wouldn't have expected an attack. But . . ."

"Go on."

"I've never stabbed anyone," I said. "Surely I wouldn't be so *good* at it."

"So you might claim. But you're an apothecary's apprentice. You know anatomy. You'd know exactly where to aim."

"I guess."

"So what are you missing?"

By now I was at a complete loss. What the witness claimed was obviously a lie, but it was plausible. How was I supposed to prove I wasn't the one who'd killed them?

Neither Tom nor I had the answer. "I'm sorry, my lord. I don't know."

"Move the bodies," Lord Ashcombe said.

I wasn't sure what he was asking. I'd already moved the bodies to examine the wounds.

"The limbs," he said. "Move the limbs."

Puzzled, I did as he asked. I took Wat's arm and bent it at the elbow. Then I did the same for Mr. Sinclair.

At least I tried to. Mr. Sinclair's arm wouldn't budge. I had to strain against the stiffness to make it move even the slightest—

Startled, I looked up at Lord Ashcombe. "The time," I said. "The *time*."

"Explain."

Lord Ashcombe knew what I was getting at, but Tom didn't. "A few hours after death," I said to him, "the muscles of the body begin to stiffen. Once half a day has passed, it's hard to move them."

"And then?" Lord Ashcombe said.

"After a further day, the muscles loosen. Mr. Sinclair was murdered yesterday; his limbs are rigid, as they should be. But Wat's are loose. So either he died only a few hours ago— which we know isn't the case—*or he died at least a day before Mr. Sinclair.*"

Lord Ashcombe nodded, satisfied. "And thus we know our witness is lying."

"So we can tell this to the court!" Tom said.

"We can do much better than that," Lord Ashcombe said. "Come with me. The spymaster has brought us a guest."

CHAPTER

7

LORD ASHCOMBE ESCORTED US INTO the palace. As glad as I was that we had concrete evidence I hadn't killed Wat and Mr. Sinclair, butterflies still fluttered in my stomach. It was one thing to have your friends know you were innocent. Getting a court to believe it was something else.

We headed to Walsingham's office. I'd spent a lot of time in this room over the last month. It wasn't much to look at: just a windowless space with a few paintings on the walls, a desk, a side table with a couple of chairs, and a bookshelf. Despite the mounds of paper and letters delivered to the spymaster at all hours of the day, his office was always tidy. Today was no exception, a neat stack on his desk, the inkwell atop it.

The chessboard on the side table was the only luxury here. The board was made of cherry and ebony, each square bordered in silver. The pieces were especially nice: white jade from the Orient, and African obsidian. The spymaster had been playing me twice a week, every Monday and Thursday, like clockwork. It had taken me several games just to get over my fear of dropping a piece and having it shatter.

I assumed we were going to meet the spymaster, so I was surprised when we found the room empty. Lord Ashcombe went around Walsingham's desk and turned to us.

"Be absolutely silent," he commanded.

We both kept quiet as the King's Warden reached beneath the painting that hung behind the spymaster's desk. There was a barely audible clack. Then the wood paneling on the right swung open.

Tom and I looked at each other in surprise. I'd had no idea that door was there. It wasn't unusual to have secret passages in places like this, built for the servants to move around behind the scenes without disturbing their masters. But something told me this wasn't intended for the help.

The secret door moved without a sound. Clearly, the

spymaster kept it well oiled. Lord Ashcombe motioned us inside.

I went first. The passage was wide enough for only a man of slight build; Tom had to angle his body to fit. Ashcombe lifted a candle overhead, lighting the darkness. He waved me forward.

Wooden joists stuck out from the stone walls, making us duck and weave our way down the corridor. We made it about thirty feet before Lord Ashcombe tapped Tom on the shoulder. He shadowed the candle and pointed. I peered through the darkness to see.

A couple of yards ahead, a pinprick of light glinted in the wall. I crept forward to discover it came from a peephole. I pressed my eye against it and looked through.

The peephole gave a decent view of the room beyond. I saw a parlor, with a carved settee and upholstered chairs, plus a deck of cards left spread out on a side table. A woman with graying hair and gnarled hands sat awkwardly on one of the chairs. Her dress marked her as a commoner: decently tailored, but nothing fancy.

The woman rubbed her knuckles nervously. She kept looking about the room in awe—and maybe a little fear. It wasn't until she turned my way that I recognized her.

I straightened in surprise. Tom took a peek; then the King's Warden led us back to Walsingham's office.

He closed the secret door to the passage behind us. "You know her?" he said.

"She lives across the way," I said, "on the other side of the alley. She's a seamstress." I couldn't remember her name. "Is she the witness?"

He nodded. "Is there any reason she would have a grudge against you?"

"No. Well . . . not really. She moved here from Portsmouth, I think, about three years ago, to live with her sister. She did complain to Master Benedict a few times after she arrived. She said the smells from our workshop were foul. And she didn't like our pigeons. She said they kept . . . er . . . making a mess on her linen, when she hung it out to dry."

"Nothing else?"

"She yelled at me and Tom once, when we were playing out back."

"I remember," Tom said. "She hit me with a spoon."

"But that was what, two years ago?" I said. "Hardly worth framing me for murder."

"That's not why she did it," Lord Ashcombe said.

"You already know the reason?" I said, surprised.

"Walsingham worked it out." Lord Ashcombe walked to the office door. "Return to the peephole and watch. And don't make a sound."

CHAPTER

8

TOM AND I HURRIED BACK THROUGH
the passage. There we huddled, heads together, spying. The
woman remained seated, still rubbing her hands, until the
door opened. Then she sprang from her chair.

Alexander Walsingham, spymaster to His Majesty,
entered the parlor carrying a small folder. Lord Walsingham
was a fairly plain man, lean, not too tall, very soft spoken.
The first time I'd met him, I'd remarked on how he wasn't
the sort of fellow one would remember—which was a rather
good attribute in a spy.

The same couldn't be said for Lord Ashcombe. As he
followed the spymaster in, the woman gulped. I could

already see she was regretting her choice to get involved.

I had no doubt Walsingham saw it, too. His manner was pleasant, designed to put the woman at ease. "Good afternoon, Mrs. . . ." He trailed off, as if he couldn't recall her name. He opened the folder, reading it from a paper inside. "Bagley."

I had no doubt that was a ruse, intended to make her think she wasn't important enough for Walsingham to remember. In the whole time I'd known him, the spymaster hadn't forgotten a single thing.

"Yes, my lord, that's me, Elinor Bagley," she said.

"I am Lord Walsingham. This is Lord Ashcombe, Marquess of Chillingham. Please have a seat."

She sat down nervously. "Did I do something wrong, my lord?"

"Of course not." Walsingham sat in the chair next to her, folder on his lap. Lord Ashcombe remained by the door, expression neutral. "It's just that we understand you witnessed the terrible murders behind your home yesterday. One of the dead was a known criminal, wanted by His Majesty for treason. Our king has asked for an account before the trial commences. May I offer you some wine?" He held up a glass from the tray on the side table.

"Ooh, yes, my lord. Very kind."

In the passageway, Tom and I glanced at each other. I suppose I shouldn't have been surprised that Walsingham could play different roles so well, but I'd never seen this side of him. He'd always been so stolid, even awkward, every time we'd met. I hadn't imagined he had it in him to be that smooth.

The spymaster sat back comfortably, prompting her to do the same. "So," he said, "please tell us what you saw."

"Oh, well, it was a terrible business, just terrible," Elinor said. "I'd started stitching a new dress when all of a sudden I see this boy lurking out the back. Now, I keep a good watch, I do, because you never know who's around, do you? Too many criminals these days, I say."

"I quite agree."

She nodded. "So I see this boy, right? And straightaway I can tell he's up to no good, just from the way he's skulking about the houses. Then I knows it for sure, because I see his face is all burned, as if he's been in a fire, like. God's punishment, I'd reckon."

"No doubt."

"Anyway, this boy goes up to the back of that apothecary, which always used to give off those terrible smells, thank goodness that's done with—"

My blood grew hot. The smells were "done with" because the Cult of the Archangel had murdered my master.

"—and he starts fiddling with the lock. Like he's trying to open it, but he doesn't have a key. You see?"

"I do," Walsingham said.

"So," she said, really getting into her story, "just then the door opens, and that apprentice boy comes out. Christopher Rowe is his name." She said it slowly, like she expected him to write it down. "And he sees the burned boy, and his eyes go all wide-like, and he says 'You! You killed my master! I'll get you for that!' And the burned boy starts to run away, but Christopher Rowe chases him down and stabs him in the back, just as you please."

"Terrible. Go on."

"Then John Sinclair, the confectioner, comes out and says, 'What's all this commotion?' And he spies what Christopher Rowe has done, and he says just that: 'What have you done? You murdered him! I'm calling the constable.' And Christopher Rowe shouts, 'I can't let you do that,' and he stabs poor Sinclair, right in the chest."

Listening to this was infuriating. Not just because it was utter lies, but because I knew exactly what she was doing.

The dialogue was ridiculous—but told to a court, it would oh-so-conveniently explain not only what I'd done, but what I was thinking, too, so I couldn't possibly claim any kind of self-defense. It would be her word against mine. And who would believe an accused murderer?

"Well, of course I was shocked," Elinor continued. "But I was scared that Christopher Rowe would see me, and come to murder me, too. So I hid in my room until he was gone. Then I went and got the constable, and they arrested Rowe right away. And let me tell you, my lord, I feel so much safer now with him off the streets."

I must have started muttering, because Tom put a hand over my mouth.

"That's quite a story," the spymaster said. "I'm glad you weren't harmed."

"Very kind of you, my lord."

"What was it you said you did again?"

"A seamstress, my lord," Elinor said proudly.

"Wealthy, are you?"

"Oh, no, my lord." She seemed a little startled by the question. Walsingham had a way of throwing you off-kilter—a fact I'd become well acquainted with since I'd entered his service. "Not at all. Just a simple woman, I am."

"Times have been hard, with the plague."

"Aye," she said. "I've not two pennies left to rub together."

"Really? Then what is this?"

Walsingham held up a necklace. Even from the secret passage, I could see sparkling jewels set in heavy gold.

Elinor turned pale. "Wh . . . where did you get that?"

"In a jewelry case, in your house. Your room, in fact."

"What were you doing in my room?"

"Looking for something like this." Walsingham spoke quietly, even as his questions drilled into her. "Why would you say you're poor when you own such a thing?"

"I—it's not—you—" She glanced at Lord Ashcombe, standing by the door. "That was . . . my mother's," she said finally. "She died three years ago, which is why I came to London. To help my sister. I didn't mention that because I still think of it as hers. I'd never sell it, you see."

Elinor seemed rather pleased with her answer. She even relaxed a bit as Walsingham nodded. "I understand completely. Could you sign this, please?"

He placed a paper from his folder on the table beside her. Then he dipped a quill in ink and held it out.

She eyed the paper cautiously. "What's that?"

"Just a document attesting that this is, in fact, your

necklace. We've had a rash of burglaries of late. We need you to swear this isn't stolen goods."

Elinor looked hesitantly from the paper to the spymaster to Lord Ashcombe. Walsingham's quick change of direction had thrown her for a loop. She wanted to refuse, but if she did, she'd be all but confessing to theft. Hand trembling, she took the quill and signed her name.

"I appreciate your cooperation," Walsingham said. "You may arrest her now, Marquess."

Lord Ashcombe unfolded his arms and stepped forward.

Elinor shrank back in terror. "Arrest me? For what?"

"Treason, of course."

"Treason?" Her voice squeaked. "I never done no treason! I never said nothing against the king!"

"You stole His Majesty's property," the spymaster said quietly. "That is, by definition, treason."

"No! That necklace belonged to my mother! She left it for me! I signed your paper! I swore it—that necklace is mine! Anyone who says otherwise is a liar!"

"You would call me a liar?" a deep voice said. "That *is* treason."

And Charles II, King of England, Scotland, and Ireland, entered the room.

CHAPTER

9

WALSINGHAM STOOD AS ELINOR
bolted from her seat. "Y-your Majesty!" she stammered.

The spymaster addressed him much more calmly. "Sire.
Are you certain this necklace is yours?"

The king made a great show of examining it. "Indeed I
am," he said. "These very jewels were stolen from Berkshire
House a month ago."

Walsingham turned back to Elinor. "So. His Majesty
says this is his. You signed a document that claims it is yours.
I wonder: Whom do you think the courts will believe?"

Elinor turned deathly white as she realized how soundly
she'd been trapped.

"Really, Walsingham," the king said, sounding bored. "I don't have time for this. Simply take her to the Tower of London and have her hanged." He turned to leave.

The seamstress flung herself at his feet. "No! Please, sire! Please! I didn't steal anything, I swear it! A man gave the necklace to me!"

"Preposterous. Why would a man give you such a gift? No, no. It's the rope for you, I'm afraid."

Charles, a great fan of the theater, really seemed to be enjoying playing this role. I admit, I was rather enjoying it myself.

"It was a bribe!" Elinor wailed. "He paid me to say I saw the murders!"

The seamstress was so desperate she didn't realize she'd just confessed to a different capital crime. Fortunately for her, no one cared about that. "Who paid you?" Lord Ashcombe said.

"I don't know." Elinor recoiled as Lord Ashcombe loomed over her. "I swear, I don't! I never saw his face! He came yesterday morning and threatened me. He said there were going to be two murders in the alley, and I was to tell the constable I saw the whole thing. He said I had to blame it on Christopher Rowe. He told me exactly what to say, and that if I didn't say it word for word, he'd gut me in the street like a fish!"

"Then how did you end up with the necklace?" Walsingham asked.

"The man gave it to me. He said he punishes his enemies, but he rewards his friends. I didn't want to take it, I swear. I was scared!"

No one believed she didn't want the necklace. I doubted she'd even been threatened. But she wasn't really important anymore. "Describe the man," Lord Ashcombe said.

"I can't," the woman said, weeping now. "I couldn't see nothing of him. He had a big cloak, and gloves, and a mask. It was one of those golden masks, with the big smile."

Lord Ashcombe frowned. "Smile?"

"Like onstage."

Charles looked surprised at that. "You mean the Muses? Thalia and Melpomene? The masks of comedy and tragedy?"

"Yes." She forgot to say "sire." "But just the smiley one."

The king exchanged a glance with the others.

"Please, sire." She begged him, her forehead to the floor. "Don't kill me."

The king was growing tired of her groveling. Fortunately

for her, Charles was well known for his mercy. "I will spare you on two conditions," he said. "First, you must recant your statement. Swear to the magistrates that Christopher Rowe had no hand in any murder."

"Of course, sire, of course."

"Second: The moment you have done this, you will leave London. You are hereby banned from the city. I expect you out by the end of tomorrow."

"But . . . I can't go back to Portsmouth. I don't have anyone to—"

Charles leaned over her, all humor gone. "Portsmouth, Plymouth—you may go to Patagonia for all I care. If my men see you again, your life is forfeit."

He waved her away. At Lord Ashcombe's command, two of the King's Men entered the room and hauled her off, blubbering. Straight to the courthouse, I hoped.

As for Walsingham, he turned toward the peephole. "At your convenience," he said softly.

Tom and I bolted from the secret passage.

CHAPTER
10

IT TOOK US A COUPLE OF MINUTES to find the parlor. Even after a month, the palace was still a maze to us.

By the time we arrived, Charles's humor had returned. He stood by the card table, idly flicking through the deck, a smile playing about his lips. "Odd's fish, Christopher. Even when you don't do anything, you find trouble."

My face grew warm. "Sorry, Your Majesty. Thank you for saving me."

"Nonsense. I'd have pardoned you regardless of the court's decision. I can't lose my most promising new spy, now, can I?"

I thanked him again, anyway. So did Tom.

"Indeed. Well, I am certainly pleased to have some of my jewelry back. Walsingham?" He held his hand out for his necklace.

The spymaster hesitated. "May I hold on to it for a while, sire? It may prove useful in our investigation."

"Oh? Very well. Just don't lose it again." He clapped his hands together. "Now I must make for the Theatre Royal. Killigrew is doing a new production of *The Parson's Wedding*. If we dawdle, I'll be late."

"No one's starting the play without you," Lord Ashcombe pointed out.

"That's true, isn't it? In that case, let's have some wine."

"By your leave, sire," Walsingham said, "Christopher and I will join you momentarily. We have some business to discuss."

"As you like. But be warned: We shall drink only one bottle. If you don't hurry, you'll have none." He turned to Tom. "Have I ever told you the story of how I escaped from Cromwell's clutches?"

"No, sire," Tom said, pleased. Actually, he had—twice. But Tom would happily listen to the king reciting the alphabet.

"Ah! Well, it starts at the Battle of Worcester . . ."

Tom walked out with the king. "Keep me informed," Lord Ashcombe said to me and Walsingham, then followed. Walsingham closed the door after them, then turned to look me over.

"Your captors did not injure you, I hope?" he said quietly.

Truth be told, I was still feeling a little worse for wear. My muscles ached from being carted about the city, my wrists stung where the manacles had chafed the skin, and my skull throbbed where the brutes had whacked me—twice. And I was beyond exhausted. Not only had I not slept a wink in jail, I'd barely slept at all the whole past month.

But at that moment, safe in the palace, the ordeal over, I felt so relieved, I was practically giddy. "No, my lord."

As usual, Walsingham changed the subject abruptly. "That was interesting, wasn't it?"

More horrifying than interesting, I thought. I thanked him for having Elinor's home searched. "How did you know she had the king's necklace?"

"I didn't," he said. "The Raven's ploy—and we can be assured, I think, that this masquerade was the Raven's doing—his ploy to keep you away from us until your trial began backfired on him. It allowed my agents time to discover who the witness against you was. Once I had her brought here, since she'd obviously either been threatened or bribed to bear false witness against you, I had her home searched for evidence. The necklace was something of a surprise."

Either way worked for me. It allowed the king to step in and stop my execution, and I said as much.

Walsingham stared out the window, into the distance. "It did not. As His Majesty stated, he would have pardoned you when the court handed down its sentence regardless. But there is something to be learned here."

"What's that, my lord?"

"What do you think the Raven's purpose was with this charade?"

His question caught me off balance. I'd already guessed the Raven—the man who'd promised revenge on me for foiling his schemes in Paris—was behind the false charges. But I'd been so worried about *how* I was going to get out of his trap, I hadn't asked what was perhaps the more important question.

Why *had* he tried to frame me for murder?

"I suppose . . . he wanted to torment me?" I said.

Walsingham waved that away. "A secondary effect. One

the Raven found satisfying, no doubt, but not his main purpose." When I didn't offer another reason, he asked, "What would have been the likely effect of the trial?"

I frowned. I'd assumed it was to have me executed. But if the king had planned from the start to pardon me . . . "The Raven wasn't actually trying to kill me," I said, surprised.

"Explain."

"Well . . . if he wanted me dead, he could have done that almost any time." He'd killed Wat and Mr. Sinclair easily enough. I might have made a harder target, spending the last month inside the palace, Tom constantly by my side. But when I'd foolishly stepped out into the alley behind Blackthorn, I'd forgotten to get Tom first. The Raven could have slipped his blade between my ribs then. Just one of a thousand opportunities.

"And even if the courts sentenced me to death," I continued, "the Raven knew from what happened with the Covenanters how valuable I was to the king. His Majesty's pardon could overrule any punishment the court could offer." Which made it a poor attempt to kill me indeed.

"Correct." Walsingham turned from the window to study the tapestry with the peephole in it. "So again I ask: What was the Raven's purpose in this?"

If he didn't want me dead, and all this wasn't just to hurt me, why bother? "I don't know."

"You are stuck in your mind."

"I . . . sorry, my lord?"

"You are thinking of *yourself*. You are focused on *your* life. Most people do the same. They wonder, and wonder only, *Why is this happening to me?* It makes them trivially easy to manipulate."

He waited for me to see what was, no doubt, right in front of me. Slowly, my face grew warm. I couldn't figure it out.

He offered me a hint. "The world turns, apprentice, and you are not the only person in it. Events rarely occur for your pleasure, or dismay. So who else would be affected by this trial?"

My mind raced. Tom, obviously, and Sally. Isaac. Lords Ashcombe and Walsingham, and—

Oh.

I understood.

CHAPTER
11

"THE KING," I SAID IN SURPRISE.

"Indeed." Walsingham regarded me once more. "You are His Majesty's new favorite subject. You stopped a plot against his life last summer, and again in Oxford in the fall. You apprehended some blackguards during the plague. Though you are a commoner, you traveled in his name to Paris, and now you live here in Whitehall. And while your apprenticeship to me is not widely known, there are a few who have become aware. Absolutely everyone is talking about you."

I was almost more horrified by that than when I'd been stuck in the dungeon. I had noticed recently that several important people in the palace had made it their business to strike up a conversation with me. I'd assumed they were just being nice.

Master Benedict had despised politics, so he'd always kept me away from things like this. I was beginning to wish he hadn't. Even after my time in Louis XIV's court in Paris, I was clearly still clueless about these people.

"So," the spymaster continued, "we already know the king would have pardoned you. What would have happened, then, once he did?"

Now I got it. "It would have been an embarrassment."

"To say the least. His newly favored child, a murderer? Not merely of a criminal, but of an innocent confectioner? It would be a disgrace."

The spymaster's test had got my mind tumbling. Now more of the puzzle fell into place. "But that wasn't the Raven's purpose, either, was it? The king's embarrassment."

"No. As with your discomfort, the Raven may well have enjoyed it. Yet it is still not his true aim. What is?"

"If I'd been convicted," I said, "even with the pardon, the king would have had to distance himself from me. I couldn't stay at the palace. I couldn't call on him for help. I probably couldn't even work with you anymore. I'd be isolated."

I stared at the spymaster. "*That* was what the Raven wanted," I said. "That was the promise he made, when he sent me that first letter in Paris."

By now, I knew the words by heart. *I am going to do to you what I should have done to Blackthorn years ago,* the Raven had written. *I am going to make you suffer. I will do this by taking away the things you love, one by one, until there is only you and me. And then, once I have stripped your life bare, you will understand.*

"This is the endgame," I said, and the realization filled me with dread. "He's finally come to finish this. He's going to take away everyone I care about and then kill me."

"He is going to try," Walsingham said. "But as you have seen, he is not infallible. We have stopped this plot. And in doing so, we have discovered he has made a mistake."

He has? "What mistake?"

The spymaster held up his hand, the king's necklace dangling from his finger. "This."

CHAPTER
12

THE JEWELS SPARKLED IN THE LIGHT
of the window. I watched them sway, uncertain what Lord
Walsingham was getting at.

I ventured a guess. "We know the Raven robbed the
secret vault under Berkshire House," I said, "so . . . the
necklace confirms he was responsible for framing me?"

"Much more than that," the spymaster said. "How
much do you think this is worth?"

I didn't know anything about jewelry. "Ten pounds?
Twenty?"

Walsingham raised an eyebrow. "It appears we need to
add 'appraisal of valuable goods' to your training," he said.

"The correct value of this adornment is closer to *five hundred* pounds. What about that strikes you as strange?"

The first thing that crossed my mind was *Why would anyone waste that much money on a few sparkly stones?* You could buy a geode just as pretty for three shillings at the fair. But that probably wasn't the answer he was looking for.

"How much," Walsingham said, "do you think it would take to bribe Elinor Bagley to claim you were a murderer?"

Considering she already didn't like me, I finally understood what he was getting at. "Not much at all."

"I would agree. My assessment of her character suggests she'd have framed you for sixpence and a keg of beer. So: What have we learned?"

I thought about it. "That despite his constant scheming, money doesn't mean all that much to the Raven. He's willing to pay—to overpay—to be sure he gets what he wants."

"Indeed," the spymaster said. "And so we have learned something critical. We now know exactly how the Raven buys his way into seemingly impossible places. His bribes are calculated to guarantee near-absolute loyalty. Who would betray a man who drops a fortune in your lap whenever he needs you?

"Knowing this," Walsingham continued, "gives us

something enormously valuable: a way to find the traitor here at Whitehall who manipulated our king into the ambush at Barnham Wood. Forty thousand pounds' worth of jewelry was stolen from the Berkshire House vault. If the Raven gave five hundred of it to a seamstress, we can be all but certain that our traitor got a much larger cut of the goods."

"So we look for someone," I said, excited, "who recently came into an unaccountable sum of wealth!"

Walsingham nodded. "Or someone with enormous debts who is suddenly free of them. This will narrow the field considerably."

I couldn't believe it. This was the first real lead we'd found since the Raven had sent me that final letter, in the box with Bridget and all that blood. When we'd discovered the jewels had been stolen from under Berkshire House while a party was going on upstairs, Walsingham had theorized there was an inside man at the ball, someone who'd helped the thieves kill the guards watching the vault.

This matched what my friend Simon Chastellain had discovered earlier. Before coming to London, Simon, who was determined to destroy the Raven for murdering his uncle Marin, had delved into the Paris underworld to try to find the man. He'd heard rumors of a mysterious thief whose specialty was pretending to be someone else. He would infiltrate some noble's house, drain the coffers dry, and then disappear into the night—though not before murdering his former master.

All this had made me wonder if the inside man at the Berkshire House party was actually the Raven pretending to be a guest—or a servant. Walsingham had agreed it was a definite possibility. After days of discreet inquiry, however, he had drawn a blank. Both guests and servants were all accounted for. But now . . .

"What if we've been looking at this all wrong?" I said. "What if the inside man at Berkshire wasn't the Raven? What if he was our traitor at the palace, attending the party as one of the guests?"

Walsingham regarded me for a moment, his expression inscrutable. "A most interesting idea," he said. "Wait here."

He left me alone in the parlor. I paced across the rug, lost in thought. Despite how tired I was, this new possibility brought a fresh surge of energy. The last four weeks had been a total failure for our investigation, and not for lack of trying.

Part of that was because I'd been kept busy with other responsibilities. Though my new apprenticeship to apothecary master Woodrow Kirby was mostly a sham, I did occasionally have to make an appearance at his side.

Ordinarily, I wouldn't have minded. I loved being an apothecary's apprentice. I loved the learning, and the work, and helping our customers get better. And though no one could ever replace Master Benedict, Kirby was a decent master, a reasonable, dedicated man.

But with the Raven hanging over my head, I couldn't afford to waste time pretending to be something I wasn't. After Walsingham's early leads had turned up nothing, there wasn't much left we could do. So the spymaster set me different tasks. Sometimes I'd study: history, politics, government, law, art. Sometimes I'd practice codes or reread Master Benedict's notes about poisons—to which Walsingham had a shocking amount of material to add.

As he was the spymaster, poisons were very much his stock in trade. And we knew well that poison was one of the Raven's favorite ways to kill. So Walsingham had me playing around with actual samples. He taught me to extract nightshade from the plant's berries, and how to identify its rank odor and sickly sweet taste. He showed me how to detect hemlock in food; though it tasted like parsnip, it carried a musky smell that could give its presence away. Most of all, we spent time with the Raven's favorite: white arsenic. The tasteless, odorless powder was nearly impossible to detect, so we focused mostly on recognizing the earliest symptoms.

Walsingham also had me play regular games of chess. Every Monday and Thursday, we spent the afternoon sitting across the board in his office. Sometimes, as we played, he'd recount what had been happening at the court or overseas. Sometimes he'd quiz me on what he'd given me to study or set me puzzles to solve while I was trying to avoid the traps he laid for me with his pieces. And sometimes we'd just play. He said the game itself would sharpen my mind, teach me to think both strategically and tactically. All I'd learned so far was that Walsingham was a much better player than me. I never even came close to winning.

Otherwise, the spymaster had me combing through letters, messages, and missives that had been intercepted or copied and sent on their way. Here, I was looking for anything and everything. Hidden codes, clandestine meetings, evidence of crimes, especially talk of treason. I'd always known there were plots against our king, but I hadn't guessed how many factions wanted Charles off the throne.

Through all this, I'd hoped to find at least some clue that might lead me to the Raven. But other than discovering a pinprick code in a ship captain's letters home—an ingenious way to send a secret message that involved punching holes through the letters in a newspaper or other correspondence with a pin; the marked letters then spelled out a secret message—I'd found nothing. The captain's code uncovered only a spicer's smuggling ring. The king was pleased with me for the discovery, which was nice, but that wasn't going to help me solve my problem.

I did have one final lead. This one, however, I couldn't share with Lords Ashcombe and Walsingham.

I'd discovered, too late, that the London chapter of the Knights Templar had been destroyed by the Raven the same night as the assassination attempt against our king. In France, I'd sworn I wouldn't tell anyone the Templars still existed, operating in secret to help defend the world from descending into chaos. And—except for telling Isaac the bookseller—I'd kept that promise. So I couldn't let anyone know that Domhnall Ardrey, the head of the London Templars, had given me one final instruction before he'd died in my arms.

Find the priest.

Of all my secrets, this was the one I wanted to share most with the spymaster. Because I didn't have any idea what it meant.

Tom, Sally, and I had met a priest in Paris, Father Bernard, who'd turned out to be a Templar. After I discovered their sacred treasure, I returned it to the knights, instead of keeping it for myself. In gratitude, they gave the three of us gifts. Sally got her beloved Saint Christopher medallion back. Tom got an ancient holy sword called Eternity. And I got a coin.

It was a Templar florin, minted in gold over four hundred years ago. It had a Templar cross on one side, and an image of King Baldwin of Jerusalem on the other. The coin was a marker, proof that I had helped the Templars. In return, I was supposed to be able to call upon the knights for help if needed.

Well, I sure needed it now. The problem was: How on Earth would I find the Templars? The London chapter was gone. The only man I knew in their order was Father

Bernard. And he'd disappeared from Paris before we left. So if he was the priest I was supposed to find, I had no idea where to start.

A different possibility had also occurred to me. When Tom and I visited Saint Paul's Cathedral, we met another priest from France, a young man come to London on a pilgrimage. He'd alerted us to an attempt on our lives right there in the church.

At the time, I'd just assumed the priest had seen the assassin draw his dagger. But after Ardrey's words, I'd wondered: Was it possible that priest's presence was no accident? Could he have been a Templar, keeping watch over us, warning us when he saw we were in danger?

It was an intriguing idea, but also no help, because we never saw that priest again. We didn't even know his name or where he was staying. If I could have told Walsingham, he'd have assigned agents to track the man down.

Instead, we were left on our own. With Tom by my side—and Sally, too, whenever her own duties could spare her—we visited churches all over London. There I inquired with the clergy if they'd ever heard of Father Bernard. When none of them said yes, I asked if they knew the young priest we'd seen at Saint Paul's: mid- to late twenties, with closely cropped brown hair, a lean build, and a slight French accent.

When they all said no, I showed them my Templar florin and told them I was looking for help. I said nothing more. If the priests were Templars or Templar allies, they'd know what the coin meant. If they didn't, they couldn't help anyway.

None of them had the faintest idea what I was on about. At every church—and we'd visited nearly a hundred to date—we drew a blank. It didn't occur to us until later that maybe I'd got it all wrong.

"What if you misunderstood what Ardrey wanted?" Sally had said the day before I'd been arrested. "What if 'find the priest' wasn't a command, but a *warning*? What if the 'priest' is actually the Raven himself?"

I sure hoped not. Because if he was, I'd made a terrible mistake: I'd given away something I knew about him. And now, in the parlor, waiting for the spymaster to return, an even more terrible idea ran through my head.

Maybe that's why the Raven is finally coming after me, I thought. *Maybe I'm starting to get too close.*

If that was the case, there was nothing I could do about it. My friends had been helping as much as they could. Every time I left the palace grounds, either Tom came with me or he made me take one of the King's Men for protection. He improved his own skills, too, by training with the soldiers himself. Best of all, he was learning once again from Sir William Leech, his first sword master, who'd taught him on our way to Paris.

Tom was in awe of Sir William, and for good reason. The man was the purest swordsman we'd ever seen. He'd taught Lord Ashcombe, and even the king when he was younger, and though Sir William didn't show it, I think he was pleased to see Tom again.

"Bailey," he'd said the first time Tom had met him on the tiltyard. "I understand you did not embarrass me in the land of pomp and cheese." He meant France.

Tom had beamed. "I've kept my training up, Master."

"We shall see. However, before I administer your daily beating"—here Tom's eyes went wide—"I understand you somehow came into possession of a sword of no small quality."

"She's called Eternity," Tom said proudly, and he pulled the great sword from its cloth and scabbard.

Sir William held the weapon with reverence. He studied the leather handle, wrapped intricately with fine gold wire; the moonstone pommel, which seemed to shine with its own inner bluish-white light; the three-foot blade of tempered steel, with words inlaid in gold. *Ego autem non exspecto aeternitatem*, it said on one side; *Sempiternus sum*, on the other. *I do not await eternity. I am eternity.*

"This blade deserves a grand master," Sir William said. "So I will make you worthy of it. This means, Bailey, that I will be hitting you much harder than I'd planned."

Which he did. Tom came back to our room every night, bruised, aching—and happy. His skill with blades grew even faster, as Sir William showed him different styles, from brutal and violent assaults intended to overwhelm the opponent, to subtle attacks of finesse to trick the unwary. He even taught Tom stealth: how to conceal a long dagger under his doublet, then creep up silently behind an enemy and thrust it into his heart, killing him quickly and quietly. It was impressive to watch—and a little scary, too.

I managed to steal a few moments of training for myself on the tiltyard, though not with Sir William; I wasn't much good with a sword. Instead, I practiced with the twin pistols I kept now always on my belt, handles forward in imitation of Lord Ashcombe. Tom said once that I smelled of gunpowder.

"Nice, isn't it?" I said.

He made a face. "That's hardly what I meant."

As for Sally, she was getting a lot of training of her own.

With Isaac hobbled by arthritis and failing eyesight, he'd finally solved the problem of who would take over his duties by bringing her into the fold. It wasn't a traditional apprenticeship. There was no official record anywhere of Sally's appointment. She didn't sleep in her master's bookshop as a proper apprentice would. And except for me and Tom, no one else knew what she was really doing with her days in the city. When she borrowed one of Berkshire's carriages, she always told them she was going to care for an ailing man who had been a friend of her father's before she was orphaned.

And while she did look after Isaac—she helped him get about, took care of his home and shop, and ran the errands he found hard to do himself, like a true apprentice would— all the while, the bookseller gave her a rapid introduction to the skills she'd need to manage the secret alchemist library buried deep beneath his home, in what had once been a Templar vault.

First and foremost was learning languages. Sally's French was excellent, but she knew very little of anything else. So Isaac started with Latin and ancient Greek, saying once she'd got better at those, she'd get an introduction to Hebrew, Arabic, and Sanskrit.

As she'd only been at it a month, she was still learning the basics. One night, she came by my room and asked if I'd help her study. I accepted—rather quickly, according to a grinning Tom. So we passed several evenings, she and I, huddled over a book and a candle in the palace's library. I found it a little hard to study, sometimes. She sat awfully close. And she always smelled of cherries. I happen to like cherries. A lot.

We hadn't spoken about the kiss she'd given me the night of the ambush. But I thought about that a lot, too, and occasionally I'd catch her blushing, which made my own face grow warm. Sometimes she'd lean into me a little, then pull away as a servant came in to tidy the tables, or one of the lords came looking for a book. One time the king himself walked in. He looked inordinately pleased to see us together.

We rose as he came to greet us. "Sally, my dear," he said. "How delightful to see you."

"And you, Your Majesty," she said.

"You really must come by Whitehall more often. Have you visited the Privy Garden? I'm sure Christopher would be willing to accompany you on a walk."

When the king makes a suggestion, you follow it. So we

spent that evening enjoying the garden in the light of the torches and a nearly full moon. Just like in the library, Sally kept brushing her shoulder against my arm as we walked. We'd definitely have to do this more often. No doubt His Majesty had an ulterior motive, too. I swear I saw him grinning down at me from the balcony above the Stone Gallery.

Besides all that, Sally did something else I really appreciated: Not only did she look after Isaac, but she was caring for my pigeon, Bridget, too.

When the Raven sent me that box with Bridget inside, unhurt but covered in blood, it was horrible proof of just how much danger everyone I cared about was in. I didn't know if the Raven knew about Isaac and the secret library, but Isaac's bookshop was the only place that could truly be a safe haven. The main door was heavy oak, banded with iron. The few windows on the upper level were small and secured with steel bars that couldn't be pried out. As long as Isaac barred the door, no one was getting inside, no matter what.

So that's where I left Bridget. It broke my heart, because it meant I never got to see her, and I knew how much she loved flying in the open air. But her trusting nature left her more vulnerable than the rest of us. And with the Raven proving he was willing to hurt even a harmless, defenseless pigeon, I couldn't take the chance. Until all this was over, Isaac's was where she'd stay. Fortunately, Sally made sure Bridget was loved and even let her out in the vast space of the alchemist library to exercise her wings. Not the same as fresh air, but it was the best we could do.

In the meantime, Sally brought me whatever information Isaac could find. There were two other leads I thought he might be able to help with. The first was about the vault itself. As it had once been a Templar treasure room, it prompted the question: Was there something there that could help us learn about the Templars? Maybe find some way to contact them?

Isaac said no. The Templars had sold the vault three hundred years ago to the ancestors of the secret alchemist group Master Benedict would eventually become a part of. There were no records left of the knights of that time, and Isaac had never had any contact with the group. He hadn't even known they still existed until we'd returned from Paris and told him.

As for the second lead, in the Raven's first letter to me, he'd said he knew my master. *No doubt Benedict never told you about me,* the Raven wrote, *so I will: He was a thorn in my side for many years.* Well, Master Benedict had kept journals. Mostly, they documented his apothecary studies and experiments, but once in a while, he would comment on something else going on in his life. Isaac, who'd known my master for years, had offered to look through them to see if any of the entries prompted an idea of who the Raven was and why he held such a grudge.

We hadn't been able to find the journals for every year. Either Master Benedict hadn't kept them or they were tucked in among the giant mess of books around the house. That was why I'd gone back to Blackthorn yesterday, to search for more.

But two weeks ago, Isaac had sent Sally with a list of who he thought were the five best candidates for the Raven. These were men who'd quarreled with my master with enough viciousness that Isaac believed them capable of such violence. I recopied the list into my own handwriting, then gave it to Walsingham, telling him I'd culled it myself from my master's notes. Walsingham thought the list promising, so he'd ordered some of his agents to look into it.

I was wondering about that when the spymaster returned to the parlor, a scroll of paper in his hand.

"This is the list of individuals who attended the party," he said. "I shall begin investigating the finances of the possible traitors here."

"Did you want my help with that?"

"Not yet."

"What about that list I gave you?" I asked. "Possible suspects for the Raven, I mean."

"It has not proved fruitful."

My heart sank. Four of our possibilities—Robert Okey, Miles Bennet, Henry Corbet, and Samuel Skippon—had been apothecaries. The fifth, John Barkstead, was a politician, a member of Parliament who'd commanded a regiment against the king in the Civil Wars. "None of them could be the Raven?" I said.

"Three of the men are dead," Walsingham said. "Corbet died of natural causes many years ago. Bennet was a member of the Cult of the Archangel; he was executed last year. Barkstead was a regicide, put to death in 1662 for crimes against His Majesty's father.

"As for the others," he continued, "Robert Okey left London for Norwich some three years ago. The agent investigating him says he has a thriving practice there and has not left Norwich in over a year. As we can be certain the Raven was in Paris when you were there last November, it cannot be Okey."

"What about Samuel Skippon?" I said.

"He's a little more interesting. He abandoned London last year when the plague came. He reportedly left to start an apothecary shop in Gloucester, in the colony of Massachusetts."

I frowned. "Your agents confirmed this?"

"No. They confirmed that the dock's records say he boarded the *Howarth*, a galleon bound for the New World. Confirmation he is actually *in* the New World would take months."

"Then all we really know is that someone wrote that record down," I said. "It's no proof he went there instead of Paris."

"True. Yet I do not think it likely. What would be the point of such a deception? Remember, at the time, none of us knew the Raven even existed. Nor could he have possibly anticipated your trip to Paris or that you would foil his plans. There would be no reason to craft such a grand lie. No, I believe our best avenue forward will be to investigate the finances of those staying at Whitehall."

He folded the king's necklace and slipped it into his pocket. But the sparkle of the jewels in his hand prompted another idea in my mind.

Maybe . . . just maybe. "My lord?"

"Yes?"

"I think I might have one more lead," I said.

CHAPTER 13

THE SPYMASTER RAISED AN EYE-brow. "Do tell."

"That necklace," I said. "So far, we've been thinking that the people working for the Raven know what they're doing. That they're either his own agents and henchmen, like Rémi and Colette in Paris, or they're his allies, like the Covenanters."

"A reasonable assumption."

"For some of them, yes. The man who attacked me at Saint Paul's, the thieves who murdered the guards at Berkshire House—they had a purpose. But what about the ones working on the fringes? The boy who handed me the box with Bridget, for example. He didn't know what he was carrying. He simply got offered a penny from a gentleman to deliver the package to Blackthorn."

In the days afterward, I'd searched for that boy. I finally found him hanging about the edges of the Leadenhall Market, trying to scrounge up a farthing or two by offering to carry groceries. He wasn't alarmed to see me, because he had no idea what he'd done.

I'd hoped he could describe the man who had given him the package. But the boy said he never saw the man's face at all. A carriage had stopped beside him, and the man had offered him the package from within. The curtained windows and a hat tipped forward had shielded the man's face. The boy couldn't even tell me anything about the man's hands; he'd worn gloves.

"Then there's Elinor Bagley," I said. "Sure, she knew what she was doing was wrong. But she had no idea where that necklace came from or with whom she was dealing. The man who bribed her was wearing a mask. A *theater* mask.

"I told you, my lord, about the four who handed me the final letter, just before the ambush. They were in costume: an angel, a plague doctor, a knight, and a ghost. We'd assumed they were the Raven's agents, like the assassin in the cathedral. The thing is, though: Those were *good* costumes. They'd been made with care.

"So what if those four didn't know who the Raven was?" I said. "What if he'd just hired them to play those roles and hand that letter to me? What if they were nothing but *actors?*"

The spymaster studied my face. "An interesting hypothesis," he said eventually. "How do you propose to test it?"

"Well, like I said, those costumes were really good. They're not something you'd make at short notice, and definitely not something you'd throw away. So I was thinking: If we could find the costumes, maybe we could find the actors who wore them."

"And they might lead back to the Raven." He considered it a moment. Then he nodded. "A solid possibility. Investigate it."

"You don't want to send one of your agents?"

"You were the only one who saw the costumes," Walsingham said. "You were the only one who spoke to the men and woman wearing them. So you are the only one who could recognize if what you see is correct. Besides, Mr. Rowe, in case you haven't noticed, you *are* one of my agents."

That startled me. I supposed he was right; I really was an agent now. It was just, after all this time, I couldn't imagine myself as anything but an apothecary's apprentice.

Walsingham ignored my surprise. "There are several playhouses in the city," he said. "You will need to check every one. It may take some time."

"Yes, my lord."

"While you're in the city, I want you to call on your friend Simon Chastellain. He contacted Ashcombe late last week, saying a ship from France will dock today, which may have information about the Raven's time in Paris. See if that messenger has arrived yet."

"I'll grab Tom," I said. "We'll go right away."

"No." He stopped me. "We need to finish clearing your name with the court. We have already seen the Raven has allies inside the jails. You are not to leave the palace grounds until everything is settled."

I hadn't even thought about that. I'd assumed the ordeal was over once the king stepped in.

"Go tomorrow," Walsingham said. "And while you're out, return to Blackthorn. Examine the scene where the bodies of Wat and Sinclair were found. You may spot something of use."

"I'd have thought the constables would have cleared the area by now," I said.

"No doubt. Yet perhaps someone was sloppy. Or someone else spotted Mrs. Bagley's masked visitor. I expect you will find nothing. But you will certainly find nothing if you do not try."

A fair point. I left the spymaster in the parlor, staring once again at the hanging tapestry.

By the time I tracked down Tom, the king had already left with Lord Ashcombe for the play. But my heart skipped a beat at seeing our other guest.

"Christopher!" Sally jumped up from the settee and ran over to me. She hugged me, burying her face in my chest. Seriously, how did she always smell like cherries?

She stepped back to look me over. I wished she'd held on a little longer. "Are you all right?" she said. "Tom told me what happened. When they took you yesterday . . ."

"I'm fine," I said. "Just a little banged up."

"That's what you always say."

"Well, it's always true."

"And yet no one thinks this is a problem," Tom said.

"I didn't *ask* to be thrown in jail," I protested.

"Who does?" Tom rose, resigned. "So what terrible place is Lord Walsingham sending us now? A lion's den? The bottom of the sea?"

"The theater, actually."

"Really?" Sally said. "You know, there's a very funny play on at the Red Bull. You should take me."

"Uh . . ." I tried to ignore Tom grinning behind her. "That's not exactly what Lord Walsingham meant." I explained what had happened, and my theory about the Raven's messengers being played by actors. "He's ordered me to stay at the palace—"

"Someone here is showing some sense?" Tom said. "Surely I'm dreaming."

"I was going to say *until tomorrow*."

Tom sighed. "No, I'm awake."

"But seriously," I said, "tomorrow we'll start checking each of the theaters for those costumes. And hopefully find the people who were wearing them."

"That'll take a while."

"Which is why we get to rise nice and early."

"Oh come on. I *never* get to sleep in anymore."

"If you have a better idea," I said, "I'm all ears."

"Actually," Sally said suddenly, "I think I do."

CHAPTER
14

THE BANQUETING HOUSE WAS PACKED.

The last time Tom and I were here, it was empty. We'd been following a trail of clues we thought were warning us of danger, but were actually sent by the Raven to trick us. This was where he first threw suspicion on Domhnall Ardrey, making us think the baron was a traitor instead of a Templar.

Tonight was a happier occasion. Guests milled about in their finery, sipping wine from crystal glasses. A troupe of musicians stood at one end of the balcony, playing a Portuguese folia on viol, harpsichord, and recorder, no doubt in honor of our queen, Catherine of Braganza.

Below, a man in a silver jacket and a woman in a gold dress danced, wearing masks of Sun and Moon, their steps changing to match the rising tempo.

"Another party?" I'd said, when Sally had told me what she was thinking. "The king sure has a lot of them." This was the second already this week.

Sally spread her hands. "That's our Merry Monarch."

"I like them," Tom said.

"That's because you stuff your face at every one," I said.

He shrugged. "If they don't want me to eat all the chops, then they shouldn't make them in sauce."

The moment Tom and I arrived at the Banqueting House, he made good on his promise. He shot like an arrow to the tables where liveried servants laid out trays of steaming meats and sugary sweets. Tom heaped two plates before returning to join me.

"Thanks," I said.

"These are mine. Get your own."

". . . Really?"

"God gave me two hands," Tom said. "It would be a sin to deny His creation."

"Well spoken, young man," said a passing gentleman of enormous girth. Meanwhile, I pointed out a problem to Tom.

"How are you going to eat those with both hands full? No, don't," I said as he bent his head down to one of them. "You're not a horse."

"I suppose not," he said. "That would be interesting, though, wouldn't it? I wonder what being a horse is like."

I wasn't so sure the king was a good influence on him anymore. "We're here to work."

"*You're* here to work. I'm here for the cream puffs."

"Speaking of which, where is Sally? She said she'd meet us by the desserts—there she is."

There she was indeed. As if by command, the crowd parted, and Sally glided toward us. She wore a gown of silk, shimmering emerald green. A band of gold wrapped in lace tied her hair, auburn curls swept over one bare shoulder. A necklace sparkled against her skin.

I stared openly. She lowered her eyes with a smile. Maybe these parties weren't so bad after all.

Sally wasn't alone. A girl I'd never seen before walked with her, wearing a gown of gold with white ruffles around the border. Her necklace was a string of pearls; her earrings also pearls, shaped into teardrops. Her fair hair was parted in the middle, framing big, black eyes.

She was a year or so older than me. I could tell she

wasn't a lady; her dress, while pretty enough, lacked the refinement of the other ladies' gowns. Nonetheless, several of the guests seemed to know who she was and complimented her on her way through the crowd. When she and Sally arrived where Tom and I stood, the girl looked me up and down in frank appraisal.

"Christopher," Sally said. "I'd like to introduce you to Nell. Nell Gwyn."

Oh—she was famous. Nell was an actress. She'd started out as an orange-girl, selling sweet China oranges to theatergoers for sixpence each, until she started getting cast in various comedies. She'd quickly won over audiences, rising to prominence in higher circles.

Like this one. During the Interregnum, the Puritans had closed most of the playhouses. King Charles had lifted those bans upon his return to the throne. Now the theater scene was popular, especially among the nobility.

Tonight, the king had invited the cast of *The Parson's Wedding*, and "witty, pretty Nell," as she'd been called, had come with them. I was a little surprised to see how familiar Sally and she were; it was obvious they'd met before. No doubt at one of the king's endless parties.

Nell held out her hand. I took it, bowing slightly. "A pleasure to meet you, Miss Gwyn."

"Likewise," she said. "Sally's told me so much about you. I feel we're already friends." She gave me a particularly bold smile, which made my face grow warm.

"And this is—" Sally broke off. "Oh, Tom, please tell me both those plates aren't for you."

"Of course not." He held one out to Nell. "Chop in sauce?"

"Er . . . perhaps later," she said. She turned back to me. "Sally mentioned you had something you wanted to ask."

"Yes," I said. "About a month ago, I saw a . . . street performance. Near Saint Paul's. It was a cast of four: three men and one woman. They were very entertaining. I thought I might hire them for a private show."

"Do you know which company they're part of?" Nell said.

"I'm afraid not. But they had really distinctive costumes. I thought maybe you might have seen them before."

I gave her every detail I could remember of that night. She scrunched her brow, thinking.

"The ghost and the angel could be anyone," she said finally. "A Templar knight . . . I don't think I've seen one in any wardrobe. But the plague doctor . . . I could swear . . . wait. Yes."

She brightened. "I know exactly where to go."

WEDNESDAY, APRIL 7, 1666

Justice was the aim of my Creator;
To build me was the task of divine power,
Supreme wisdom, and eternal love.

CHAPTER
15

IT WAS A BLEARY-EYED KIND OF MORNING.

The party had gone late into the night, as the king liked.
Time meant nothing to him, of course, since he could get
up whenever he chose. For the rest of us, it meant dry eyes,
and heads feeling like they'd been stuffed with cotton. My
gut was protesting, too. It wasn't so much the chops in sauce
Tom kept foisting on me as the absolute raid we'd made on
the sweets. I ate so much honey, I didn't think I could ever
look a bee in the face again.

Tom's iron stomach spared him the day-after troubles,
as usual. But he always grumbled at rising early, and today
was no exception.

"Mnnggh," he said, and covered his head with his pillow. "You promised you wouldn't wake me until seven."

"It's seven thirty," I said.

"Stop telling lies."

To his dismay, it really was seven thirty. He dragged himself out of bed. "Let me have breakfast, at least."

Even the thought of eating made me sick. We stopped by the kitchen for Tom to grab three turkey pies, which he juggled as we saddled Blossom and Lightning and headed off to Berkshire House. Sally had said she wanted to come, which I was glad for.

She was already up, waiting by the carriage Lord Clarendon had given over to her use. "Don't you two look a pretty portrait," she said.

"I'm fine," Tom said, stuffing the last bit of pie in his mouth. "He's the one that kept getting up in the night."

"I told you to stop eating," Sally said. "Four sticky buns, Christopher, really."

"I thought it was six," Tom said.

I tried to shush him. "It's . . . whatever. I couldn't sleep. Bad dreams."

"Again?" Tom said, frowning.

"It's nothing. Can we stop talking about this?"

I was glad when they let it go. We headed out. Our first stop: north of Covent Garden Market.

The Cockpit theater was a house in decline. Once a staging area for cockfights—that was how it had got its name—it had been converted to an indoor playhouse some fifty years ago. Like many of London's theaters, its troubles had begun during the Interregnum, when Puritan soldiers raided the playhouse during a performance and imprisoned all the actors.

When the king returned to the throne in 1660, the Cockpit's owners hoped their theater would once again stage great plays. But the two most important acting troupes—the King's Company and the Duke's Company—moved their productions to newer, more fashionable venues. When the Theatre Royal opened on nearby Drury Lane, the Cockpit simply couldn't compete.

The place showed it. It was in desperate need of repainting, the old colors faded. Inside the front door, the steps down into the seats were chipped, the slabs wobbling. I wondered how many patrons had taken a tumble.

This morning, the stage was the only section of the theater that was lit. The set was half built with a garden backdrop, trees already in place on the right. A burly man with rolled-up sleeves grabbed another tree from a pile near the back steps and lugged it across the floorboards.

"Excuse me, sir?" I said.

He nearly dropped his tree. "What? Who's there?" he said, startled.

"Apologies," I said. "We're looking for George Gifford."

"That's me." He put the tree down gently, adjusting its position with care. When he was satisfied, he turned and squinted, trying to see who addressed him. "If you're look-ing for work, I don't have any. All the roles are filled, and I already have plenty of—oh."

He broke off as we came into the light. He'd spied our clothes. In particular, his eyes fell on the sword strapped to Tom's back, and the twin pistols in my belt. The only posi-tive thing about my arrest was that, since I'd been refilling the vials in my apothecary sash, I'd taken both it and my pistols off, so I wasn't wearing them when captured. If I'd had them on when the constable nabbed me, I'd have never seen them again.

As only guards and lords were permitted to walk around the city armed—and I was obviously no guard—the actor took me for a noble and changed his tune. "My apologies, young sir. I couldn't see you in the darkness. How may I be of service?"

No doubt he was hoping for a commission of some sort—which was exactly what I wanted him to believe. "It looks like you're setting up for a show," I said. "Is your company booked at the moment?"

"A short production of *Love and Honour*." He slapped his hands to shake off the dust. "We open tomorrow night. But if you have need of a most excellent band of players, I assure you, we can accommodate whatever you require." He'd already begun his performance trying to sell me his troupe, theatrical voice and everything.

"I've written a play," I said, trying to sound like I knew what I was talking about. "A tragedy of sorts, set in the time of the Black Death. I'd like to hire you to show it."

I jingled the coin purse Lord Ashcombe had given me for expenses. Gifford eyed it eagerly.

"Absolutely, young sir," he said. "Do you have the play with you? I'd be keen to look it over."

"I have some questions first. I was hoping to stage the performance soon. And I don't want any cheap-looking costumes. Which means you'd have to have what I want already on hand."

"Then you've come to the right place, sir. We have an extensive wardrobe, collected over fifty years of productions. If you could tell me what you're looking for, I'm sure I already have it."

"Excellent," I said. "First, it's a plague story, so obviously we'll need a plague doctor, with the mask and everything. Then we'll need a crusader knight. The tragedy is that he loses his beautiful young wife, she becomes a ghost, and he pleads with an angel to bring her back from heaven."

Gifford started out nodding, commenting as I spoke. "We have a plague doctor. . . . I've played a knight myself. . . . It's not hard to costume a ghost, just makeup and . . ."

He trailed off.

His eyes widened slightly as he peered at me. We stood a moment in silence.

"You know," he said thoughtfully, "It just occurred to me . . . I'm afraid I won't be able to help. We probably—I mean, we do need to focus on *this* production for the moment, you see. . . ."

He'd recognized me. And that made me realize I recognized him, too. When he said he'd played a crusader knight before, it knocked something loose in my memory.

This was the man who'd dressed up as the Templar. The

knight had worn a beard, and this man was clean-shaven, but the voice was the same.

"You know who I am," I said.

"Me? No. No, not at all. I'm sorry, I hate to be rude, but I really have to finish the set—"

"Yes, you said you had your first performance when, tomorrow?"

"That's right."

"So you wouldn't have time to make new scenery before then."

"No, but . . . why would I need new scenery?"

"Tom?" I said. "Think that sword of yours can chop down a tree?"

Tom drew Eternity from her scabbard. "Rather easily, I'd wager."

Gifford's eyes went wide. "Now wait. Wait a minute—"

"As for me," I said, drawing one of my pistols, "what do you bet I can hit that statue from here?"

"Oh, can I have a try?" Sally said.

"Of course." I handed her my second gun. "Whoever shoots off the biggest piece wins. Er . . . I'd move if I were you, Mr. Gifford."

"No! Stop!" he cried.

I lowered my pistol. "Are you prepared to tell us the truth?"

"I don't . . . there's no . . . I don't know who you are—"

"Aim for the nose," I told Sally. "Use the bead as your sight, like this."

He looked frantically between the mad children with the guns and the giant with the sword, about to hack his future into kindling. "Why are you doing this?" he wailed. "We meant you no offense!"

"No *offense*?" I said. "Do you have any idea what trouble you caused? Why did you hand me that letter?"

"I was paid to," he said, confused. "Commanded to, actually."

"Commanded? By whom?"

"Why, His Majesty, of course," he said.

CHAPTER
16

I STARED AT HIM IN DISBELIEF.

"His Majesty? King *Charles*?"

Gifford looked baffled. "Who else?"

"You spoke to the king?" Sally said.

"What? No, of course not."

"Then explain yourself," I said.

Gifford relaxed a little as we lowered our weapons. "Our instructions were plain," he said. "We were told that the king was very pleased with a young lord in his service—er, you—and he wished to create a masquerade for your entertainment. We were told there were certain puzzles involved and that you'd be solving them around the city with the help of letters and clues."

Tom and Sally looked just as startled as I was.

"Our job was to play the role of apparitions you encountered in the alley," Gifford said. "We were given specific instructions about how to dress and ordered to follow them to the finest detail. We were then to wait for you in the alley. Once you appeared, we were to ask you, over and over again, 'Do you have a coin?' Then, when you showed it to us, I was to hand you that letter and say 'You must hurry. Time is running out.' So that's what we did."

He described it exactly as I remembered. "Do you know what the coin I showed you was?"

"We were told it would be gold," he said. "Beyond that, he said nothing."

"Who said? And how do you know he was speaking for the king?"

Gifford looked surprised at that. "The message was delivered by Lord Arthur Pembry."

"Who?"

"The Earl of Branstoke. Surely he wouldn't fabricate such a tale?"

Arthur Pembry, Earl of Branstoke. I'd never heard of him. But my heart beat a little faster at his name.

Was it possible Mr. Gifford had just handed us our traitor?

Tom wouldn't know Pembry any more than I would. But Sally might. As the king's ward, she spent a lot more time in the upper circles. She shook her head slightly at my look and asked, "Can you describe the earl?"

Puzzled, Gifford said, "Shortish man. He was wearing tall heels, but his actual height was at least four inches less than mine. Slight build—a little gaunt, even. Perhaps forty years old. He has a mole on his neck, here, near the clavicle." He pointed at his own collarbone to show me the spot.

Gifford's description of Arthur Pembry revealed the eye of an experienced actor, practiced in studying the traits and mannerisms of the people around him. The details would be extremely helpful. It was possible, of course, that whoever had delivered the "king's" message wasn't the actual Earl of Branstoke, or had used an entirely false name. But this was a better lead than any we'd uncovered before.

Something else occurred to me. "You said you were paid. How much?"

"Thirty pounds," Gifford said.

He sounded almost embarrassed by the amount, and with good reason. Thirty pounds was an outlandishly large sum for an easy evening's work. But it made his story very credible. First, who but a king would pay so generously for something like this? And second, the overpayment perfectly fit Walsingham's hypothesis of how the Raven got others to do his bidding so easily.

"We'll check on this," I said, both as a farewell and a warning.

I guessed then that Gifford *was* telling the truth, because, worried, he stopped us. "Does this mean there's to be no patronage?"

"What are you talking about?"

"It wasn't just money I was promised. The earl said if we did a good job, the king would award us a license to perform serious works." He waved at the set pieces on the stage. "I've gone into debt. . . . I staked my whole theater on it."

His face fell when he saw my expression. I didn't even have to speak for him to realize he'd been tricked. I suddenly felt bad about the way I'd threatened him earlier. Like so many of the Raven's dupes, he hadn't known any better.

"I'm sorry," I said.

He sat on the stage, cradling his head in his hands.

CHAPTER 17

I WANTED TO HURRY BACK TO THE palace and tell Walsingham what we'd discovered. But he'd ordered me to collect the message about the Raven from Simon and also to examine the crime scene behind my house, so I needed to take care of that first. We continued north to Great Russell Street, where Simon had found new lodgings.

When he'd first arrived in London, Simon had been stabbed in the back by one of the Raven's assassins just outside my home. I'd taken him in, letting him stay in my bed to recover. I'd tried to convince him to remain at Blackthorn until he was healed.

But when the Raven sent me the box with Bridget drenched in blood, Simon was appalled. He'd believed the Raven was dead. It was all I could do to stop him from leaping out of bed and hunting him down. As it was, he refused to stay at Blackthorn any longer. On this, he wouldn't be budged.

"I'm clearly a danger to you here," he fumed. "And I can't protect myself, either."

He'd moved to a large house rented in the fashionable and growing Bloomsbury district northwest of the city. He took his brutish bodyguard, Henri, for protection. He also arranged for another six servants to stay in the house with them—two of them brutes themselves.

I worried about those new men. The Raven was adept at placing agents among the servants anywhere he pleased. But Simon knew how to foil that.

"You forget that while I am French," he said, "I spent most of my life here in England, in Nottinghamshire. Except for Henri, everyone in this house is a longtime servant brought down from my family's estate. I trust them all with my life."

Given the Raven's skill at bribery, that didn't reassure me. Yet when I protested, Simon asked a very good question.

"Well, who *can* we trust?" he said, frustrated. "Can you guarantee anyone? Even the King's Men?"

I couldn't.

And the thought gave me a chill.

I hadn't been to visit Simon much. As guilty as he felt about bringing trouble to me, I felt the same about him. Maybe we were both being silly; after all, the Raven already knew we were friends. But I couldn't get his taunt out of my head.

I am going to make you suffer. I will do this by taking away the things you love, one by one, until there is only you and me.

The Raven's words weighed on me day and night. I slumped in my saddle as we rode, feeling every lost minute of sleep. The more often I came here, the more danger Simon would be in.

Fortunately, he had a new companion in London. Dr. John Kemp, who'd arrived from Newcastle in the wake of last year's plague, had taken up residence at the Missing Finger, the inn across from my home. A former soldier, Kemp was the physician who'd stitched Simon up after the assassin had stuck a dagger in his back. Kemp and Simon had taken to each other, and soon the two spent more time talking, playing games, and drinking brandy than tending to Simon's wounds.

Both the medical care and the friendship continued after Simon moved. I was glad, and not just because I wanted Simon to have someone looking after him. While our French vicomte was a hothead, the doctor was a calming influence. If it wasn't for Kemp, Simon would already be rampaging around town.

The doctor was there when we arrived. Daniel, the oldest of Simon's servants, let us in and directed us up to Simon's bedroom. We passed Henri, who was lounging in the hall, chewing a piece of straw like a toothpick. We said hello. He grunted.

Upstairs, Simon and Kemp were playing cards. Simon was lying in bed on his stomach, Dr. Kemp in a chair beside him. Each had their usual dram of brandy on the bedside table. A mix of English and French coins lay scattered on the bedsheets; they were gambling.

"Christopher!" Simon's face lit up. "Tom and Sally, too! Come in, come in. Daniel, some chairs for our guests, please. Join us, we'll deal another hand."

"I wouldn't, if I were you," Dr. Kemp said to us. "The Frenchman cheats. As do all of his sort."

"The Englishman lies," Simon said. "As do all of *his* sort. Er . . . with apologies, friends."

It was all in good fun. Daniel returned with two other servants: Mary, a pretty girl of around seventeen, and Michael, who was nearly as large as Henri, though he smelled much better. Each carried a comfortable chair.

"No need for them all," Dr. Kemp said, standing. "One of you can use mine."

"Out of money again, Kemp?" Simon said.

"Don't worry, vicomte. I'll steal some silverware on the way out."

Simon laughed—then cut off quickly with a grimace of pain.

Dr. Kemp sighed. "Are you going to listen to me or not?"

"Yes, yes, doctor. Leave me alone."

Simon said it with humor, but there was an edge to his voice. As Dr. Kemp donned his waistcoat, he called for his apprentice, and Jack, a quiet boy of sixteen, came up the stairs. We exchanged pleasant hellos as Jack collected the doctor's things, and then I noticed something curious.

The boy's shirt cuffs were wet, like he'd just been washing his hands. That in itself wouldn't have meant anything. But I also noticed there was blood on one of the sleeves.

Again, that was hardly a surprise; both the doctor and his apprentice would naturally get blood on themselves through the normal course of their duties.

Except this blood was bright crimson. Which meant it was fresh.

Jack had got blood on himself *here*. And as I thought of Kemp's resigned tone, and the edge to Simon's voice, I started to get alarmed.

Had Kemp operated on Simon *again*?

A month after the stabbing, Simon's back should have been entirely healed. "What—"

Dr. Kemp cut me off. "Good to see you as always, young master apothecary. In fact, your arrival reminds me: I need more of your honey balm. Will you be at your shop anytime soon?"

He sounded casual enough, but he gave me a meaning-ful look. The doctor wanted to speak to me—in private.

"Actually, we're going there this morning," I said, also trying to sound casual.

"Excellent. I'll await you at the Missing Finger."

Sally must have caught the doctor's look, because when she asked Simon, "How are you feeling?" it came with more than the usual interest.

"I'm fine," he near growled. "You didn't come here to mother me, too, did you?"

"Not at all," she said. But as Simon winced reaching for the cards, Sally stepped in to collect them. Tom scooped up the coins and dumped them into a bowl beside the bed.

"We're not going to play?" Simon said, annoyed. "You want me to die of boredom, then?"

"Sorry," I said. "I wish this were a social call. I'm actually on an errand for—" I almost said *Lord Walsingham*, but I'd been ordered to keep my new apprenticeship to the spymaster a secret. The only one I'd told outside the palace was Isaac.

"For Lord Ashcombe," I finished. "He said you contacted him about a message from Paris?"

"Ah. Yes."

A letter rested on the nightstand. Simon reached for it and immediately grunted in pain.

Sally, sitting beside him, gave him an innocent look. "Would you like me to get that for you? I wouldn't want to mother."

He glared at her—then broke into a sheepish grin. "My apologies. To all of you," he said. "I am . . . frustrated."

Sally passed me the letter.

"There's not as much in it as I'd hoped," Simon said. "Though perhaps it will still be useful."

Simon had already broken the seal. Inside was a short letter, written in French.

"It's not from Paris," he said. "It's from the Val de Loire. You remember the vicomte I told you about, Guy d'Auzon? He shot Rémi, when Rémi and Colette attacked him?"

I nodded. When Simon had heard about it, he'd gone to see Rémi's body. At that time, we'd all thought Rémi was the Raven.

"After we learned the Raven was still alive," Simon said, "I wrote to d'Auzon, warning him. I also asked him if he'd ever caught Rémi doing anything that in retrospect might have seemed suspicious. Or if he'd ever seen Rémi speaking to a stranger. As it turns out, he had. D'Auzon said he twice saw Rémi speaking to a man out near the barn. A man he'd never seen before on his farm."

I sat up. "What did the man look like?"

"He doesn't remember. D'Auzon saw him only from the back and didn't pay him much attention at the time. In his defense, there wouldn't have been any reason to do so. He thought the man was a trader, come to discuss the sale of the milk."

Inwardly, I cursed. Once again, we'd run into that problem Sally had long ago pointed out: No one ever pays attention to servants.

"If d'Auzon didn't know who the man was," Sally said, "why does he remember him at all?"

"Ah. That's the interesting part. He overheard very little of the conversation, but what he did hear stuck in his mind. The man spoke French fluently, which, of course, is hardly remarkable. But his style of French was very formal. What's more, d'Auzon thought he might have had a slight accent. An *English* accent.

"Now, it's not unheard of for English traders to travel through France, even in the countryside. But we may have actually discovered something interesting here. If Rémi's unknown contact *was* the Raven—"

"Then we know the Raven can't be French," I said. "He's *English*."

"Who speaks formal Parisian French," Simon said. "If that's true, then we know even more about him. The Raven isn't just an Englishman. He's an English *noble*."

CHAPTER
18

MY MIND WAS CHURNING.

An English noble, I thought.

Could it be true?

The notion that we might have stumbled on a new clue to the Raven's identity made my blood race. Yet I couldn't help but think of Walsingham's warning about assumptions leading us down the wrong path.

It was true that formal French would fit an English noble's education. And Master Benedict wasn't the type to have been cowed by a title; he could certainly have made a bitter enemy of one of the peerage.

But the nobility weren't the only ones who might learn

that style of French. Any well-educated person would learn a more formal sort of speech. In fact, my own education, both at Cripplegate orphanage and with Master Benedict, had tended toward that. D'Auzon could have heard me speaking like the man he'd overheard and would have thought we came from the same place.

But an English accent *did* mean an Englishman. If the man who visited d'Auzon's farm was the Raven, then we'd just narrowed down our list. Not to the point of identifying him, maybe, but to know the Raven was a fellow countryman cut out a lot of possible suspects.

So I counted this a small victory. I tucked the letter under my doublet. "Sorry we have to go," I said. "Lord Ashcombe is waiting for this. I promise we'll have a proper visit soon."

"If boredom hasn't carried me to the grave," Simon said wryly.

We said our goodbyes. I hesitated at the door, thinking of that blood on Jack's shirt. "Are you sure you're all right?" I said.

"*Go* already." The edge returned to Simon's voice. "If I want a lecture, I'll call for Dr. Kemp."

• • •

I forced us to pick up the pace on our way to Blackthorn. I needed to find out what was really going on with Simon. And only Dr. Kemp could tell me what it was.

It was the strangest feeling, going home. Before, I'd always welcomed the sight of Blackthorn. Though I missed Master Benedict terribly, I had such good memories of the time we'd had together. Being surrounded by his things made me feel like he wasn't really gone.

The Raven had ruined that. He'd stained my memories by attacking Simon here, then bruised them even worse by hurting Bridget. Now that she was locked up at Isaac's, for the first time, Blackthorn truly felt empty.

And I hated that.

This isn't yours, I thought. *I won't let you take it. No matter what I have to do. This I swear.* Shouting defiance, even in my own head, made me feel a little better. Not much, but for the moment, it would have to be enough.

Tom and I left our horses with Sally's coachman, and all three of us went inside. "Do we need anything from here?" Tom asked.

"You didn't find any more of Master Benedict's journals the day I was arrested, did you?" I said.

Tom shook his head.

"Why don't you look for them, then? I have to go out the back and see if the Raven's left any clues."

"Oh, no," Tom said. "I'm coming with you this time."

"Yes, he is," Sally said firmly. "I'll look for the journals. And if Master Benedict has other books that will help with my studies with Isaac, can I borrow them?"

"Of course," I said. "Anything that's mine is yours."

She went upstairs.

"That's good," Tom said.

"What's good?" I said.

"You should get used to sharing your things with Sally."

I punched him in the arm. He laughed.

The alley at the back was empty.

Normally, I wouldn't have thought anything of it. Now, however, the silence seemed sinister. As if the air itself had changed.

Mr. Sinclair died here, I thought.

As for Wat . . . I'd been trying not to think about him since we'd seen his body in the palace. But I couldn't stop the memories coming back now. Every image I had of him rushed into my head.

Wat smirking by the window when Master Benedict

slapped me to make the Cult of the Archangel believe I knew nothing of what they wanted.

Wat and the apothecary Nathaniel Stubb tearing apart my home.

Wat and the other apprentices, Martin and the Elephant—I never did learn that one's name—trapping me at Blackfriars, in the Apothecaries' Guild.

And finally, the worst of the memories. Wat looming above me, down in the alchemists' secret laboratory. His face melted by fire, clothes still smoking—

Master Benedict broke through the image. *Wat's gone,* he said in my head. *You don't have to worry about him anymore.*

He deserved it, I said. *He deserved everything he got for taking you away.*

Let it go, child. Let it go and grant yourself some peace.

He was right. As usual. What I needed more than anything was to keep Master Benedict in my heart. And rid Wat from my mind for good. "So let's get this done," I muttered.

"Pardon?" Tom said.

"Nothing."

We searched the alley. It was a good place for a murder. The narrow path and high buildings kept it shadowed even in daylight, offering plenty of dark corners where the Raven could hide.

The bodies had been carted away days ago. But two dried, dark brown splotches still stained the stones behind Mr. Ralston's grocery. I guess no one had bothered to wash away the two victims' blood.

No—only one victim, I thought. Wat was dead well before he was brought to the alley. He wouldn't have still been bleeding. Which meant the second stain was deliberately left by the Raven, so the lack of blood under Wat's body wouldn't look odd. He'd clearly thought out just how to frame me. I wondered: How had he drawn Mr. Sinclair into the alley? And was Sinclair chosen on purpose? Or was the man taken at random?

You're missing something, Master Benedict said.

I did have a nagging feeling there was something important here. But I was so *tired*, and trying to make my sleep-deprived mind work was like trying to peer through heavy fog. I slapped my cheeks a couple of times to try to wake myself, but it was no use. I couldn't think.

I stared up at the windows of Elinor Bagley's sister's house. If only that woman had been a true witness instead of a crook.

· · ·

With no more clues to discover, we went back inside. Sally called down the stairs. "Find anything?"

"Not really." I turned to Tom. "Why don't you go upstairs and help her look for the missing journals? I need to talk to Dr. Kemp about Simon."

Tom looked annoyed. "How many times do I have to say it? I'm staying with you."

"Actually, that's a good idea. Dorothy will be working now. I'm sure she'd love to see you."

Tom paused. Dorothy, the innkeeper's daughter, had a thing for him. "Er . . . do we really have to?"

I grinned, ready to drag him along, when fate spared him. The bell on the front door rang as Dr. Kemp, having seen our mounts outside, came into the shop.

"You're lucky today," I said to Tom.

He breathed a sigh of relief. "Should have played cards with Simon after all," he said, and he went upstairs.

Dr. Kemp looked around the room. I'd barely had the chance to speak to him since Simon moved out. "Nice to see you back," Kemp said.

"Well . . . I'm not really back. Not yet."

"Are you feeling well?"

"Me?" I said, surprised. "Why?"

"You look a little worn down. And your eyes are red."

"Oh. I haven't . . . I don't sleep much, these days."

"Bad dreams?"

I paused. I'd expected him to say something about me being too busy. Instead, he'd guessed right. "It happens."

"Something in particular bothering you?"

Yes, there was. But I didn't want to talk about it. It was stupid, I know, but I had the terrible sense that if I said what troubled me out loud, it might just make it come true.

So I changed the subject. "What's going on with Simon? He looks worse than ever."

"You noticed." Kemp leaned on the counter. "What's 'going on' is that our favorite Frenchman is an idiot."

If I hadn't known how blunt the good doctor could be—and how stubborn Simon was—I might have been offended on the vicomte's behalf. As it was, I had to agree. "His wound isn't healing?" I said.

"It would if he'd stop acting the fool. Instead, he's torn his stitches. *Again*. That's three times now."

"Simon's not the sort to sit around and do nothing," I said ruefully.

"Not sitting around is one thing," Dr. Kemp said. "Swordplay is another."

I blinked. "Swordplay?"

"Did you know that two of those servants he brought from Nottinghamshire aren't actually servants? They're guards."

Simon had told me that. Though I wasn't sure how much he'd revealed to Kemp. "Someone did try to murder him a month ago," I pointed out.

"And guards are perfectly normal for a lord like him, yes. Except they're not standing around keeping watch. He's been sparring with them."

"What?"

"Just what I said. It wasn't only the stitches he tore. He's reinjured his back."

Oh, Simon. "How bad is it?"

"Very. Do you know what's going on?"

I hesitated. The more people we brought into our troubles, the bigger the chance they'd become targets for the Raven. "What's Simon told you?"

Kemp snorted. "About as little as you have. Simon said an old enemy he thought was dead is still alive. That's who was responsible for the attempt on his life. And apparently, this same man was also behind the ambush on the king at Barnham Wood."

The assassination attempt, and the explosion at Niall Ramsay's house, where the Raven had eliminated the Templars, were events too big to keep quiet. The palace had blamed both on Covenanter rebels, and all the news pamphlets had printed that story—along with calls for reprisals against Scotland. Only Lords Ashcombe and Walsingham and the king knew of the Raven's involvement. And only Tom, Sally, and Isaac knew the London Templars were all dead.

I shook my head. Simon really shouldn't have told Dr. Kemp that the Raven was tied to the ambush. If that got out, it would be dangerous. Most of all to the good doctor.

"You haven't spoken to anyone else about it, have you?" I said, trying to sound casual.

Dr. Kemp gave me a wry look. "I know when secrets should be kept. I don't really care, either way. I'm concerned about my patient. Because Simon told me in no uncertain terms that he will bury his sword in this man's guts if it's the last thing he does. And if I try to stop him, I need not visit his house again."

That was Simon, the hothead. I tried to explain. "It's not just the attempt on his life. This . . . man . . . murdered his uncle."

Kemp shrugged. "I have no objection to revenge. If the

man deserves it, send him to the devil. But the longer that wound remains unhealed, the greater the risk of reinfection. If the wound gets truly foul, it'll go into his abdomen. I don't have to tell you what that means."

"Have you seen signs of deeper infection?" I said, worried.

"Not yet. But I've been slathering that honey balm on the wound like I've been buttering the king's bread."

That reminded me; Kemp had said he needed more. I gave him the last of my stock, a single pot. At the rate the doctor was using it, that wouldn't last a week. I sighed. I needed to make another batch. Though God only knew when I'd get the time.

"This will help," Dr. Kemp said, "but as I said, infection isn't the only danger. Simon's sword practice has retorn the muscle in his back. It's hanging together by a thread at this point."

"What happens if he tears it completely?" I said, not wanting the answer.

"He won't be able to stand. He'll be in excruciating pain for the rest of his life—what little of it will remain. I've never seen anyone with an injury like that survive for long."

The doctor tucked the honey balm away in his jacket. "Whatever powers of persuasion you can bring to bear, Christopher, I'd use every one. Because if Simon doesn't stop all this nonsense, I promise you: He will die."

CHAPTER
19

AFTER DR. KEMP LEFT, I LINGERED
in the shop, totally lost as to what to do.

Simon's wrath could be frightening. The very first
time we'd met, when he'd thought I was an assassin come
to kill the French king, Simon had put a sword to my guts
and threatened to run me through if I didn't tell him the
truth.

He'd been perfectly apologetic about it afterward. But
when Simon's fury ran high, he wouldn't listen to reason. I
knew I couldn't get him to stop chasing the Raven. The best
I could do was keep him in the dark. I promised myself I'd
tell him nothing of what we learned from now on.

The bell above the door dragged me from my thoughts again. I half expected Dr. Kemp with more bad news. So I was pleased instead to see Dorothy, the innkeeper's daughter.

She, on the other hand, looked worried. "Is everything all right, Christopher?"

"Yes. Why wouldn't it be?"

"I heard you were arrested."

Oh. Of course. I should have realized word would get around. Elinor Bagley had probably told her lies to the whole parish. "A misunderstanding," I said. "A *big* misunderstanding. All a mistake."

She sighed, relieved. "I knew it was. You wouldn't hurt anyone."

That's not exactly true, I thought. And if I'd gone to trial, her sentiments wouldn't have swayed the court one bit. But I found myself deeply grateful that she said it.

Dorothy and I had never been close, exactly. She was nearly three years older than me, and though we'd lived across from each other ever since Master Benedict had taken me in, our duties kept us busy. I'd mostly spoken to her only when my master took us to the Missing Finger for the occasional stew or slab of roast beef.

But she'd always been friendly to me. I was almost surprised to realize how much it mattered that someone who didn't know the real truth believed in me anyway.

"I'm glad we're friends," I said.

She smiled, flattered. "Me, too."

I'd once told the king that Dorothy was pretty, when I'd revealed to him that she'd been chasing Tom. And she was. But Tom had told me afterward that what he most wanted was something else. *A kind girl, who'll make a kind home,* he'd said. I'd always teased him about Dorothy, and he'd never really considered her. Now I was starting to think maybe he should.

"It isn't true about Mr. Sinclair, is it?" she asked. "Was he really one of the men who were murdered?"

I nodded. "He died in the alley behind his shop."

She bit her lip. "Is this something to do with what's happening to you?"

I hesitated. "Why would you think that?"

"Well . . . your friend was stabbed outside, last month. And you're staying at the palace now."

Dorothy knew I'd been keeping company with Lord Ashcombe. What she didn't know was why. And I had no intention of telling her, for the same reason I wanted

Dr. Kemp kept out of it. Even talking to her could make her a target for the Raven.

So what she asked next gave me a chill. "Did Mr. Sinclair find you before he died?"

"Find . . . *me*?" I said. "For what?"

"He wanted to talk to you about something."

"What about?"

"I don't know. He didn't say."

I frowned. "Tell me everything that happened."

Dorothy started from the beginning. "Mr. Sinclair came back to London early that morning. I saw him arrive through the window, and I was going to say welcome back, but the dining room was so busy, I sort of forgot about him until around noon. That's when I saw him step out of his shop. He looked . . . I don't know. Puzzled? Like something unexpected had happened, and he didn't know what to make of it."

"What did he do?"

"At first?" she said. "Nothing. He just stood there in the doorway, looking down the street. Like he was watching something. Or someone, maybe."

My heart thumped a little. Had Mr. Sinclair seen that masked man Elinor said had threatened her? "Did you see who?"

"No. But after a minute, Mr. Sinclair went to your shop. He tried the door, but it was locked, of course. He peered through the shutters, trying to see inside. Then he came to the Missing Finger. I said hello, but he seemed kind of distracted. He asked if you were around. I told him you were staying elsewhere at the moment. I wasn't sure if you wanted people to know you were at Whitehall." She paused, wondering if that was correct.

"You did the right thing," I assured her. "What happened next?"

"I told him you did stop by every once in a while, and if I saw you, I'd let you know he was looking for you. I asked if there was something I could help with, and he said no. Then he went back home. And then . . . well."

I stood there, mind racing.

"Christopher?"

"Sorry. Just thinking. Thanks for telling me. But, um . . . look, please don't take this the wrong way, but I think you should stay away from me and Blackthorn for a while."

Dorothy was shocked by my request. "Why? What's going on here?"

"I can't tell you that," I said. "Still . . . I'm sure you've noticed a lot of bad things have been happening lately. Especially to people around me."

"Like your friend Simon," she said slowly. "And Mr. Sinclair."

"Like that." I sighed. "You've been very kind to me. You deserve to be safe. So . . . stay away. Please? For me?"

She regarded me for a moment. Then she nodded and went to the door. She turned before she opened it. "So many awful things have happened to you this past year," she said. "You are going to be all right, aren't you?"

I lied. "Sure."

She left.

Once she'd gone, I ran upstairs. Tom and Sally were sitting on the floor in one of the spare rooms stuffed with books, sorting through the piles.

"Anything?" I asked.

"No journals yet," Sally said. "But we've barely touched this stack."

"Forget it. We need to go back to Whitehall."

Tom sprang to his feet. "What's happened?"

I told them what Dorothy had said.

"I don't understand," Tom said. "Mr. Sinclair was looking for you. What does that mean?"

"It means maybe we were wrong about his murder," I said. "I don't think he was murdered to frame me. I think the Raven killed Mr. Sinclair because he saw something he shouldn't have."

CHAPTER
20

LORD WALSINGHAM WAS AT HIS
desk. When I arrived, he was peering carefully through a
magnifying lens at a parchment. He made no comment at
my somewhat disheveled state, just bade me take the chair
opposite him. I smoothed my hair and sat down.

As usual, the spymaster wasted no time with pleasant-
ries. "So?"

I launched right in to what I'd discovered. The conversation with Dorothy fresh on my mind, I started with the
fact that Mr. Sinclair had been looking for me when he was
murdered.

"Interesting." Walsingham placed the lens on the desk.

"Was the confectioner in the habit of checking on you?"

"Not usually," I said. "I mean, he didn't ignore me; he was always friendly. And he called on me a couple of times after my master died, to see if I was doing all right. From what Dorothy said, though, I don't think that was it. I think he might have seen something that alarmed him. And for some reason it made him think of me."

"What might that be?"

"I don't know," I admitted. "At first, I thought maybe he'd seen Wat and recognized him as the apprentice who'd murdered my master. But that wouldn't fit the timeline, would it? Wat was already dead by the time Mr. Sinclair returned."

The spymaster listened patiently. He never seemed to mind when I thought out loud, giving me as much time as I needed to work out the problem.

"Then," I said, "I thought that maybe he'd seen the man in the golden mask who'd bribed Elinor. Though if he had, while that would have been strange, why would he specifically come looking for me?

"No, it had to be something to do with me. Or maybe . . . Master Benedict? What if Mr. Sinclair saw somebody who my master had had trouble with in the past? The Raven did say Master Benedict had been a thorn in his side. And Mr. Sinclair's confectionery was already there when my master bought our home and turned it into an apothecary. Of all our neighbors, Sinclair was the only one who's lived there the whole time."

Walsingham pressed his hands together and pondered what I'd told him. "An interesting hypothesis," he said finally. "Unfortunately, the Raven left us no way to test it. Which, as you pointed out, may well have been his purpose in murdering Sinclair. We will keep this in mind. What else?"

I handed him the letter Simon had given me, sent to him by Guy d'Auzon. "Simon said—"

Walsingham held up a hand. "I will draw my own conclusions first."

I sat silently until he finished reading. Then I sat some more as he thought about what the letter meant, until he said, "Go ahead."

I told him what Simon thought about the Raven being a noble and how I wasn't sure about that.

"I agree with you," Walsingham said. "It seems likely that the Raven is English, but the theory that he is part of the peerage is not yet supported by what we know. What else?"

Finally, I told him about my conversation with George Gifford at the Cockpit. I told him about Gifford's claim that he was paid by Arthur Pembry, Earl of Branstoke—and if it was really the earl, that we may well have found our traitor.

Walsingham, never a fidgety man, grew even more still. After half a minute of staring at me, he opened a drawer in his desk, pulled out a sheet of paper, and handed it over.

It was a series of names, written in a hand I didn't recognize. "What's this?"

"The guest list," Walsingham said, "for the Berkshire House party. Read it carefully."

I recognized a few of the names, including Sir Thomas Killigrew, the knight whom Tom and I had originally displaced. But it was near the end that I found what he wanted me to see, eight lines from the bottom.

A. Pembry, Earl of Branstoke

I looked up, pulse racing. "He was there. He was at the party."

"Indeed." The spymaster nodded slowly. "And Mr. Gifford's description of the earl . . . well. If it wasn't Pembry, then it was an extraordinarily well-crafted likeness."

"So Pembry *is* our traitor," I said.

"Almost certainly."

I could barely keep my seat. "And maybe even the Raven himself?"

Walsingham considered it. "We cannot assume that yet. I do not know if he was in Paris when you were. Like most of those with means, Pembry fled London with the plague. He was not with the king in Oxford, but whether he went home to Branstoke or elsewhere, I do not know."

"Can we find out?"

"I shall assign an agent to that. What I *can* say, however, is that Pembry has been throwing money around since he returned to London. Even more so since the attempt on the king's life. He's held three parties in as many weeks at his estate outside the city. All reportedly quite lavish."

"So it has to be him," I said.

"Caution, apprentice. We still need to investigate. I do not know if such largesse is normal for Branstoke, as I have never had any reason to look into him before. Have you told anyone else about this?"

"No. Tom and Sally were with me at the theater, so they heard what Gifford said. I was going to tell Lord Ashcombe when I saw him—"

"Don't."

That surprised me. "But—"

"We will keep Branstoke's name to ourselves for the moment."

"I . . . yes, my lord." I clamped my mouth shut.

He saw it. "You have something to say?"

"Well . . . shouldn't Lord Ashcombe know, at least? I mean, if the earl is the traitor, then isn't there a danger to His Majesty?"

"I doubt Pembry will act against the king again anytime soon. The original treason of the Raven, after all, was solely a ploy to rob the vault at Berkshire House."

"I suppose," I said.

The spymaster spoke patiently but firmly. "I do not choose this course out of any wish to keep Ashcombe in the dark. But you must understand that the King's Warden is, at heart, a soldier. So when he sees a threat, he reacts as a soldier: He kills it.

"If Pembry is our traitor," Walsingham continued, "he may lead us directly to the Raven. What is called for, then, is subtlety. What would Ashcombe's reaction be, do you think, if you told him what Gifford had said?"

That was easy to answer. "He'd arrest the earl, throw

him in the dungeon, and . . . um . . . interrogate him."

"Indeed. Perhaps Pembry would talk. Perhaps he would deny everything. Either way, the Raven would be alerted—and he would almost certainly go on the run. No. We will glean much more information if we allow the earl to continue about his business. We will watch him all the while. And that will give us our greatest chance of cutting off the head of this particular serpent. Do you not agree?"

"I do, I guess. It's just . . ."

"Speak your mind."

"I don't like the idea of lying to Lord Ashcombe," I said. "He's put so much trust in me. It's like I'm betraying him."

Walsingham nodded. "I understand. Nonetheless, there is something you must realize. Lying is part of being a spy—lying, even to friends. It is regrettable, perhaps. But it is the nature of the role.

"If it makes you feel more comfortable, then I will make it an order. You are not to tell Lord Ashcombe, or anyone else, about Arthur Pembry. You are to inform Tom and Sally that the Earl Walsingham has commanded the same of them. Understood?"

"Yes, my lord."

"Then you are dismissed."

I'd never left Walsingham's office feeling this bad. Plenty of times I'd been confused, or exhausted, or downright dizzy with the mental effort he demanded of me. But I'd never actually felt *awful*.

Yet that was exactly how I felt now. For the first time since I'd moved into the palace, I found myself hoping I wouldn't see Lord Ashcombe.

Which meant, naturally, that I ran into the King's Warden right away.

Tom and Sally had said they'd wait for me in the Privy Garden. I was just making my way there when I spied Lord Ashcombe talking to another gentleman in a cross corridor. I hurried on, hoping he wouldn't notice me.

No such luck.

"Christopher."

I halted at the sound of his voice. He spoke for a moment more to the other man, then approached me. "Walsingham said he'd sent you to collect Chastellain's letter. Did you get it?"

I relaxed a little. This I could answer. "Yes, my lord. It's with Lord Walsingham now." I told him what the letter had said, and what both Simon and I thought it meant. I also told him about Mr. Sinclair looking for me, and the possibility that he'd seen someone from Master Benedict's past.

Lord Ashcombe nodded. "Could be valuable. Anything else?"

Why? Why did he have to ask me that?

My stomach churned. But like it or not, my master had given me an order. There was only one thing I could do.

"We're still investigating," I said.

Technically, that wasn't a lie. But in my heart it absolutely was.

"Very well," he said. "Carry on."

Lord Ashcombe left me there. As I watched him go, I thought, *Pembry's not the only betrayer. Now I'm a traitor, too.*

That's unfair, Master Benedict said. *It wasn't your decision.*

Didn't matter. It still felt like a betrayal. I was ashamed of myself.

And—maybe worse—I couldn't shake the feeling that, by keeping silent, I'd just made a terrible mistake.

CHAPTER
21

OUR EARLY START MEANT I'D FIN-
ished that morning's duties by noon. Tom, Sally, and I had
a light lunch—at least Sally and I did; by the time we'd
finished, Tom was still working on the second half of a
roast beef—then I went off to Master Kirby's apothecary.
Since Tom had training scheduled with Sir William that
afternoon, he made me take a pair of the King's Men for
protection. Given the events of the last two days, he didn't
need to insist.

Truth be told, I'd rather have skipped the trip entirely
and taken a nap. My lack of sleep was really weighing on me;
it was all I could do not to push my lunch plate aside and

snooze right there at the table. But I hadn't gone to Master Kirby's in over a week, and while I wasn't truly the apothecary's apprentice, Walsingham wanted me to keep up appearances. It wouldn't hurt to keep in Kirby's good graces, either. So I headed over to the workshop to put some time in.

Kirby had two other apprentices, David and Edward, twelve and eleven years old. They couldn't quite decide what to make of me. I didn't live in the workshop, as they did, nor did I ever put in more than one day's work at a time. I didn't wear my pistols in the lab, but they'd seen them in my belt, and weapons of any kind were strictly forbidden to apprentices. They knew I spent most of my time at the palace, but I wasn't a noble. No doubt I was an enormous source of gossip.

So I did my best to make sure there wasn't any resentment. I was always friendly, sneaking them apple tarts from the tables at Whitehall, which the younger apprentice, Edward, enjoyed especially. I took on my fair share of the work while I was there, even the drudgery like carting water from the river and cleaning up spills. I also helped them with their studies, sometimes teaching them one of Master Benedict's own tricks.

Working with them made me think of my own future, and how much I'd like to be a master apothecary, running

Blackthorn with apprentices of my own. It wasn't that I didn't like my time with the spymaster. But doing simple, honest work made the lie I'd told Lord Ashcombe weigh heavier—and the shame burn a little hotter. There'd be a reckoning for that at some point, and I was dreading it. It made me sigh and wonder if my life would ever be normal again.

At least things were going smoothly here. I was glad that Master Kirby didn't resent me, either. There was nothing he could do, of course—I'd been placed here by the king himself—but I made sure to always be respectful and to praise Master Kirby to His Majesty whenever Charles asked me how it was going. After my first few appearances in his laboratory, then, Master Kirby and I came to a reasonable enough arrangement. I did what I could for his shop, and he let me decide what I wanted to work on.

Today I made some honey balm, as Dr. Kemp had taken the last of mine. Curious to see what I was doing, David and Edward came over to watch, and even Master Kirby looked over my shoulder and quizzed me as to the herbs I infused in the pot. I didn't want to give away all of Master Benedict's secrets—they'd be my secrets one day, when I ran my own shop—but if one or two recipes bought me goodwill, it was worth the price.

It was a satisfying afternoon being an apothecary's apprentice again, and by the time I left to meet Tom for dinner at Whitehall, other than the lingering discomfort about lying to Lord Ashcombe, I was feeling pretty good about a productive and peaceful day.

Then a new message arrived.

The letter came well after eight. Tom and I were lounging about in one of the palace's many parlors. I was holding a quill, trying to keep myself awake while searching for hidden messages in some correspondence Walsingham had intercepted. Tom, having stuffed himself at dinner, halfdozed on the couch. He'd run into the king's spaniels at some point; his stockings were covered in dog hair.

Dobson, my favorite of the palace servants, who'd helped Tom and me learn our way through the maze that was Whitehall, entered. "Pardon me, sir," he said, in that ponderous way of his. "A letter has arrived for you at the palace gates."

He carried it in on a silver tray. I sort of wished he wouldn't be so formal with me all the time, but Dobson would rather have slit his own wrists than relax his manners. I thanked him as he departed.

"Who's it from?" Tom said, rubbing his eyes.

I broke the seal on the letter—then sat up sharply when I read the name at the bottom.

Your Hopeful New Friend

"'Your Hopeful New Friend'?" Tom said, confused.

I read the letter, growing more amazed. "This must be . . . it is," I said. "It's from George Gifford, at the Cockpit. Listen to this."

My dear sir,

I write to you in some desperation. After our discussion today, in which I assured you of my complete lack of knowledge and ill will in playing the role I was hired to play, I received another visit from the gentleman we spoke about.

"He must mean Arthur Pembry," I said.

Tom frowned. "*Pembry* went to see him? Today? That's an awful coincidence."

"I'm not sure it is a coincidence." Was it possible that we'd been followed?

The idea had been in my mind ever since the ambush. It was why I'd rarely gone to visit Simon, and why, after dropping off Bridget, I hadn't seen Isaac at all. Anyone I spent time with was marked for danger.

This letter was proving me right. Gifford may not have understood how much trouble he was getting into when he first accepted Pembry's job, but he knew how bad it was now. He was making a real effort not to name any names in his message—not even his own. Just from the opening paragraphs, he sounded alarmed, if not downright scared.

This gentleman asked a curious series of questions. He had a particular interest in you, and whether you and I had discussed him at all. I said no, as I feared the truth might land me in no small amount of hot water. I assure you once more that I acted only in good faith on what I believed was a genuine request on the part of our mutual friend.

"That has to mean the king," I said.

I fear now I am not only deeply in debt, but equally out of my depth. I am hoping you might provide a certain protection against any malfeasance that might come my way. If you would be so kind as to gain the genuine promise of our mutual friend's goodwill, then I believe I may be of valuable service to both of you with knowledge and information.

If this is possible, please come to visit me at the same place as before. My cast and I will be preparing for tomorrow's grand opening until nine o'clock tonight.

I beg of you to consider my humble request.

Sincerely,
Your Hopeful New Friend

Tom stared at me, wide-eyed. "He's in trouble."

"And he knows it," I said.

"What do you think Pembry said to him?"

It must been pretty bad for Gifford to risk writing

such a letter. But, as Walsingham had once explained to me, opportunities like this were one of the ways in which he acquired agents. Helping someone in trouble could turn them into a valuable long-term asset.

And with the contact Gifford had with Pembry—and through him, the Raven—he might well make an excellent agent indeed.

"Come on," I said. "We're going to see Lord Walsingham."

CHAPTER

22

HE WASN'T IN HIS OFFICE.

That was unusual for this time of night. The spymaster was pretty much always at his desk at this hour, going through the last of the day's correspondence. He reminded me a lot of Jean-Baptiste Colbert, Louis XIV's closest advisor, whom we'd met in Paris. That man's favorite thing to do was work, too, from morning till night. It was part of what made him so effective.

It was unlikely that Walsingham was in his quarters, but we tried them anyway. No luck there, either, which meant the earl was out in the field somewhere. That wasn't too uncommon—the spymaster often spent time down at the docks, keeping tabs on the war with the Dutch, or at the Guildhall or Parliament, keeping a personal eye on the political machinations of both the city and the country as a whole.

Or, I realized, he could be following Pembry himself.

If that were the case, he might already know that Pembry had visited my "Hopeful New Friend." Either way, the letter was too good an opportunity to pass up.

"Let's hurry," I said to Tom, and we ran to the stables to get our horses.

"Where are we going?" Tom said.

"To the theater," I said. "We'll bring George Gifford in ourselves."

We made it to the Cockpit after nine. As the theater was close to Whitehall, it took only a few minutes to arrive. I just hoped we weren't too late.

That didn't seem to be the case. There were a few windows on the outside of the theater, all of them tiny; the stage was intended to be lit by footlights, lamps, candles, and torches. A soft glow showed someone was still inside.

Gifford's letter said his cast would be with him until nine, going through the final rehearsal before the opening performance tomorrow. I hoped they'd already finished and had headed home. It would be hard enough to recruit Gifford as an agent without other people around.

"We'll go in quietly," I said to Tom.

He placed a hand on my arm. "How do we know this isn't a trap?"

We didn't. But I wasn't sure what options we had. "Gifford asked us to come here. If we want to keep him on our side, we can't abandon him. The longer he feels exposed, the less he'll trust us." And the bigger the chance the Raven would learn what he was doing.

"What about getting some of the King's Men?" Tom said. "They'll come if I ask them."

I knew they would. Our stand at the king's side at Barnham Wood had increased the soldiers' respect for us enormously—especially for Tom, who'd stood shoulder to shoulder with Lord Ashcombe, fighting off Covenanters with his holy blade. Since then, he'd become like one of their own. Whereas before he'd had to search for someone to spar with him, now the King's Men invited him to join their contests. His being a pupil of Sir William Leech— even though Tom was just a commoner, same as them— only made the soldiers like him more.

But that worked against me now. "The King's Men report to Lord Ashcombe," I said. "When they tell him we needed them here, he'll ask me why. And I won't be able to answer that."

Tom didn't like it any more than I did. But orders were orders. So he drew Eternity and made me draw one of my pistols. I felt its weight in my hand and thought that was a pretty good idea.

We went inside.

The theater looked empty.

The set was complete now. The painted wood, canvas, and statues gave the impression of a pleasantly landscaped retreat, not unlike the Privy Garden at Whitehall. Lamps burned at the foot of the stage, the source of the glow we'd seen through the windows, casting the trees in shadow, a play of light and dark.

But none of the actors were there.

Tom put a warning hand on my shoulder. I raised my pistol.

"Mr. Gifford?"

Though I'd called softly, my voice carried past the empty seats and filled the hall. For a moment, we heard nothing. Then footsteps came from the back of the stage.

A man stepped out from behind one of the painted trees. At first, I couldn't tell who it was, as he moved in and out of the shadows cast by the lamps. But I knew it wasn't George Gifford. This man was stockier, and there was something familiar about the way he walked—

"Dr. Kemp?" Tom said, surprised.

Dr. Kemp came forward, into the light. He was holding his hands up, facing us. And he had a grim look on his face.

"Doctor?" I said. "Why are you . . . ?"

I trailed off as I caught a glimpse of a figure behind him. It was a man. At least, I think it was; the figure was so shrouded, I couldn't tell. He wore a heavy cloak and boots, and thick gloves that showed not an inch of his skin. The hood of the cloak and the trees kept his face in shadow. I caught a flash of yellow as he moved, until he came fully into the lamplight. Yet still I couldn't see his face.

He was wearing a mask.

It was gold. The mask smiled, so wide as to be grotesque. Thalia, the Muse of Comedy. The mask of the man who'd bribed Elinor Bagley to frame me.

And now, too, I saw why Dr. Kemp had his hands up.

The masked man held a pistol to the back of his head.

CHAPTER
23

I COULDN'T TAKE THE SHOT.

The masked man stepped forward carefully, keeping Dr. Kemp between us. He offered too small a target. The only part visible was that mask of his, leering with its awful grin.

I'd hit targets that size before. The stage was about thirty yards away; I practiced regularly with my pistols at twenty-five and could shatter a bottle at that distance three times out of four.

That fourth one was what worried me. If I missed a bottle, nothing got hurt but my pride. If I aimed wide now, it was Dr. Kemp who would take the bullet.

And there was a big difference between shooting a bottle and shooting a man. On the tiltyard, my hand didn't shake. Now it trembled with the blood racing through my veins. I'd used my pistols well enough at Barnham Wood, but those Covenanters had been a few feet away. I couldn't risk killing Dr. Kemp. I just couldn't.

The masked man gave me no opening. Still holding his pistol to the doctor's head, he grabbed Kemp by the collar, halted him in the center of the stage, then leaned forward, whispering.

It was Dr. Kemp who spoke aloud. He tried to make a joke, but the tension in his voice told me he was scared. "How's your evening been, boys?" he said. "Up until now, I mean."

Neither Tom nor I had any reply. You wouldn't figure I'd be more scared than the good doctor, but I was.

The masked man shook Kemp by the collar. He leaned in closer, practically hissing now. I still couldn't hear any of it.

"My, um, companion," Dr. Kemp said, "wants me to speak for him. Everything I have to say from now on will come from him. Do you understand?"

My voice cracked. "Yes."

And so Dr. Kemp became the masked man's voice. "Put your weapons down," he said.

We hesitated.

"If you don't want to comply, just say so. I'll shoot the doctor and leave."

Kemp paled as he was forced to utter the threat. Tom looked to me, but we had no options. I placed my pistol on the floor of the theater. Tom followed suit with Eternity. The masked man gestured at my belt, and I removed my second gun as well.

"That's better," he said. "Less chance of someone getting hurt now. Wouldn't want that, would we?"

The man shifted so we could see more of him, though he was still too well covered to identify. He looked like he was taller than the doctor by a couple of inches, but that could have been his disguise as much as anything—his boots had heels, while the swell of his cloak allowed him to hunch over.

I glanced down at my pistols. In stepping out from behind the doctor, the masked man had exposed enough of himself for me to take a shot. Except I'd never reach my guns in time.

He did that on purpose, I realized. He was taunting me. *So close, and yet so far.*

"Do you know who I am?" he said, still speaking through Dr. Kemp.

I did. Standing across the theater, I knew this was no impostor. "You're the Raven."

The man bowed his head behind the mask's leering grin. "And so we finally meet."

"Not really," I said. "I'm just talking to a mask. You could be a fraud."

"And yet you know I am not," the Raven said. "Don't worry. There will be plenty of time later to meet properly. In the meantime: You have *vexed* me."

The word triggered a memory in the back of my head. *You've heard it before,* Master Benedict said.

In Paris. It was said by Aphrodite, the chambermaid who'd plotted against the royal family to get the lost Templar treasure. *You have vexed me,* she'd said. *Ruined carefully crafted plans at every turn.* And she'd been working for the Raven.

"I haven't done anything to you," I said.

"But you have, Christopher. You have. I went to a lot of trouble to set up our next game. Then you cheated."

"What are you talking about?"

"The deaths of Wat and Sinclair. All that effort to put you on trial. But along comes Ashcombe, and Walsingham, and the king, to pull you from the fire. I ask you: If that's not cheating, then what is?"

"You didn't seem to think it was cheating," I spat, "when you schemed against the whole palace a month ago. When you murdered innocent girls, when you killed the King's Men—"

The smiling mask couldn't change its expression. But the muzzle of the Raven's gun pressed harder into Dr. Kemp's head.

"Er . . . Christopher," Dr. Kemp said, and this time he was speaking for himself. "Perhaps I could persuade you not to be rash."

I shut up. The Raven whispered in the doctor's ear again.

"The game I'd planned was to be between you and me," the Raven said. "*Only* you and me. *You* brought others in. So now your friends will have to play, too."

He shook the doctor by the collar. "A new contest, then," he said. "You won the first round, in Paris. I won the second, here in London. So we will play a deciding round. The final round between you and me. And the winner will take it all.

"Our game starts tomorrow, bright and early," the Raven said. "The rules are as follows: Tom and Sally will accompany you. You may also keep your horses; you'll need them to have a chance. All of the king's other resources you are denied. No Ashcombe, no Walsingham, no King's Men. *Nothing.* If you break this rule, you will forfeit the game immediately.

"I would also deny you your other allies, the Templars," he said, "but then I don't need to do that, do I? I've already removed those pieces from the board. Nonetheless, if their charred corpses are of use to you, by all means, bring them along."

The Raven was still whispering in Kemp's ear, so it was only the doctor's voice I heard. But I could tell by the Raven's shaking shoulders he was laughing at me.

I glanced again at my pistols. I'd have given anything to have one of them in my hand.

"What do I get if I win?" I said.

"Me, Christopher. You get to meet me. Face-to-face, no mask."

"And if I lose?"

"Then you and your friends will die."

"No," I said. "This is between you and me. It's always been you and me. So leave the others out of it."

Tom began to object. It wouldn't have made a difference. "I have told you the rules," the Raven said. "I have given you the stakes. I couldn't care less what you wish."

"Then I won't play."

"Oh, but you will." He pressed the muzzle deeper into the base of Dr. Kemp's skull. "You will play, or you will forfeit. And your friends will die just the same."

The Raven's grip tightened on the doctor's collar. "And just in case you don't believe me," he said, "let me demonstrate. I will now—"

Dr. Kemp's eyes went wide as he heard what the Raven whispered. "NO!" Kemp shouted.

Then the Raven pulled the trigger.

CHAPTER
24

I SAT, HEAD BOWED, ON THE EDGE of the stage.

Tom sat beside me, just as miserable. We'd collected our weapons, my pistols now back in my belt. Lord Ashcombe stood behind me, supervising the King's Men. One of them stood over Dr. Kemp's body. The others were searching the theater, but I knew there'd be nothing to find. The Raven had disappeared.

Watching him murder Dr. Kemp was the worst thing I'd ever witnessed. I could hear Master Benedict in my head.

This isn't your fault, he said.

It was hard to accept that. But whether it was my fault or not, I understood: We'd learned something from it, nonetheless.

The Raven had killed the doctor for more than one reason. He'd proved—once again—that he could strike at anyone, anywhere. Now I would have to take the Raven's game seriously. Kemp's death ensured I didn't dare break the monster's "rules."

But it told me something else as well. Something I don't think the Raven intended.

It told me that I'd met the man before.

If all the Raven wanted was to kill Dr. Kemp, that would have been easy. But he'd also forced the doctor to speak for him. There was only one reason to do that.

He didn't want me to hear his voice.

The Raven was worried. He was worried that if I heard him, I'd recognize him. That Dr. Kemp wouldn't know who he was, *but I would.* And then there wouldn't be any game at all.

"You are unharmed?" a quiet voice said.

I looked up to see the spymaster. He'd finally arrived.

The Raven had fled as soon as he'd killed Dr. Kemp. Before I could reach for my pistols, before I could recover from the shock of watching a decent man die, the Raven had bolted, disappearing behind the smoke of black powder into the false garden on the stage, vanishing through the back exit into the night.

I couldn't just leave Dr. Kemp there. Tom and I had ridden back to Whitehall and informed Lord Ashcombe that we'd discovered a body.

The Raven's shot had burned his rules into my brain. So I didn't tell Lord Ashcombe what had really happened. Instead, I showed him the letter from George Gifford— which, I realized too late, had probably been forged by the Raven. Then I said that Tom and I had come to the theater and found Dr. Kemp already dead.

I'd tried to find Walsingham at the palace, too. As before, no one knew where the spymaster was. I left a message with Dobson to pass to him when he returned. Walsingham must have received it, because he'd finally come.

"You are unharmed?" Walsingham asked again.

I nodded, not trusting myself to speak. Beneath my despair, I felt anger. *Why weren't you there?* I thought. *Where were you when I needed you? If you'd sent an agent to the theater instead of me, then the Raven couldn't have started his evil game.*

It was irrational, I knew. Master Benedict knew it, too. *It's no more his fault than it is yours, child,* he said. It cooled my anger. But every bit of despair remained.

The spymaster looked beyond me to the body at Lord Ashcombe's feet. "What happened?"

I showed him the letter from "Gifford" and told him the same lie I'd told the King's Warden. *No Ashcombe, no Walsingham, no King's Men. I heard you, you monster.*

Lord Ashcombe joined us, frowning. He'd recognized the body right away. He'd met the doctor once, the day Simon had been attacked. "Why would the Raven kill Kemp?" he said.

"Punishment," I said, as if I was just guessing. "He wanted to punish me by killing a friend. It's retaliation for foiling his plot to have me tried for murder."

That was partially true, at least. It made me wonder: How many more lies would I tell Lord Ashcombe, who'd been as good to me as anyone since Master Benedict died?

Walsingham watched me as I gave my answer. His face, blank as always, was impossible to read. Did he know I was lying? I thought he might.

One of the King's Men called out. "More bodies back here, General."

A pit growing in my gut, Tom and I followed Ashcombe and Walsingham behind the scenery. A door in the darkness backstage led to a small room where the actors could prepare for their entrance. A King's Man held a lantern, revealing the rest of the Raven's handiwork.

There were four more corpses here. All were actors, in costume for the roles they'd never get to play. There was one woman, young and pretty, with long black hair. The other three were men. One was little more than a boy; one was much older. The last of the bodies was George Gifford.

I recognized two of the others. The young man had played the angel outside Saint Paul's. The woman had been the ghost, the legendary White Lady of Devonshire. I had no doubt that the older man had worn the plague doctor mask, completing the group.

They had no wounds; there was no blood. It was none-theless clear what had killed them. Every one of them had thrown up. And a shattered glass lay beside each of them. Smears of red wine stained the floorboards. A pair of bottles rested on a sideboard, one empty, one halfway there.

They'd been poisoned. I knew by what. The vomit that spattered their clothes smelled faintly of garlic. The wine had been laced with arsenic. The Raven's favorite.

Here was the confirmation that Gifford had never sent me that letter. Instead, worried about what I'd told him, he must have contacted Pembry, to see if the earl had lied as I'd claimed. Pembry must have then told the Raven, said Gifford was making trouble. And so the Raven had arrived to smooth things over with a gift of poisoned wine.

Lord Ashcombe turned to me with a baleful eye. "Explain this," he growled. "Why would the Raven poison these actors? And why did Gifford write to you, anyway? What did that letter you showed me mean?"

I'd never felt so much like a traitor. "I—"

Walsingham cut me off, his eyes still on the bodies. "Christopher had a theory that the Raven used actors to pass him the final letter a month ago. This was the troupe who did it."

"They'd met the Raven?"

"No. Their contact was Arthur Pembry."

"*Branstoke?*" Lord Ashcombe's eye burned. "Where is he now?"

"Dead."

I looked up in shock. "*What?* When? How?"

"This very evening," Walsingham said. "He was found in his quarters at the palace. It was made to look like griping in the guts, with flux and vomiting. But, like here, we can be certain it was poison. Arsenic, as the Raven favors."

Lord Ashcombe looked from Walsingham to me. "How do you know all this?"

I couldn't bear the shame that gnawed inside. "I visited George Gifford this morning," I said miserably. "He told me Pembry had paid him and promised him His Majesty's favor."

I stood, head bowed, as Lord Ashcombe clenched his fists. "You kept this from me?"

"On my orders," Walsingham said quietly. "Christopher was commanded to say nothing. I wished to track Pembry's movements in secret. It was our best chance of finding the Raven."

Which the Raven himself must have known. In one brutal day, he'd killed both Pembry and Pembry's agents, leaving no link that could lead back to him.

"And how clever are you feeling now?" Lord Ashcombe snarled.

"It was a mistake," the spymaster acknowledged.

Ashcombe shook his head in disgust. "You're a fool, Walsingham," he said, and he stalked from the room.

He didn't even look at me when he left. I'd never felt so small. I wanted to run after him, beg for forgiveness, tell him I was sorry, so sorry, I had to keep the secret, I *had* to.

I didn't. Not just because I couldn't face him. Because I was *still* keeping a secret—now from everybody. I already felt like a traitor. Lying to him again would just prove it true.

As for Walsingham, he continued to stare down at the bodies. He spoke quietly to himself. "A mistake," he said thoughtfully. "A mistake." He paused. "Is there anything else you discovered?"

It took a moment to realize he was talking to me. Time to betray him, too. "No."

Walsingham looked over at me. He studied my face for what seemed like a long while. Then he said, "There is nothing more for you to do here tonight."

So I was dismissed. By the time I returned to the stage, the King's Men had removed Dr. Kemp's body. Nothing left of him but a bloodstain on the wood.

And the shame I felt inside sparked and smoldered, then burned into fury.

The Raven didn't have to kill Dr. Kemp. He could have used George Gifford as his voice, or Arthur Pembry. He was going to get rid of them anyway.

But Dr. Kemp? This was pure cruelty. *He killed the man just to get at me.*

"All right," I whispered. "You want to play? Then we'll play."

Tom waited for me in the seats, out of the way. He stood as I stepped down from the stage.

"Let's go," I said.

He glanced around at the King's Men filing in and out of the theater. They'd just begun to carry the bodies from backstage. Tom followed me out. There were a half dozen horses here other than our own. Lord Ashcombe's wasn't among them. He must have already left for the palace.

We mounted Blossom and Lightning. "Where are we going?" Tom said.

"Berkshire House."

We had to tell Sally what had happened. In truth, I didn't want her with us tomorrow. I knew there would be danger. But the Raven had set the rules. Tom and Sally would play whether I wished it or not.

"What did you tell them?" Tom asked. He meant Lords Ashcombe and Walsingham.

"Nothing," I said. "I told them nothing."

Tom didn't like it. But he knew the rules as well as I did. *No Ashcombe, no Walsingham, no King's Men.*

Those rules weren't the final thing the Raven had given

us. When he'd fled, he'd left a letter on the stage beside Kemp's body. No forgery in this one, no lies. Just one last taunt before the game started.

Tom and I had already read it. When we arrived at Berkshire House, we told Sally what had happened. We let her sit for a moment, let her grieve for the loss of so many innocents. Then she read the Raven's message, too.

Three friends joined. Three souls wagered.
One day to find the warrants that grant salvation.

The Sun marks the clock. Our game begins
at dawn.

THURSDAY, APRIL 8, 1666

Before me things created were none,
save things eternal.
And eternal I endure.

CHAPTER

25

I WAS ALREADY AWAKE WHEN IT
arrived.

The same nightmares that had plagued me for weeks came that night with a vengeance. They burrowed into my mind and gnawed at me, waking me with a start, over and over again. Eventually, I just gave up and lay there, listening to Tom's slow, steady breaths.

At the first sliver of light, I rose and dressed. Then I sat in the one chair we'd managed to squeeze into our tiny room and waited. It didn't take long.

A small beige rectangle slipped under our door. I sprang up immediately and flung the door open.

A servant, a young woman, stumbled away, startled. "Oh!"

I stared at her, taking in every one of her features, etching her face in my brain. Rattled, she said the obvious. "Letter for you, sir."

"Where'd you get it?"

"I—the gate. The guards."

"Who gave it to them?"

"I . . . I really wouldn't know, sir."

She took a step back. I'd frightened her. It made me feel something of a fool. I'd hoped to catch one of the Raven's agents, perhaps, passing on his messages. But he hardly needed a man—or a woman, in this case—in place for that. A simple runner could hand it in at the palace gate, then ride away, impossible to be traced.

"Sorry," I said.

By the time I closed the door, Tom was sitting up. "A little jumpy today, are we?" he grumbled.

He swung himself out of bed and began to dress while I examined the letter. There were only two markings on the outside. The first was my name.

Christopher Rowe
Apprentice to Master Apothecary Benedict Blackthorn
Palace of Whitehall

Apprentice to Master Apothecary Benedict Blackthorn, I thought.

That wasn't true anymore. And yet . . . it was. In my heart, it would always be true, more true than anything else I would ever become.

It was also the first time the Raven had called me by that title. Was it significant? Was there a hidden meaning? A clue in the words?

Calm, child, Master Benedict said.

Tom was right. I was jumpy. Looking for significance in everything, everywhere.

That's the game the Raven wants to play, I argued.

You cannot win playing his game, Master Benedict said. *You can only win by playing yours.*

That was a good point. I needed to keep my mind clear. I took a deep breath, trying to settle my nerves.

"So?" Tom said. "What does it say?"

The second marking on the letter was the seal. Just a featureless circle pressed into red wax. I broke it open, and we read it together.

Begin where the ground drinks the blood of queens.
Visit the House where their bones rest, and pray
for the path to be revealed.

"That's it?" Tom said.

"That's enough," I said, heart racing. "Let's get Sally."

"Wait . . . you know what this means?"

"I do. And so do you," I said. "After all, we've visited the place before."

CHAPTER 26

SALLY WAS WAITING FOR US IN THE courtyard of Berkshire House when we arrived to collect her. She'd dressed today in a practical riding doublet and skirt, which allowed her to ride sidesaddle: left leg in the stirrup, right hooked over the pommel, the knob snugly behind her knee.

She knew the basics of riding but was nowhere near an expert. While Tom and I took Blossom and Lightning everywhere, Sally had mostly stuck to her carriage. Since we weren't certain if that would break the Raven's rules—he'd said we could have horses but made no mention of other transport—Sally had borrowed a palfrey named

Beatrice from Berkshire's stables. The whole thing put her on edge.

"What if we have to sprint somewhere?" she said nervously.

"You can do it," I said encouragingly. "And if worse comes to worst, we'll leave Beatrice behind and you can ride with me."

She gave me a speculative look, as if she wouldn't mind that at all. Watching her mount Beatrice made me wonder about the logistics of riding double. She'd have to wrap her arms around my waist and lean against my back . . . and come to think of it, I didn't mind the idea, either. I flushed as I caught Tom grinning at me.

"Say nothing," I muttered.

"Who, me?" he said innocently.

He whistled as we rode into the city.

Tom was not an especially musical person. Which was a nice way of saying he couldn't hold a tune. Nonetheless, he grew edgy about what awaited us as we rode. So he switched from whistling to singing, chanting an old war song we'd heard from the King's Men. Though he might have changed the lyrics a bit.

Here we go, brothers we,
Riding into battle.
I have my arm, I have my sword,
I fight now for my king!
Yet I haven't had any breakfast,
Not even a simple bun
With maybe some butter and cheese.
If I have to be up so early
I don't think it's right I should starve.

Sally covered her face, laughing. "All right, Tom," I said. But he made me laugh, too. And that made me think, *Maybe, just maybe, we can do this after all.* So he turned our moods from gloomy to hopeful as we approached the Tower of London.

I'd once had good memories of this place. Master Benedict had brought me here first, not long after I'd become his apprentice, to see the king's menagerie. Tom and I had gone there a couple of times, too, on the king's birthday, when admission was free to all.

Then things changed. The Tower was where I'd stayed after I'd stopped the Cult of the Archangel, when Lord Ashcombe got injured and almost died. It was where Tom and I had come, too, during the plague, looking once again for Lord Ashcombe to help us when someone had broken into my shop. Now, as the towers rose above the city, I knew that whenever I thought of this place, I'd always think of the Raven—and also remember that after everything Lord Ashcombe had done for me, I'd let him down.

The outer stone walls were surrounded by a moat 125 feet wide. The main entrance to the complex was over a bridge to the Lion Tower, which stood separate from the main defensive structure.

The Lion Tower had got its name because the menagerie was housed here. There were several big cats; besides the three lions, there were a leopard, a tiger, and my favorite, a panther named Maisie, all kept in cages one could view from above. Other animals rooted about in smaller cages nearby, including a raccoon, a porcupine, and an ape. There was something of an aviary here as well, with vultures, eagles, and warwovens.

And then, of course, there were the ever-present ravens. They weren't kept at the Tower. They just lived around it, swooping down opportunistically to snatch food wherever they could.

I watched one now, perched on the edge of the bridge to

the main gate. It eyed us as our horses passed by. They were frightfully intelligent birds, ravens, known to play pranks on people—and also to forever hold a grudge. Maybe that's why the Raven had taken that name.

Thinking of birds made me think of Bridget again. And that reminded me of the only clue to the Raven's identity that he'd ever given me: a pigeon feather.

We'd found it under Marin Chastellain's mattress, after the Raven had murdered him, but we'd never discovered what it meant. Once again, I tumbled it over in my mind, trying to find some link.

I knew ravens hunted pigeons. And ravens liked to flock around the Tower. The Tower was where I'd brought Lord Ashcombe . . . and the Raven had tried to lay the blame for the king's ambush on him. To paint the King's Warden as a traitor.

I shook my head. None of that got me anywhere. In fact, lately, I'd begun to wonder if the pigeon feather was a clue at all. Maybe it was meant to throw me *off* the scent. Left there as a ruse, so I wouldn't see something else.

I sighed. That was the problem. I never knew if I was moving toward discovering who the Raven was, or if he was leading me around in circles. The Raven, like the

Templars, had proven to be a master of misdirection—

I drew in a breath.

The Raven is good at misdirection, I thought.

And so were the Templars.

Did that mean . . . Was it possible that the Raven was a *Templar*?

A knight gone rogue? It would explain how he knew so much about them. How he'd known who was in the London chapter. How he'd known I'd found the true treasure in Paris.

On the other hand, if he *was* a Templar, it wouldn't make sense that he'd attack his own organization. He'd be getting rid of his most valuable resource. And if there was one thing the Raven was good at, it was making use of resources.

No. The most likely answer was that *the Raven had a traitor inside the Templars.* Someone he'd turned with a ridiculously large bribe, like he'd done in the palace with Arthur Pembry.

That might turn out to be a valuable clue. But at the moment, it was no help at all, since I didn't know how to contact the Templars. Which wouldn't have done us any good anyway, since the Raven had already destroyed the London chapter.

I urged Blossom on, over the bridge.

. . .

It was a most unusual place, the Tower of London. Once it had housed England's rulers. Now it was used for different purposes. Besides the menagerie, the crown jewels were kept inside, along with an extensive library. The Royal Mint was here, as well, occupying the buildings between the outer and inner walls, where they hammered out the coins of the realm. And, of course, it was also a prison for the king's own captives. Those who displeased His Majesty by committing crimes great and small were held here—but then sometimes, so were honored guests.

Most interesting to me, the Tower housed the Royal Armory, storing a vast amount of England's arms and artillery. There were said to be hundreds of tons of gunpowder, with dozens and dozens of cannons. Some were supposed to be as much as thirty feet long, capable of firing twenty-four-pound cannonballs—

A hand grabbed my collar. "Hey!" I protested.

"No," Tom said.

"I didn't say anything."

"You were thinking it."

"How would you know what I was thinking?"

"Because you have that dreamy look in your eyes," Tom

said. "That look that says *I wonder if that blows up.*"

"No, Christopher," Sally said firmly.

I grumbled and rode on.

The entrance to the central keep, the White Tower, was on its western wall, ten feet above the ground, a wooden staircase leading up to it. I hopped off Blossom and tied her to one of the crossbeams. "We're here," I said.

The others dismounted. "Are we going inside?" Sally asked.

"No. Somewhere else."

I pulled out the riddle the Raven had sent us.

Begin where the ground drinks the blood of queens.
Visit the House where their bones rest, and pray
for the path to be revealed.

Tom looked around, puzzled. The inner grounds of the Tower were mostly earth, with small patches of grass that hadn't yet been worn down by boots tramping across it every day. Supplies destined for our navy lay bundled about in stacks, waiting to be shipped out. Directly north of us stood the barracks of the Yeoman Warders who lived in the complex.

"So where does the ground 'drink the blood of queens'?" he said.

"You're looking at it," I said. "In all of history, four English queens have been executed. Three of them—Anne Boleyn, Catherine Howard, and Lady Jane Grey—were beheaded right here, outside the White Tower, over a hundred years ago."

"'Visit the House where their bones rest,'" Sally quoted. "Is that the Tower itself?"

"Just one specific part of it." I led them through the bales to a chapel west of the Tower's barracks. "The church of Saint Peter ad Vincula—Saint Peter in Chains. They're buried in here." So this was where we'd pray for the path to be revealed.

Whatever that meant. Stomach fluttering, I took a deep breath and went inside.

CHAPTER 27

IT WAS A SURPRISINGLY ORDINARY church.

Maybe that shouldn't have been a surprise. Back when the Tower was the royal palace, our kings and queens would have prayed in their own private chapels on the upper floors of the White Tower. No need to mix with the commoners who ran the daily business of the grounds.

Saint Peter ad Vincula, then, was just a squat, almost-rectangular stone building with arched glass windows, a flat roof, and a single short bell tower at the west end. The inside was equally plain, the pews showing their age, with only a few private boxes for the Tower's senior officers. The altar was low, covered with a heavy cloth that hung down to the stone. A pair of candles rested at opposite ends of the altar, unlit.

There were a few people praying in the pews—a pair of servants and a Yeoman Warder, by his dress. "What now?" Sally whispered.

"We need to find—there."

A middle-aged man in a cassock stood bent over in the far corner, removing linens from a low cupboard. We approached him. "Father?"

The man peered up at us. He wore a pair of spectacles with glass so thick it made his eyes goggle. "Yes, child?"

"I was wondering: Do you happen to know where Henry the Eighth's wives are buried? The ones who were executed in the Tower, I mean."

A look of boredom crossed his face. He'd obviously answered this question a thousand times before. "By the altar. There's no memorial. They're just under there some-where."

He returned to rooting around in the cupboard, but I needed to pester him about one more thing before we left. This wasn't one of the churches I'd visited since the ambush.

"Father? Sorry to disturb you again, but . . . um . . . you

wouldn't happen to have a visiting priest staying here? From France, maybe? He's a young man, mid- to late twenties, with closely cropped brown hair, a lean build, and a slight French accent."

The priest blinked. "We're Church of England. French are Catholics."

"Er . . . yes. But . . ." If the priest we saw in Saint Paul's was a Templar—or the Raven—he wouldn't have had any problem pretending to be one or the other. "How about a Father Bernard? He's much older, also French."

"There are no Frenchmen here at all," he said, slightly irritated.

"Right. Sorry, one more thing: Does this mean anything to you?"

I dug into my apothecary sash and brought out my Templar florin. Whether he'd seen either priest or not, this was the true test. If the man was allied with the Templars, he'd recognize it instantly and know I was to be helped.

Except I wasn't sure he even could see it. He bobbled his head back and forth, squinting through his absurdly thick spectacles. "Is this a donation?" he said, and he reached for it.

"Um . . . no." I jerked the coin away.

My quick movement startled the priest. He frowned,

getting cross. It must have looked like I was playing a prank on him.

"This was what I meant to give you," I said hastily, and I reached into my coin purse for a guinea. That made it a very *big* donation, but now was not the time to be cheap. He was already irritated with me; I couldn't afford to have him kick us out of his church.

"Bless you, my son," he said, mollified, but still a little puzzled. "If you'd like to pray, go ahead."

That was the next step in the Raven's riddle. The three of us went to the front row, as close as we could get to the altar, and knelt in the public pews. Tom, always devout, actually started praying. Sally leaned in and said, "Is that really what we're supposed to do?"

I didn't know. Us "praying" might be a signal for someone in the church to hand us a message. With no other ideas, we joined Tom, quite literally praying for the path to be revealed.

After a few minutes, I started getting antsy. After ten, I'd had enough. *The Sun marks the clock,* the Raven had said, which meant we only had until sundown to play his game.

"I don't think this is it," I whispered to the others.

"Then what?" Tom said.

I still didn't know. "Look around for anything that doesn't seem right."

"None of this is right," he muttered, but he and Sally did as I asked.

I kept wondering if I'd got part of the riddle wrong. I was pretty sure we were in the right place. There was nowhere else I knew of associated with "the blood of queens," and this was "the House where their bones rest." But we'd prayed, and nothing had happened.

I glanced behind me. Different people now sat in the pews. Gone were the Yeoman Warder and servants. Instead, a new couple prayed, a young husband and wife, plus a man who had to be one of the prisoners. He was decently dressed and in good spirits, but a burly guard stood politely behind him, waiting.

The prisoner, maybe? Or the guard? Whatever the Raven's plans for us were, he wouldn't come in person to play them out. He'd have bribed someone, either directly or indirectly, just as he had with Pembry and Gifford. But how was I to identify—

"Christopher."

Sally was staring at the altar. "Look," she whispered.

I did, but had no idea what she was trying to point out.

"Slide over this way," she said, and the three of us squeezed closer to the wall—

There.

On the right side of the altar, an object of some kind peeked out from under the cloth that hung down. Something was hidden there.

"Go get it," I whispered to Sally. "Tom and I will make a distraction."

"Oh no," Tom said.

"Not *that* kind of distraction. Come on."

We shuffled out of the pew and moved toward the back. As soon as we passed the other worshippers, I turned to Tom and said loudly, "Wait. Where's my—did you forget to bring the letter?"

"What letter?" Tom said, puzzled.

"The letter for Colonel Legge," I said, voice rising. William Legge was the master of the armories at the Tower; I'd heard his name once from Lord Ashcombe. "You were supposed to bring it." I cursed at Tom, with a silent apology to our Lord for swearing in His house.

The fact that I hadn't told Tom what I was going to do made his reaction totally realistic. He cringed at the curse, and also at being dressed down in the middle of a church, just like a real servant would.

Everyone turned to stare at us, shocked at my words. The priest we'd spoken to earlier came over, frowning. "Sir," he said sternly.

Sally joined us, clutching what looked like a slab of wood to her chest. Our distraction had done its job.

Which meant it was time to go. I apologized profusely for my language and gave the priest another guinea as penance. Good thing Lord Ashcombe had given me this purse—

I froze.

I'm not supposed to use any of the king's resources, I thought in a panic. *I just broke the rules.*

Had I? I couldn't decide if that was true. *The king gave me a pension,* I argued. *That could be my money.*

Tom and Sally regarded me, puzzled, not sure why I'd stopped moving. Now I was drawing even more attention to myself.

I couldn't help it. Had I ruined everything from the start?

But you do *have money of your own,* Master Benedict said.

Of course. He'd left me his savings, along with his shop. That gave me the out I needed.

"I'm so sorry," I said humbly to the priest, making sure all the bystanders were listening. "Please accept these donations in my name, Christopher Rowe, as offerings for your prayers for my beloved master, Benedict Blackthorn."

There. I'd just declared in God's own house that this was from me, for Master Benedict's soul. And it wasn't even a lie. I'd just have to make sure I stopped at Blackthorn and replaced the coins with my own, hidden in the mattress of my bed.

The priest was grateful for the additional donation. But his expression said he'd had enough of us. With another quick apology to the other worshippers, we went outside and around the corner.

Tom was still offended I'd cursed in a church. "Odd's fish, Christopher."

I spread my hands. "At least I didn't set anything on fire."

"This is what it's come to," he said to Sally. "Not burning a church to the ground counts as a victory."

"Can we move on?" I said. "The clock is ticking."

Sally looked wary. "This riddle might take some time," she said. And she showed us what she'd found beneath the altar.

CHAPTER
28

TOM STARED AT IT IN CONFUSION.

"What is that?"

Sally held out a thin piece of cedar, a foot long and eight or so inches wide. On one side, it was flat and unmarked. On the other, it looked like a frame for a portrait. Except that inside the frame was a slab of dark wax with numbers carved into it.

"A wax tablet," I said, surprised.

"A what?"

"An old writing device." Master Benedict had told me all about these. We even had one tucked away somewhere among his things. "It goes back to ancient times, the Greeks and Romans, when paper was too expensive to be used for anything you didn't want to keep forever. Say, for example, you were a student working on arithmetic problems. Instead of wasting valuable paper, you'd use a stylus to scratch your calculations into the wax. They'd stay there as long as you left it alone. But you can also reuse it, like a slate. You just erase what you've written by heating the wax and smoothing it out. Then the tablet's blank again, and you can write something different on it."

"So what do these numbers mean?" Sally said.

"Must be a code of some kind."

"Do you know which one?"

I didn't. There were a lot of ways to set a number code.

This one was nearly forty digits long—assuming both lines were even the same cipher.

Tom frowned. "It looks familiar," he said. "Like the one you solved to get the recipe for gunpowder. Just before . . ."

He trailed off, glancing awkwardly at me. He was about to say *before Master Benedict was murdered.*

I remembered the code. Thinking about it now brought up that terrible memory—but also some good ones. The time he'd spent with me, teaching me things like this. That's what I tried to focus on now.

"That code for gunpowder," Tom said. "Didn't it tell you exactly how to solve it?"

I even remembered what it was: ↓M08→. Which meant "replace M with 08, and work forward: N is 09, O is 10, et cetera."

I looked at the tablet, frowning. The wax displayed the numbers, but there were no markings on the back. "I don't see the key to the code here."

"Maybe it's supposed to be that old one you two are talking about," Sally said.

I didn't see how the Raven could have known about that. Though maybe that was the point: to show how deep he'd got into my head. It was worth a shot, anyway, since I had no other idea what to do.

I started by using the quill and ink from my sash to write out the ↓M08→ cipher on the back of the riddle the Raven had sent this morning.

A	B	C	D	E	F	G	H	I	J	K	L	M
22	23	24	25	26	01	02	03	04	05	06	07	08

N	O	P	Q	R	S	T	U	V	W	X	Y	Z
09	10	11	12	13	14	15	16	17	18	19	20	21

Below it, I wrote out the code on the tablet.

2542454144543514152425424541441524.33

Then I got to work. Tom and Sally leaned over my shoulder as I began matching two-digit pairs with the letters of the cipher. "25 is . . . D." I wrote it down. "Next is . . . wait a minute."

I frowned. "Next is 42," I said. "But there can't be a 42. There are only twenty-six letters in the alphabet."

"Could the numbers be shifted?" Sally said.

"Sure. You could set the numbers to be anything, really. But if the Raven's done that, I'll have no idea where to start."

"Maybe the numbers aren't two digits," Tom said. "Maybe they're just one: *2, 5, 4, 2, 4*, like that."

"It's possible, but then we'd only have ten letters to work with." I frowned. "Actually . . . we'd only have five. Look." I pointed to the string of numbers in the wax. "There's only *1, 2, 3, 4*, and *5* here. None of the other numbers—"

Then it hit me.

"I know," I said suddenly. "I know what the code is."

CHAPTER
29

"WHAT IS IT?" TOM SAID.

"The Polybius square," I said.

"You mean . . . Vigenère's square?"

"No. From way earlier." I scratched out the ↓M08→ code. "Polybius was an ancient Greek historian. He wrote about a code developed by two other Greeks, Cleoxenus and Democleitus. It's a way of writing the alphabet as—"

"Oh!" Sally said. "I know this one!"

I blinked. "You do?"

"Isaac taught me," she said, pleased. "It was a way of remembering the Greek alphabet. Can I do it?"

I handed her my quill.

"You make a grid," she said to Tom, drawing lines on the paper. "Five rows and five columns, with the numbers one to five on each side. Like this."

	1	2	3	4	5
1					
2					
3					
4					
5					

"Then," she continued, "you fill it in with the letters of the Greek alphabet. Um . . . don't tell Isaac if I get this wrong."

Reciting to herself, she filled in the grid.

	1	2	3	4	5
1	α	β	γ	δ	ε
2	ζ	η	θ	ι	κ
3	λ	μ	ν	ξ	ο
4	π	ρ	σ	τ	υ
5	φ	χ	ψ	ω	

"You got it," I said. "That's the Polybius square."

"So what do you do with it?" Tom said.

"You match each letter with the numbers for its row and column—row first, column second—to get a two-digit number. For example, the letter in the top left, alpha, is in row 1 and column 1, so alpha is 11. The letter next to it, beta, is in row 1 and column 2, so beta is 12. Right below alpha is zeta—column 2, row 1—so zeta is 21. Like that."

He understood. "This looks a lot easier than Vigenère."

"It is," I said. "And best of all, we don't need a key to solve it. All we have to do is swap the letters for the numbers."

Sally wanted to finish it, so I had her write the numbers out again, this time as pairs.

25 42 45 41 44 54 35 14 15 24 25 42 45 41 44 15 24 33

"Now we replace the numbers with the letters in the square." She began writing them down. "*25* is κ . . . *42* is ρ . . . that's the Greek rho, not *p* . . . *45* is υ, upsilon . . ." She continued until the whole message was written out.

25 42 45 41 44 54 35 14 15 24 25 42 45 41 44 15 24 33
κ ρ υ π τ ω ο δ ε ι κ ρ υ π τ ε ι ν

I stared in amazement. "Do you know what that says?" I asked her.

"Um . . . no."

I took the quill back. "Write it like this."

κρυπτω ο δει κρυπτειν

"Well . . . I can sort of read it," she said, and she sounded it out. "*Krypto ho dei kryptein*. Which means . . . um . . . *krypto* is . . . 'to hide'?"

"'I hide,'" I said. "The literal translation is 'I hide that which must be hidden.' In other words: '*I hide a secret.*'"

"Who hides a secret?" Tom said.

"I think it means the tablet itself."

Sally turned it over, peered at it, ran her fingers carefully over the wood. "I don't see anything here."

I didn't, either. But my master knew the answer. *Where might a wax tablet hide a secret?* he asked.

Long ago, he'd shown me, on our own tablet at home. He'd asked that same question then. I'd looked it over for a long time until I finally gave up. *I don't know,* I admitted.

He'd smiled slightly and said, *You can't see it.*

No, I said.

And so that will be your hint. You can't *see it.*

I'd gone away, even more confused. How was "you can't see it" a hint? If I couldn't see it, how could I find it?

And then, the very next day, out of nowhere, the answer had come to me.

"Don't get alarmed, Tom," I said, "but we're going to need some fire."

His eyes narrowed. "Why?"

There were plenty of candles in Saint Peter ad Vincula, but it was best if I didn't go back in there. I gave Sally a penny to go and buy one from the priest, with a mental note to add one of my own pennies to the purse. When she returned, I surprised both of them by flipping the tablet over and holding it upside down above the candle's flame.

"Are you burning it?" Tom said, surprised.

"Not the wood," I said. "The *wax.* I'm melting the wax. Master Benedict showed me, once. He said it was something the ancient Greeks used to do, to hide a secret. You write your hidden message on the wood itself—and then cover it with wax. Once the wax dries, you can't see through it. So an enemy who searches the wax tablet won't even know the message is inside."

This isn't a coincidence, my master said.

He was right. Secrets under secrets. Ancient Greeks. And the Raven had made the code to find it in Greek. Just like Master Benedict had shown me.

The smoke from the tablet pulled me from my thoughts. The wax had softened and was starting to drip. I started to pry out the slab.

"Hold on," I said. "There's something under here."

"Wasn't that the point of melting the wax?" Tom said. "To see the message underneath?"

"It's not just a message, though. I'm saying there's *something* under—"

The whole slab of wax fell out. I managed to catch the biggest chunk, which had a piece of paper folded and sealed behind it. Another letter.

Something else fell out, too, tucked inside the letter. It fluttered down, landing at Sally's feet. She picked it up.

Then she stared at it, not quite able to believe what she was seeing.

CHAPTER

30

"WHAT'S WRONG?" TOM SAID.

"It's . . . *me*," Sally said in alarm.

She showed us what had fallen from inside the letter. It was a playing card, oval in shape. It had one of the queens on it. Except printed above the queen was a name: SALLY.

She stared up at us, wide-eyed. "What does it mean?"

This card had to be part of the Raven's game. But what—

"The warrants!" I said.

"What warrants?"

I pulled the Raven's original letter from beneath my sash. "Right here. Look."

We huddled together to read it.

Three friends joined. Three souls wagered.
One day to find the warrants that grant salvation.

The Sun marks the clock. Our game begins
at dawn.

"'One day to find the warrants that grant salvation,'" Tom quoted.

"The *warrants*," I said. "We've been wondering what that means. This card has to be it."

"So finding this means . . . Sally is safe?" Tom said.

I wasn't sure. *Three souls wagered.* Did we have to find all three warrants to save us? Or was each one good enough to spare that person?

And would the Raven let us live regardless? Even if we won his stupid game, I didn't believe he'd actually let us go. He had to have something bigger planned for us. Or at least for me.

But this was a promising start. We'd figured out what the warrants were. We were looking for playing cards.

"Hey," Tom said. "There's something on the back of it."

He showed us the other side of the card. Instead of a decorative design, it was blank—except for a single symbol printed in the center of the oval.

"What is that?" Sally said.

"It looks like an alchemical symbol," I said. Maybe. I couldn't remember them all.

I shook my head, upset with myself. The Raven had

used symbols like this before. I should have anticipated that and memorized the list Master Benedict had made. Now we'd have to go to Isaac's to get the key, which was down in the secret library under his bookshop.

Tom broke apart the rest of the wax. He was hoping to find more cards inside. "Where are ours?"

"There won't be any more," I realized. "Not here, anyway. We'll have to find the other two somewhere else."

"How do you know?" Sally said.

"Because I'm starting to understand how the Raven set up his game. He told us last night: I won in Paris, he won in London. This is the deciding round. He's going to make me run the same gauntlet as last time. Three of us, three places to go, three cards to find. I'm sure of it."

"So where's the next place?" Tom said.

"It has to be in this letter." Like the others, this one was sealed with a circle pressed into red wax. I broke it open, and we all read the new riddle together.

The master becomes a traitor. The traitor becomes a thief. The thief is condemned, rejected by all except the cowards you thought could save you. Visit his refuge and gaze from on high upon his face.

"What does *that* mean?" Tom said.

Whatever it was, it didn't sound good. Master, traitor . . . thief? Was it talking about Arthur Pembry?

I didn't think so. Pembry might have been condemned by taking poison, but that was the Raven's doing. And the rest of the riddle didn't fit.

Cowards you thought could save you. Who would the Raven call that? The king and his friends?

No—wait.

"The Templars," I said.

"What about them?" Tom said.

"The cowards. The Raven must mean the Templars. I'd hoped they might help me—save me from the Raven—but they couldn't stop him."

It seemed to fit, at least. Not that it told us who this master, traitor, and thief was. Or where I was supposed to go to "gaze from on high upon his face."

"Maybe this other symbol is a hint," Sally said.

The Raven had included a new glyph below the riddle. It was a long vertical line, with four shorter lines branching out from it. It looked a bit like an awkwardly jumping stick man.

"Is it alchemical?" Sally said.

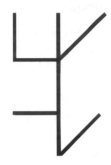

"Doesn't look like any I've seen before," I said. "Though there's *something* familiar about it."

"It looks a little like a map," Tom said. "Could these be roads?"

It did look awfully similar to a road map. "Does anyone recognize it? Say, a main avenue with cross streets?"

No one did. "So what do we do now?" Tom asked.

I could think of only one thing. "We'll have to go to Isaac's."

Sally hesitated. "Can we do that? I thought the rules said no one else could help."

"Actually, they didn't," I said. "The Raven told us we couldn't use the *king's* resources. His Majesty has nothing to do with either Isaac or the library."

I still wasn't thrilled about going. I'd hoped to keep Isaac out of this, but he had the table of alchemical symbols we needed. "Maybe he'll know who this riddle is talking about, too," I said.

I sure hoped so. Because if he didn't, the Raven's game would end for us right here.

CHAPTER
31

ISAAC KNEW OUR VISIT COULDN'T
be a good thing.

When the Raven had revealed he was still alive, I'd told Isaac I wouldn't be back until this was over. Sally, as his unofficial apprentice, was how he and I kept in touch. She'd not only passed messages between us, she'd also let us know that the other was well.

But now that I saw him again, I realized Sally hadn't been entirely honest about Isaac's health. It wasn't just that he moved so carefully; I already knew he had arthritis, plus a cloudiness in his eyes that hampered his vision.

But today he seemed even more worn down. His skin was terribly pale, sunken cheeks above a rumpled collar. He looked like he hadn't been sleeping.

"I haven't," he admitted when I asked him. "I've been poring over Benedict's journals, trying to think who the Raven might be. Did Lord Walsingham have any luck with the list I sent you?"

Before I could tell him no, another old friend came swooping down the stairs into Isaac's bookshop. "Bridget!" I said.

She flew past my open hands to land on my shoulder. Wings flapping in excitement, she brushed against my face, hopping up to my head, then to my shoulder, then back again, poking her beak into my hair and cooing.

I cupped her in my palms and stroked her feathers. She wouldn't sit still, fluttering her wings and hopping back onto my shoulder, burying herself against my neck. I let her stay there.

In the meantime, I told Isaac why we'd come. I ran through everything the Raven had done. When I got to the end, I showed him the riddle we'd found at the Tower. "Do you have any idea who this might mean?"

He read the message carefully.

The master becomes a traitor. The traitor becomes a thief. The thief is condemned, rejected by all except the cowards you thought could save you. Visit his refuge and gaze from on high upon his face.

He frowned, thinking. "You believe the 'cowards' are the Templars?"

"It's the closest thing that fits," I said.

"Templars," he mused. "Master . . . then traitor . . . then thief. I . . . oh." He looked up at us. "You found this riddle at the Tower?"

"In Saint Peter ad Vincula, yes."

His eyes lit up. "I believe I do know the answer. Sally, we're going to need that blue book with the alchemical symbols to match them to this card with your name on it. While you're down there, bring up another tome. I'll tell you where to find it."

I hid a smile as he gave her instructions. I liked seeing her as an apprentice. She'd been so worried when she'd injured her hand in Paris that no one would ever employ her. Now, not only was her hand mostly working, but she'd found a lifelong career. Best of all, with her becoming the keeper of the secret library, it meant we'd always be connected, no matter what. Tom saw me watching her and smirked.

Caught again. I shook my head and played a bit more with Bridget, taking advantage of what little time we'd have together. I'd really missed having her around. It made my spirits sink knowing I'd have to leave her behind again when we left.

As for Tom, he had his own request. When Sally ran down to the secret library, he asked hopefully, "Isaac . . . I don't suppose we could beg something to eat? I have a feeling this is going to be a long day."

"Of course," Isaac said, and he showed a delighted Tom to the pantry. Tom returned with his arms full of bread, sausage, butter, and cheese. "It's for everyone," he said, somewhat defensively.

In truth, the sight of it made me realize how hungry I was. We set a small table and began filling our plates.

"You never told me if those names I gave you were useful," Isaac said.

"Oh. No, sorry. Only one of them is even a possibility

for the Raven. And that's if he didn't go to the New World," I said glumly.

Isaac was disappointed, too. "I'll keep looking. But the Raven may not be in Benedict's journals at all. The gaps in the books we have span quite a few years."

Tom was just getting into his food when Sally arrived with the books. "Found them," she said. "I—oh, Tom. What is that?"

Proudly, he showed off his creation. "You like it? It's bread with butter, then sausage, then cheese. Then another slice of bread, and more butter, more sausage, and *more* cheese. Isn't it beautiful?"

"How are you even going to eat that?" I said. The thing was eight inches tall.

"I . . . hmm." He pondered it for a moment, scratching his cheek. "Maybe I didn't think this through."

As Tom tried to decide how best to attack his tower of gluttony, Isaac began leafing through the book Sally had brought him. I munched my own food, feeding bits of bread to Bridget on my shoulder, as I studied the key to the alchemical symbols my master had drawn up.

Sally leaned in close, her arm against mine.

VOCABULARIUM ALCHEMIAE

THE THREE PRINCIPLES

⊖ salt *the contractive force*	crystallization, contraction
⚷ sulphur *the expansive force*	dissolution, evaporation
☿ mercury *the integrative force*	balancing salt and sulphur

THE FOUR ELEMENTS

▽ earth	cold and dry	melancholic
▽ water	cold and wet	phlegmatic
△ air	hot and wet	sanguine
△ fire	hot and dry	choleric

PLANETARY METALS

☉ gold / Sun		
☽ silver / Moon	♃ tin / Jupiter	
♂ iron / Mars	♀ lead / Venus	
☿ mercury / Mercury	♄ copper / Saturn	

TERRESTRIAL MINERALS

⦶ saltpeter	♈ realgar	
♅ quicklime	cinnabar	
✳○✳ sal ammoniac	tartar	
litharge	marcasite	

CORROSIVES

aqua fortis	aqua regia
✝ vinegar	distilled vinegar
⊕ oil of vitriol	

WEIGHTS & MINERALS

M℔ one pound	℈ one scruple
℥ one ounce	P℔ one pinch
ℨ one dram	O℔ one pint
ANA equal amounts	

INSTRUCTIONS / PROCESSES

calcination	sublimation	sugar	honey
congestion	separation	spirit	wax
fixation	ceration	essence	powder
solution	fermentation	still	distill
digestion	multiplication	take	mix
precipitation	caput mortuum	alcohol	compose
purify	oil	retort	receiver
digest	filter	night	boil
		day	

I glanced down at her. She kept her eyes on the paper. "Anything match?" she said.

This was distracting. "Er . . . sort of. Look at marcasite."

I turned the page so everyone could see and placed the card facedown to compare the symbols.

"It's not *exactly* the same," I said. "Marcasite has a curving top, and this symbol is flat. But that could just be the way this one is drawn."

"What's marcasite?" Tom said, mouth full of food.

"Pyrite. It comes in a few different forms. Fool's gold is one of them."

"It's used for jewelry, too," Sally said.

"Right, the polished stones."

She frowned. "But why is it on the back of *my* card? What does it have to do with me?"

"Do you own any marcasite jewelry?" Tom asked.

"Everything I have is borrowed from the ladies at Berkshire House."

Knowing the symbol's meaning didn't make the card clearer at all. "Maybe we're getting ahead of ourselves," I said. "If I'm right, there should be two more cards, one for Tom and one for me. I'm guessing they'll have symbols, too. Once we have all three, we might see the point of this."

"Aha," Isaac said.

"You figured it out?"

"Not your symbol puzzle," he said. "The riddle. I know to whom the Raven is referring."

"Who?" Sally said.

Isaac turned the book around so we could see it. It was written in a very old hand, transcribed in a monastery years ago.

"This tells the story of Geoffrey de Mandeville," Isaac said.

Tom added more sausage to his plate. "Never heard of him."

"There's no real reason you would have. Geoffrey de Mandeville was the first Earl of Essex, awarded his title by King Stephen five hundred years ago. More important—

at least for our purposes—is that, in 1140, Stephen also awarded Geoffrey a different office: constable of the Tower of London.

"Now, Geoffrey was a schemer," Isaac said. "And at the time, Stephen was fighting his cousin, Matilda, for control of the kingdom. When it looked like Matilda would win, Geoffrey switched sides and supported her. When the tides turned once more, Geoffrey switched his allegiance back to Stephen. But it was too late for that. The angry king stripped Geoffrey of all his titles, and had him dragged from the throne room, kicking and screaming.

"Furious, Geoffrey launched a rebellion. For a whole year, he raided the countryside, robbing everything he could and burning everything he couldn't. He was only stopped when, besieging Burwell Castle, someone hit him with an arrow."

I sat up as I listened to Isaac's tale. "Master of the Tower," I said. "Then traitor to King Stephen. And then—"

"Thief," Tom said. "Master, traitor, thief. That's the riddle."

"But what do the Templars have to do with it?" Sally said.

Isaac leaned back in his chair. "That's the interesting part. For his crimes against king and people, the pope had Geoffrey excommunicated. So when he died, Mandeville was not allowed to be buried in consecrated ground.

"But earlier in his life, he'd supported a fledgling organization of brother knights: the Templars. In recognition of that support, the Templars took Geoffrey's bones and buried them in the grounds of their own church. In thanks, Geoffrey's son paid for an effigy of him to be made and placed nearby."

"That's it," I said, half rising. "Gaze upon his face. That has to mean Geoffrey's effigy."

"So where is that?" Tom said.

"In what used to be the heart of Templar London," Isaac said. "You'll find Mandeville's remains in the Temple Church."

CHAPTER

32

"WE'VE BEEN THERE," I SAID, SURPRISED.

"We have?" Sally said.

"Me and Tom. When we started looking for the priest Domhnall Ardrey told me to find. After Saint Paul's Cathedral, the Temple Church was the second place we checked."

Even though we'd known the London chapter of the Templars was gone, I'd hoped to find at least some remnant of the order there. The place had, after all, once been their headquarters in the city. But I'd made just as much of a fool of myself when we'd gone as I had this morning at the Tower. No one knew anything of a visiting French priest,

Father Bernard, or the Templar florin I'd showed them.

Suddenly, I had a thought. "Master Benedict's journals never happened to mention a priest, did they?"

Isaac shook his head. "As far as I know, other than attending church, your master never had any connection with the clergy. But there were many things in Benedict's life he kept to himself. He was a very private person, even with his closest friends."

How well I knew it. I'd learned more about his past in the year since he died than I had in the three years I'd spent as his apprentice. Still, now we had the answer to the second riddle. "We have to go."

"Be safe. And take those alchemical symbols with you. No doubt you'll need them for the other cards."

I stuffed the papers beneath my sash. I wished I could take Bridget with me, too. As we gathered our things, she flapped about frantically. That was the problem, having such an intelligent pet. She always seemed to know when I was going.

I tried to take hold of her, but she kept fluttering through my fingers, cooing desperately. *Don't leave me!* she seemed to be saying. *Take me with you! I can help you!*

There's not much that feels worse than leaving someone

you love behind. "I know you can," I said quietly as I finally caught her and held her close. "But I can't take the chance of the Raven hurting you again. I need to know, at least, that you're warm and safe."

Tom stuffed the last of the cheese in his mouth. "But *we're* just fine running around," he muttered. "Bridget's probably the safest of all of us."

"The Raven already hurt her once," I protested.

"Actually, he didn't," Tom said. "He scared her, sure, by stuffing her in that box with all that blood. But otherwise, he didn't harm a single feather."

Tom had a point. Considering what the Raven could have done to Bridget, she'd basically come out unscathed. It was something I'd never really understood.

One the one hand, I could see a purpose to it. The Raven hadn't stuck her in that box to hurt her. He'd done it to hurt *me*. To give me that scare when I opened it.

Yet he could have done much worse. How awful would it have been if he really *had* hurt Bridget? As upset as I'd been to find her bound like that, it wouldn't have compared to my grief at seeing her dead.

It had never made any sense. The Raven was a traitor, a poisoner, a mass murderer. So far, he'd been responsible for dozens of deaths—and those were just the people I knew about. Why had he spared Bridget's life? Why would he show me such mercy?

I finally managed to calm her. I held her to my cheek for a moment, then passed her to Isaac. "Maybe the Raven just likes pigeons," I sighed. "Maybe he keeps them himself. Maybe that's what that pigeon feather he left for me in Paris was supposed to mean. A way in which we're alike."

We made to go.

Then Isaac spoke.

"Pigeons," he said.

We turned back. Isaac was staring down at Bridget. She was struggling in his hands, trying to follow.

He looked up at me, eyes wide. "Pigeons," he said again. "The Raven likes *pigeons*."

Tom blinked. "Is that a real clue?"

"Not just a clue. An *answer*." Isaac stared at us. "I think . . . I think I might know who the Raven is."

CHAPTER
33

WE ALL STARED BACK. "WHO?"

Isaac looked lost. "But . . . it can't be," he said to himself. "Can it?"

"Isaac," I said. "Who are you talking about?"

"Peter," he said. "Peter Hyde."

Tom and Sally looked at each other in confusion. They didn't know who that was.

But I did.

"Who's Peter Hyde?" Sally said.

"Master Benedict's old apprentice," I said, stunned. "The one he had before me."

My master had had four apprentices in his lifetime.

The first was a boy named George Staple, who'd died in the plague of 1636. The second was Hugh Coggshall, who'd become a lifelong friend of Master Benedict's until Hugh's passing last year. The third was Peter Hyde.

I knew almost nothing about Peter. All my master had ever told me was his name; he'd refused to say any more. I'd caught a further glint of trouble in one of Master Benedict's old journal entries. I knew the passage by heart.

For two years, Hugh has been pressing me to get a new apprentice. With my private experiments, and the past trouble with Peter, I have been reluctant to do so. Finding someone with the necessary aptitude for the job is hard enough. Because of my own work, I must also choose someone who, when they are older, can be trusted.

And when faced with an unknown boy, how can one know what he will become? Hugh insists that Peter's descent into darkness was not my fault. But the boy was mine to shape, and I failed him. One more failure, of so many in this life.

My master had got past his reluctance. He'd gone to the testing at the Apothecaries' Guild and chosen me. But Peter Hyde . . . "What happened to him?" I said.

Isaac gave me a sad look. "I think we'd better sit down."

Bridget flapped back into my hands as we returned to the table. She calmed as I stroked her feathers, and we listened as Isaac told his tale.

"Your master, as you know, traveled to Paris in 1652, staying with his old friend Marin Chastellain—that's when he met young Simon. Benedict had gone there to study the latest outbreak of plague. In those days, he was obsessed with finding a cure.

"When he returned, Benedict was in as low spirits as I'd ever seen him. He'd failed to find anything that could stop the sickness, and it weighed terribly upon him. Normally, when he fell into those moods, he'd isolate himself. But this time he surprised us all: Just a few months later, he took on a new apprentice."

Isaac shook his head. "To say I was shocked is an understatement. With Benedict deep into his secret experiments in alchemy, keeping a child around was somewhat risky. He said he hadn't planned on taking an apprentice, but he happened to be at Apothecaries' Hall during the test, and this boy—Peter Hyde—caught his eye. He said the child's answers were remarkable, showing keen intelligence and a willingness to learn. So on a whim, your master chose him."

Isaac frowned. "I always had the sense something more was going on. That there was some other reason he'd chosen Peter, something else about the boy that made him stop and watch the examination. But he never said what, and I knew better than to pry.

"Regardless of the true reason, Benedict was right about one thing: The boy *was* brilliant. Beyond brilliant, in fact. Your master once said he believed Peter would outshine us all in the future. And considering what a genius Benedict himself was, you understand the magnitude of his claim.

"But there was trouble inside Peter, too. Something . . . wrong. A darkness, Benedict once called it."

I shivered. My master had written those same words in his journal. "What did he mean?"

"At first, it was little things," Isaac said. "Technically, Peter was turning into an extraordinary apothecary. But he didn't seem to care about *people*. He was completely indifferent to the patients he and Benedict treated. What interested Peter was how remedies were made, what they did, and why they worked—and even more so, why they *didn't*. A dead patient wasn't a tragedy to Peter. It was merely a puzzle to work out.

"What's more, Peter would regularly get into fights with boys on the commons over what seemed the most trivial slights. And the grudges he kept were vicious. One time, early on, Peter came home crying. Some older boy had shoved him down playing at ball—nothing unusual, just part of the game. Benedict consoled him and imagined that would be the end of it. Certainly Peter never mentioned it again. Until seven months later, when, in another game, Peter deliberately stomped on the same boy's knee, breaking it.

"Of course Benedict was horrified. The child would never walk right after that. Benedict told Peter their lives were dedicated to healing people, not hurting them. Peter just shrugged and said, 'Then he shouldn't have pushed me.'

"He was trouble in other ways, too. Always clever, he figured out your master was up to something all those nights he went to the secret laboratory. One time, Benedict caught the boy following him. He scolded him, but Peter wasn't contrite. If anything, he grew resentful. Peter's attitude was that Benedict was denying him knowledge, keeping him down. And over time it only grew worse.

"Benedict was at a loss for what to do with the boy. But as the months passed, he noticed something. When Peter had time to himself, he'd go up to the roof and watch the birds flying overhead. He'd even steal little handfuls of grain to feed them.

"Benedict saw this as an opportunity to teach the boy compassion. Always having enjoyed birds himself, your master built the coop on the roof, then bought pigeons to keep. And he assigned Peter to look after the birds."

Isaac nodded toward Bridget. "It was an enormous success. Peter cared for those pigeons with as much love as you did. He'd take a candle up in the evenings and do his nightly studies next to the coop, just to be with them. And he still stole handfuls of grain to feed other birds that might come."

Pigeons, I thought in amazement. I stroked Bridget, nestled in my arms. "If Peter is the Raven . . . that explains why he didn't hurt her."

"And the pigeon feather as a clue," Sally said.

"Indeed," Isaac said. "It is a direct tie back to your master, the man who gave Peter the first thing he cared about. He never would have hurt any bird. Not even to torment you." Isaac sighed. "But whatever was in Peter that made him care for these creatures, it never transferred to anything else. If anything, his wrath only got worse. A year later, Peter poisoned a child."

We gasped. "What?" I said.

"It was again over some slight or another," Isaac said wearily, "too small to even remember. But Peter made a tincture of madapple and gave it to the boy, telling him it was spirits he'd stolen from his master's stash. It wasn't enough to kill the child, but it gave him terrible hallucinations for days. Benedict found out because the father of the boy was a regular customer and called your master over. Benedict recognized the symptoms right away, of course, and found the empty vial hidden in the child's clothes.

"Your master realized immediately how the boy had got the poison, and why. And that was a step too far. For Peter to actually use the knowledge Benedict had taught him to hurt people . . . it was beyond the pale."

No betrayal could have hurt Master Benedict worse. *These ingredients,* he'd once told me, *are the gifts the Lord has given us. They are the tools of our trade. What you must always remember is that they are only that: tools. They can heal, or they can kill. It's never the tool itself that decides. It's the hands—and the heart—of the one who wields it. Of all the things I'll teach you, Christopher, there's no lesson more important than this.*

"What happened next?" Tom said.

"Benedict was torn," Isaac said. "He still felt responsible for Peter. But he knew he couldn't let something this grievous stand. He confronted the boy and told him he'd have to confess and accept whatever punishment the law and the Apothecaries' Guild set forth.

"Peter was furious. He accused Benedict of betraying him and said your master would regret this someday. Then he fled from the house. That was the last time Benedict ever saw him."

I couldn't believe it. The pigeons, the grudges, the poison—*all* of it fit. "Why didn't you tell me about Peter before?"

"It never would have occurred to me," Isaac said, apologetic. "Even now I don't see how it's possible."

"Why not?" Sally said.

"Because Peter is dead."

CHAPTER
34

"DEAD?" I SAID, CONFUSED.

Isaac nodded and continued his story. "After Peter fled Blackthorn, after all he'd done, even then, Benedict wouldn't give up on him. It was true that Peter would have been expelled from the guild, and he likely would have had to spend some time in prison. Benedict still said he'd stand by the boy, help him get back on his feet afterward, regardless of what punishment was doled out.

"But Peter was nowhere to be found. Benedict checked with his colleagues first. Peter was cunning, and he had real charm. He knew well how to lie, how to paint himself as the victim even when he was at fault. Benedict believed Peter might run to the guild with a story that your master had poisoned the boy by accident, and was blaming his mistake on an innocent apprentice.

"But Peter never contacted the guild, and none of the other apothecaries had seen him. Benedict further inquired with the boys on the commons, with ingredient merchants, with aviaries, to see if Peter had tried to find a job in the areas he was familiar with.

"Your master found nothing. He even went to Cambridge, where Peter was born, and spoke to the boy's parents. They had no idea what had happened. In fact, not only had they not seen him, they hadn't received a letter from him in months. Benedict had allowed Peter to take paper as he needed and had given him a few coins to pay for post to his parents. It appeared the boy had just pocketed the money.

"Still Benedict searched," Isaac said, "contacting guilds in various towns, trying to find the child. Then one day he received a note from Peter's family. They'd got a letter from an herb merchant in Brighton. Peter had apparently fled to the coast and taken a job at the market. The merchant sent his regrets with the news that Peter had been stabbed to death.

"Benedict was devastated. He traveled to Brighton, but what was there for him to do? He found the merchant, who told him that Peter had come to work for him a few months ago. Recently, he'd begun to suspect Peter was stealing his stock and selling it himself, but that wasn't what did him in. Apparently Peter liked to gamble, and he got in a fight with some sailors down at the dock after they'd accused him of cheating at dice. They stabbed him, and he bled to death on the wharf.

"Benedict visited his grave, but that never brought him any peace. He only told me this because one night, when he and Hugh were over, we all had a little too much wine, and the story came pouring out of him. He swore to both of us that he'd never take on another apprentice. And you know how stubborn he could be. Even though he needed the help, he kept that promise for six years." Isaac nodded at me. "Until you."

My heart broke for my master. If he'd cared even a fraction for Peter as he had for me, Peter's death would have crushed him.

And that made me sit up, startled.

It would have crushed my master, I thought.

And maybe . . . that was the whole point.

"I don't understand," Tom said. "If Peter's dead, how can he be the Raven?"

"He can't," I said slowly. *"Unless Peter's not actually dead."*

Tom looked confused. "Is that possible?"

I turned to Isaac. "You said Master Benedict visited his grave."

"That's what he told me," Isaac said.

"So he never actually saw Peter's body."

"I suppose not."

"Did he check with the constables in Brighton? See if they had a record of Peter being stabbed to death?"

Isaac paused. "He didn't say he did. But I can't imagine he would have. What would be the point?"

"Right," I said. "Why would he? He had no reason to doubt the story."

"But the herb merchant said it happened," Sally said.

"What merchant? Who was he? Did Master Benedict look into him? What if the man he spoke to in Brighton was a fraud? Paid to tell him a story, make him go away."

Sally wasn't convinced. "Why would Peter go to all that trouble?"

"Because he didn't want to go to prison." I stood, pacing. "Peter knew Master Benedict. He might have thought my master's search was about bringing Peter to justice, but that wasn't the issue. He *cared* for Peter. He wouldn't have let him just disappear. He'd keep looking, no matter how long it took. There was only one way Master Benedict would ever stop."

"If Peter were dead," Tom said, surprised.

"Yes," I said. "So Peter makes up a story—and most important, he makes it *believable*. He gives Master Benedict proof he's dead. My master goes away. The constables stop looking for him. And he's free. Free to start a new life, where no one even knows he exists.

"We know the Raven is an expert at setting traps," I said. "Telling lies. Getting people to do his dirty work for him. If Peter really is the Raven . . . this might be the first con he ever pulled."

We looked at each other in stunned silence.

"So—wait," Sally said, suddenly eager. "If it is Peter . . . what does he look like?"

Isaac was surprised at the question. "I never saw the boy."

"Not once?" I said, disappointed.

"Benedict kept his apprentices away from his secret work. Especially me, because of the library downstairs. You know that better than anyone. I never saw you, either, until he sent you here, after his death."

"So then who would—" I gasped. *"Mr. Sinclair."*

"The confectioner?" Tom said.

Now I understood. "Mr. Sinclair lived next door to Blackthorn for decades. He knew every one of Master Benedict's apprentices. And remember what Dorothy said? *Sinclair had been staring down the street, as if watching someone.* Then he'd gone to my shop and asked if I was around.

"What if the person Sinclair saw was *Peter*?" I said. "And he recognized him, so he came to tell me. What if it really *wasn't* random, the Raven killing Mr. Sinclair? What if it had a purpose: to stop him from telling me what he knew?"

It all fit. In fact . . . maybe that's why the Raven killed Dr. Kemp, too. Kemp wouldn't have recognized Peter, but if the doctor had seen someone snooping around Blackthorn . . . and if I asked him about it . . . ? The Raven would need to silence Dr. Kemp as well.

"Is there anyone left in London who knows what Peter looks like?" Sally asked.

Isaac shook his head. "If there is, I don't know who it would be. Peter joined Benedict in 1653, then stayed with him for three years. Sinclair was the only neighbor who lived there when Peter did."

The troubles with the Commonwealth, then the return of the king, meant a lot of people had moved in and out of London in the last decade. *Someone at the Apothecaries' Guild might know,* I thought. Though they weren't particularly friendly to me these days.

"Is there anything we *do* know about Peter?" Tom said.

"Well," I said, "if he was Master Benedict's apprentice ten years ago, he'd have to be in his twenties today. So we can say for sure that he's young—the *priest!*"

"Which one?"

"From Saint Paul's. The one who warned us about the assassin. He was exactly the right age!"

"But Peter was from Cambridge," Tom said. "That priest was French."

"Says who? He had a French accent, but that's easily faked. Especially for someone like the Raven."

"This is an interesting theory," Isaac said, "but we don't know if any of it is true. Peter Hyde may well have died in Brighton."

Possibly. But too many of the pieces were falling into place. Even a fake death matched what we knew about the

Raven. I wished desperately that I could talk to Walsingham; his agents could investigate Peter Hyde easily. But the Raven's rules prevented me from doing so. And we couldn't do it ourselves; it would take too much time, and time was the one thing we didn't have. We'd stayed here too long already.

"We have to go," I said. I looked down at Bridget. If the Raven really was Peter, then Tom was right; she was perfectly safe. But we couldn't know that for sure. "Sorry, girl," I said softly. "Just one more day."

I handed her back to Isaac. We said our goodbyes, listening at the door after we were outside to make sure Isaac had bolted it. Then we headed to the Temple Church, where the second riddle sent us.

We didn't quite make it.

CHAPTER
35

THE THOUGHT THAT WE MIGHT

finally know who the Raven was—even if we had no way of finding him—had my blood racing. To keep my mind occupied, I studied the second letter as we rode. Not the riddle itself, but the strange symbol below it.

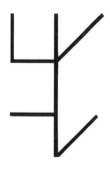

"Does it match the route we're following?" Tom asked.

I was finding it hard to concentrate; I kept thinking about what Isaac had said. "I can't really tell."

"Maybe it's not here," Sally said. "It could be a map of something near your home."

That was an interesting idea. At the moment, we were headed down Fleet Street. Though the road was busy, I forced myself to still my mind and closed my eyes, knowing Blossom would follow Lightning as Tom led the way. In the darkness, I tried to picture the streets around Blackthorn.

I couldn't make them match. Adding the alleys didn't help, either.

Maybe it was Whitehall? Last month, the Raven had given us a route that had led us through the palace. I took the map Dobson had given us from beneath my apothecary sash and tried to compare them. If there was a match to the symbol, I didn't see it.

"It's probably based on something around the Temple Church, then," Sally said.

That would make a certain sense. Though at this point, I was starting to think it wasn't a road map at all. Something nagged at the back of my mind—I'd swear I'd seen something like this somewhere before. And I wouldn't put any trick past the Raven.

Peter, I said to myself. *I should start thinking of him as Peter Hyde. It will help me get inside his head.*

Yet even as I thought that, I could hear the spymaster warning me. *The human mind,* he'd once said, *is exceptional at recognizing patterns. So good, in fact, that when there are no patterns, we invent them to fill the gaps. Once a man's mind is fixed on what he believes is the truth, nothing else can be real. If he finds evidence that supports his theory, then he is correct. If he finds evidence that refutes his theory, does he rethink his beliefs? Very rarely. Instead, he dismisses the evidence or finds some way to twist it so it will fit his view of the world. He simply refuses to see.*

It was a caution against making assumptions—which was exactly what I was doing. And, in particular, it was a caution against *fixating* on those assumptions.

And you know the Raven is skilled at misdirection, Master Benedict said.

The sound of my master's voice made me think of him. How sad he must have been when Peter turned to darkness; even more so when he believed Peter had died. It made me angry to think that anyone could be so cruel to someone so kind.

You're doing it again, I told myself. *You don't know Peter is—*

My thoughts were broken by someone shouting. In French.

"Ça alors! Que faites-vous?"

Then someone fired a gun.

I recognized the snap of flint striking a frizzen even before I heard the powder burn. The air thumped with the boom of a pistol.

Sally's horse, Beatrice, reared in alarm. Sally, riding sidesaddle, was thrown backward. She held desperately on to the reins, and the leads twisted Beatrice's neck as she fell. They both went down in the crowd.

"Sally!" I shouted.

Another gun boomed. I heard the *zzzzzz* of a bullet buzz past my head, and that made me slide from my saddle, too. One foot got caught in the stirrup, and I lost my balance, slamming a shoulder hard onto the cobblestones.

A third shot rang out. *"Un assassin!"* a voice shouted in French. *"Un assassin!"*

The crowd began to panic. Blossom neighed in alarm, eyes rolling, searching for the source of the danger. If she bolted with my foot stuck in the stirrup . . .

Tom saved me. He jumped from Lightning's back and seized Blossom's reins, keeping her from fleeing. He grabbed Beatrice's reins, too, wrapping them around his wrist as the mare struggled to rise. He didn't have to worry about Lightning; the old warhorse had no intention of running anywhere. Lightning snorted, stamping his hooves, welcoming the fight.

I finally managed to free my foot from Blossom's stirrup. "Sally! Where—"

I spotted her on the other side of Beatrice. "The alley!" I shouted. "Take cover! Go!"

She fled through the stampeding crowd. I pushed myself from the cobblestones, shoulder throbbing, watching until she slipped safely into the shadows. Then I drew my own pistols and turned.

Two men stood in the emptying street, shoulder to shoulder, facing away from us. From the clouds of smoke rising above them, I knew they'd fired at least two of the shots. One man had already jammed his pistol back into his belt, ammunition spent. The other still held his, but both of them had drawn their swords: rapiers, with long, thin blades and ornate basket hilts.

"Le vois-tu?" one of them asked the other. *Do you see him?*

They continued in French. "He ran through there," his companion said, pointing toward an alley to the north. "Keep watch; I'm going to reload."

The man tucked the blade of his rapier under his arm and began filling his smoking pistol with powder from a horn. Tom and I backed away, Tom using the horses to block the alley Sally had hidden in.

I called to them in French. "What are you doing?"

The man reloading his gun glanced back at me. Though I was holding both my pistols, he didn't seem to consider me a threat. "An assassin, stalking us, monsieur. He fled when we fired. Are you injured?"

"No. What do you mean, an assassin?"

"Well, what would you call a man skulking through the alleyways, holding a pistol and wearing a mask?"

I stared at Tom in alarm. He didn't know any French, but it wasn't too hard to understand the word *masque*.

We backed farther toward the alley, using the wall as cover. "What mask?"

"Something gold," the man said. He tucked away his own pistol, then yanked the one from his companion's belt, reloading that next. "I couldn't see it well under his hood."

He didn't have to. I was sure it was the same mask Elinor Bagley had described. Thalia, the Muse of Comedy. The Raven. Or his agent.

Now I looked around, too, but I couldn't spot anyone. It seemed as if our French allies had scared him off.

Why would the masked man be stalking you? Master Benedict said.

He must have been following us. I'd been wondering for some time if one of the Raven's agents, or even the Raven himself, was watching. It would have been easy to shadow our horses once the streets got crowded and we could no longer ride at speed.

But why would the man have his gun out? my master pressed.

That made me pause.

Why *would* he have his gun out? Was he going to shoot us?

No, that didn't make sense. We had one day to play this game. I knew the Raven couldn't be trusted, but I was pretty sure he wouldn't break his own rules. Beating me by using them was the whole point.

Wasn't it?

Had I got it wrong? Maybe this was punishment. Did

the Raven think *I'd* broken the rules? I had given away those guineas, though I'd covered for that.

Or maybe this wasn't aimed at me at all. But then . . . was the masked man planning to shoot someone else?

In my head, my master kept prodding me. *Why would the Raven do that? What purpose would that serve?*

It would cause chaos, I answered.

What else?

I thought about it. *It would slow us down, because I'd stop to treat anyone who was wounded.*

What else?

Um . . . *To alert someone to something?*

What else?

Master Benedict's question rang in my head. I didn't know what else.

What else is the Raven good at? he asked.

A . . . distraction?

Misdirection, I thought. But what would he be trying to direct our attention away from—

I stopped. And a sinking feeling gripped my stomach.

Sally.

As soon as the bullets had started flying, I'd sent Sally to the safety of the alley.

Or had I?

"Sally!" I shoved my way through our horses. They shied away from my panic. "Sally!"

I made it into the alley. I looked through the shadows.

She was gone.

CHAPTER
36

"SALLY!"

I sprinted into the alley.

"Christopher! Wait!" Tom was still stuck behind the horses. It was too narrow here for all three of them, and Beatrice balked at entering the shadowed passage. It took all of Tom's strength to hold her. "Wait for me!"

I couldn't. Sally had disappeared.

On some level, I knew this was a perfect trap. The masked man causes a distraction for the Raven to grab Sally. Then I come running trying to find her. And the Raven takes me, too.

That's against his own rules, I tried to tell myself. But I wasn't sure I believed that anymore. "Sally!"

Suddenly, I came to a crossroads. Going straight would lead me through Whitefriars, toward the Thames. Right and left the alley ran behind the shops. There were plenty of nooks and crannies to hide in.

Which way?

"Sally!"

If the Raven wanted to carry her away, he'd choose the street or the Thames. But if he just wanted to hurt her . . . then a darkened alley would be the perfect place to dispose of a body.

Which *way*?

I looked around desperately for some sign that she'd been here. Something she'd dropped, maybe, in the dirt—

The dirt.

Most of Walsingham's instruction to me had been about finding secret messages. In the few weeks we'd had together, we hadn't covered other aspects of spying, like how to track someone. But the earth might still tell me the way.

It was covered in footprints; plenty of people had walked through here. Yet Sally's print would be much smaller than most. I scanned for the tread of her shoes: low, flat heel—

There.

It was faint, but I could see her footprints pressed into the other tracks in the alley. She'd gone left.

I followed them, faster now. "Sally!"

Why wasn't she answering?

If her footprints are there, Master Benedict said, *then she must be moving of her own accord.*

That heartened me a little. I hadn't seen any evidence of her being dragged, at least. Though she could have been gagged. A blade to her throat.

I ran, looking anyplace a person might be hidden. "Sally!" I called one more time.

Then I saw her.

She was sitting on the doorstep behind a house, slumped over, head between her knees. I ran to her, crouching, pistol grips slick with sweat. No one else was around.

"Sally? What's wrong?"

She lifted her head, blinking. "Christopher?"

Guns still in hand, I hugged her to me. She wrapped her arms around me, resting her head on my shoulder, breathing slowly.

"Are you hurt?" I said. "Why didn't you call out?"

"I . . . I don't feel well," she said.

Had she been shot? With rising dread, I looked her over,

front, back, everywhere. I saw no blood. "What happened?"

"I don't know."

We were a fair distance from Fleet Street. "How did you get here?"

"I . . . you told me to hide," she said.

I supposed I had. Though I'd meant for her to find cover against flying bullets, not hide from *us*. "Did you hit your head?"

"I . . . don't know. I'm dizzy. I . . . can I go back to Isaac's?"

I ran my hands carefully through her hair, pressing against her skull. I couldn't feel anything out of the ordinary. There was some scar tissue underneath, near the back, a reminder of when she'd nearly been killed in Paris. But I felt no fresh wounds, no lumps or hot spots, and my fingers came away unstained by blood. So what could be wrong with her—?

Oh no.

"Sally? Sally, look at me."

She did. Her eyes were so green.

"What have you eaten?" I said.

"What?"

"Food. Drink. What have you had?"

She looked a little puzzled. "Nothing. I mean . . . just what we ate at Isaac's. What are you—?"

She stared in shock as I leaned in close, my mouth next to hers. I think she thought I was going to kiss her.

I smelled her breath.

Garlic.

"Christopher!" Tom called from the alleyway.

"Here!" I shouted back, and Tom came running. I was already rummaging in my apothecary sash.

Tom arrived alone; he must have found somewhere to hitch the horses. His sword in his hand, he saw me crouched next to Sally. "Is she all right?"

I found the vial I was searching for and uncorked it. "Drink this," I said to Sally.

She seemed flustered, first by my leaning in, then by my pulling away. "What is that?"

"Ipecac and charcoal dust."

"Ipecac?" Tom said. "Isn't that the stuff that makes you throw up?"

"Yes. Drink it."

Sally recoiled from the open vial. "Why?"

"Because I think you might have been poisoned."

CHAPTER
37

SALLY STARED AT ME, CONFUSED. "What? No. I didn't . . ."

Tom turned white. "How could she be poisoned?"

I put the vial to her lips. "Drink it."

"I don't want to," she said.

"Don't be foolish."

"I can't be poisoned. I didn't have anything you didn't. We all ate the same food."

"We did," Tom said, worried. "What makes you think she's poisoned?"

"She doesn't feel well," I said.

"I probably just hit my head," Sally said.

"And her breath smells like garlic. Arsenic poisoning can smell like that."

"Your breath smells like garlic, too. It was in the sausage."

"*I* ate the sausage," Tom said, alarmed. "I ate a *lot* of it!"

"Do you feel sick?"

"Well, now I do." His lip trembled.

The truth was, I didn't feel sick, either, and I'd had my fair share of the food. But I didn't know what else could be wrong with her. "Just drink the ipecac," I said.

Resigned, Sally swallowed the contents of the vial. "Can we go back to Isaac's now?"

Tom looked at the empty vial. "What about us?" he said.

"I don't have any more." I had some at Blackthorn, but that was too far away. Ipecac needed to be taken immediately. By the time we got Sally back on a horse and rode home, it would be too late for it to do us any good.

We'd have to hope Isaac had some on hand. I helped Sally up, holding her close as we walked back through the alley toward Fleet Street. She seemed steady enough on her feet, but she clung to me anyway.

Tom was still worried. "If it is poison, why would it affect her so badly, but not us?"

"She's smaller than we are," I said. "It would take less to affect her. A lot less, in your case."

"And you don't feel sick?" he said hopefully.

Other than with worry? "No."

That seemed to relieve him. But he was still troubled, and for the same reason I'd been troubled earlier. "The Raven gave us a day. Why would he poison us now?"

That was what I didn't understand. It was possible that attack in the street wasn't a distraction—though if not, then what was its purpose? If Sally had been poisoned, it hadn't happened here. So what was the point?

And, as Tom had asked, why poison us, anyway?

What if the poison wasn't meant for you? Master Benedict said.

That puzzled me. If it wasn't for us, then who . . .

I trailed off.

Isaac.

Oh, please, no.

I rushed Sally back to the horses as fast as I could.

We were close enough to Isaac's that the trip didn't take long. I held Sally's hand as we rode, keeping her steady in the saddle. She didn't seem so dizzy anymore, which was good. She had gone a little pale, and she was sweating, but that could be the ipecac. And indeed, by the time we reached the bookshop, the potion had done its work. Sally vomited copiously against the wall.

"Does that feel better now?" I said.

She wiped her mouth. "I *hate* throwing up."

Isaac was surprised to see us back so soon—and dreadfully worried to see Sally unwell.

"What about you?" I asked him. "Are you feeling sick?"

He was even more surprised at the question. "I'm fine. Other than the usual aches and pains. What's going on?"

I told him all that had happened on Fleet Street. He listened, shocked, then furrowed his brow as I told him my suspicions that Sally might have been poisoned.

"I can't see how," he said. "We ate and drank everything the same."

"The wine was watered, wasn't it?" I said. "Where did you get it?"

"The water? From the well downstairs."

That was as secure a water source as could be. "What about the food?"

"Sally brought it to me herself three days ago. I've been

eating from those groceries ever since. I've had no trouble."

"And you're sure no one's been in here?"

"How could they be? Except for Sally, you're the first visitors I've had since you brought me Bridget."

With one barred entrance and all the barred windows, it really was impossible to get inside Isaac's home. That meant for Sally to be poisoned, there was only one person who could have done it.

Isaac himself.

Suddenly, it occurred to me: Isaac had disappeared for months. He claimed he was quarantining himself during the plague, I thought. But I never actually saw him doing it. He could have been anywhere. Even in Paris.

What if he told me the story of Peter Hyde to throw me off the trail? The real trail . . .

It took only a second for that idea to run through my head. That was how little time it took me to feel ashamed.

What's wrong with me? I thought, spirits sinking. *How did I ever become this person? A boy who looks at his closest friends and wonders if they're enemies?*

That's what the Raven does, Master Benedict said gently. *It's what he promised he'd do to you.*

His words made me think of the Raven's first letter

once more. *I am going to make you suffer,* he'd said. *I will do this by taking away the things you love, one by one, until there is only you and me.*

And finally, finally, I understood.

I'd assumed the Raven meant he was going to kill them all. But there was more than one way to take a friend.

He'd made me lock away Bridget so I couldn't see her.

He'd made me see less of Simon, and nothing of Isaac.

He'd made me doubt Lord Ashcombe, wonder if the man could be a traitor. The king's most loyal servant. The man who'd lent me his name for our mission in Paris. Who'd come hunting for me when our ship was wrecked on our return.

Now, even if just for a moment, he'd made me doubt Isaac. Master Benedict's oldest, dearest friend.

And, it seemed, all for nothing. Sally looked like she was already feeling better. If she'd been poisoned, the ipecac might have saved her life, but it wouldn't have made her that well that quickly.

Thinking she'd been poisoned wasn't crazy—arsenic was, after all, the Raven's favorite way to get rid of someone— but she'd also told me she thought she'd hit her head. Even with no visible wound, a knock could have made her dizzy and nauseous. To say nothing of the fright of getting shot at. I hadn't listened because the Raven had my head all mixed up inside.

The attack on Fleet Street had been a distraction; I was certain of that. But if the purpose wasn't to harm Sally, then what? Direct our attention where the Raven wanted it, instead of where we needed it to be?

Or maybe its only purpose was to delay us. Traveling through city traffic was painfully slow, and running back and forth from one end of town to another chewed up a frightening amount of time. Bringing Sally back here had probably cost us another hour. It was already pushing one o'clock; by the Raven's rules, we had only until sundown to solve his puzzles and find the warrants—the playing cards—that spared our lives.

And all the while, he was using the time—and my worries—against us.

Enough. "We have to go," I said, rattled.

"I think I should stay here," Sally said. "I'm feeling better, but . . ."

I was glad she'd suggested it. It spared me an argument about leaving her behind where she'd be safe. "We'll come back and check on you."

"No," she said. "Solve the riddles first. Just because I have my card doesn't spare the two of you."

She was right, of course. She usually was.

But I still planned to return.

CHAPTER
38

AT LEAST THIS TIME NO ONE SHOT
at us.

Tom and I rode as swiftly as we could through the
crowds to the Temple Church. As with the last time I'd
been here, the place made me think of Paris.

While searching for the Templars' treasure in France,
we'd gone to Saint Mary's, in the Marais. It was the first
church the knights had ever built. And the complex that grew
around it would remain the world headquarters of their order
until King Philippe le Bel had the Templars all cast down.

The Temple here was built in the exact same fashion.
Its original section was a perfect circle, in imitation of the

Church of the Holy Sepulcher in Jerusalem. It had a high base, with stone buttresses and narrow, arched windows six feet from the ground. A smaller tower stood atop the round, its top crenellated like castle defenses.

As the power of the Templars had grown, the need for more space resulted in a chancel being built on the east side. Its shape was more traditional, a rectangle with a three-peaked roof and large stained glass windows. The altar and pews were in the chancel now, the Round Church still housing the effigies of the knights entombed on the grounds.

So the Round was where Tom and I went straightaway. It was nearly twenty yards in diameter, with six giant pillars of Purbeck marble, a baptismal font, and a stone coffin against the north wall. And there we stared down at the figures we'd come to find.

There were nine effigies, each a remarkable likeness of an armored knight in mail and tabard. The statues had been carved as if lying down, and set into the floor. Eight lay within the central circle formed by the pillars, in two groups of four. The ninth rested against the wall on the south side.

Nine, I thought. Just like the nine knights who'd founded the Templars, long ago.

These weren't the same nine knights, of course. Geoffrey

de Mandeville hadn't even been part of their order. Still, it left us with a problem.

None of the effigies was marked. "Which one is Geoffrey?" Tom said. "The one that's separate?"

I wasn't sure. Would Mandeville be that important? Or was the ninth knight placed away from the others because he wasn't a Templar? "Maybe the priests will know."

I found one of them in the chancel. He was irritated that I'd interrupted his praying, doubly so when I asked which knight was which.

"I have no idea," he said dismissively.

I probably shouldn't have tried his patience—I'd already inquired here a month ago, with no results—but I asked him about visiting priests from France. Not only did he not recognize the young priest or Father Bernard, when I brought out my Templar florin, he looked like he was about to strangle me. I apologized for disturbing him and backed away.

"That is the most bad-tempered priest I've ever met," Tom whispered.

It also left us with no way of knowing which of the figures was Mandeville. Unless . . .

"The symbol," I said.

"What symbol?"

"Underneath the second riddle. The one that looks like a road map. Maybe that's a hint."

We pulled it out and tried to compare it to the layout of the effigies.

The master becomes a traitor. The traitor becomes a thief. The thief is condemned, rejected by all except the cowards you thought could save you. Visit his refuge and gaze from on high upon his face.

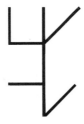

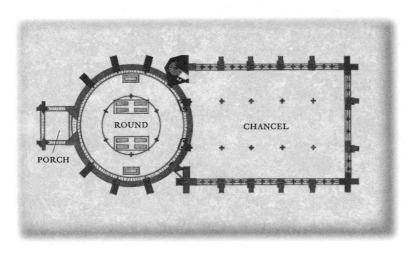

I turned the symbol this way and that. "I can't make sense of it at all," I said.

"Wait," Tom said. "We didn't follow the instructions." He pointed to the last line of the riddle. "We're supposed to 'gaze from on high.' Does that mean the roof?"

We looked up. The giant pillars ended in broad, pointed arches, curving above us to support the small turret we'd seen outside. There were narrower pillars all around the upper section—and small open interior windows between them.

"Hold on," I said. "There's a triforium up there."

"A what?"

"A gallery. On the upper level. That must be where we're supposed to go. We can look down on the effigies from there."

The stairs up were on the north side of the chancel. Watching carefully to see that the priest's back was still turned, we sneaked up the stone steps. I was pretty sure we weren't allowed up here.

The broad, circular gallery surrounding the open center was paved with ancient medieval tiles. Some were geometric shapes, but others showed figures of legend: Templar knights on horseback, rearing lions, birds with fleur-de-lis-feathered tails. Our shoes clacked sharply on the surface.

We walked as softly as we could, more sliding our feet than stepping. Tom went to the right as I poked my head out one of the windows, looking down into the round. "I can see the effigies from here," I whispered. Though I spotted nothing to indicate which was the right one.

Then Tom whispered back. "Christopher."

I crept to where Tom was standing. He'd gone far enough around the circle that we couldn't be seen from the stairs. "Did you spot something?" I said.

He pointed to the window in front of him. Just below it, set against the wall, was a box.

Gaze from on high, I thought. That instruction got us to come up to the triforium—and so we'd found what the riddle had sent us to discover. I was sure of it.

Because the box's lid was sealed with a simple circle of red wax.

CHAPTER

39

"THIS IS IT," I SAID.

I bent closer to examine the box.

Tom put a hand on my shoulder. "Careful."

"It's a box," I said. "What do you think it's going to do to me?"

"Maybe it'll explode. Or fling poisoned daggers at us or something."

The Raven had made Tom even more paranoid than me. But now Tom had made *me* nervous, so carefully, I sliced the seal with my knife and used the point of the blade to tip it open.

Nothing happened. Feeling foolish, I looked inside.

Tom joined me. "What's in there?"

It looked like a sheaf of papers, each one folded in on itself, like we'd found beneath the wax tablet at the Tower. Tom took one out and peered at it.

"There's something inside," he said.

It was another of the Raven's letters; I could see the red seal as Tom cracked it open, and the handwriting underneath. As he tilted the paper, an oval card slipped out. Tom caught it in midair, then turned it around to look at its face.

His eyes went wide. "It's me!"

Sure enough, we'd found the second warrant: a playing card, identical in make to Sally's. Except this one was a knave, with the letters TOM printed clearly on the face.

"Does this mean I'm safe now, too?" Tom said.

I wasn't sure any of us were safe. I didn't know what the Raven had planned with these cards, but I was pretty sure there'd somehow be a catch. Nonetheless, this did look like what we'd been sent here to find. But if that was the case . . .

"Then what are all these other papers for?" I said.

I took the second one from the stack and opened it. It was another letter, the same seal in red wax. More puzzling, there was another playing card inside the folds, identical to the first. *Totally* identical, in fact. A knave, with TOM printed on its face.

I'd found a second TOM.

"Another?" Tom said. "Why do I get two?"

He reached out to take it.

And suddenly, I understood.

This *was* a trap.

"No!" I said.

Tom froze as I pulled the card away from him. "What's wrong?" he whispered.

"Where's the letter your card came with?" I said.

It had fallen behind him. Tom picked it up.

"Put your card back inside," I said.

"Which one?"

"The one you're holding."

He slipped the card he'd found back into the paper. I did the same. "Now give me yours," I said.

When he handed it over, I put both letters aside. Then I looked in the third letter in the box, then the fourth, making sure they remained in the right order. As I'd guessed, they also contained TOM cards. And there were four more letters to go.

"I don't understand," Tom said. "What's going on?"

"Every letter in this stack has a TOM card. That's the trap. Seven of them will be the wrong warrant, I'm sure of it. Only one of those cards will spare your life."

He paled. "How are we supposed to know which is the right one?"

As cruel as the Raven was, I knew he wouldn't just make me guess. This had to be another puzzle. "There must be some identifying mark," I said, "either on the card or the paper. That's why I didn't want to get them mixed up."

Now that the letters were safely back in order, I chose the one on the top and checked it over. "Here," I said.

On the back of the paper was a number: 1773.

I examined the second one. Another number. "'9612,'" Tom read.

We flipped through them all. Each had a different four-digit number on the back. In order, the list looked like:

1773

9612

6076

4296

2384

3142

8617

5054

But there wasn't any indication which was the right one.

"Maybe that's what we need Geoffrey de Mandeville for," Tom said. "Choosing the right effigy. Would that fit with the numbers somehow?"

I looked down again through the window into the round. I could see the eight effigies in the center well enough. The ninth was blocked from view by the wall.

"I don't see anything that suggests numbers," I said. "Do you?"

"That's not exactly my specialty," he said, but he looked anyway. "There's nine knights . . . for the nine numbers?"

"There are only eight numbers in the stack."

"No, I meant one, two, three, like that, up to nine."

"There are ten digits," I pointed out. "You forgot the zero."

"Oh." He scratched his head. "Wait—what about that road map that came with the riddle? Maybe that points to the right numbers?"

I looked down at the symbol.

And as my mind began churning, the voice in the back of my head got louder. Now it sounded like Master Benedict.

You've seen this before, he said.

I have? I thought, only half a question.

Yes. I showed it to you. And that's the whole point.

He showed it to me? That's the point?

Numbers, I thought.

And the voice in my head finally came through.

"Tom, you've done it again," I said.

"As usual," he said, "I have no idea what you're talking about."

"Numbers." I took out the letter we'd found at the Tower and opened it. "*That's* what this symbol is. It's not a road map at all. It's a *number.*"

CHAPTER

40

TOM FROWNED. "HOW IS THAT A
number?"

"It's a code," I said. "It was invented by some monks.
Um . . ."

What was their name? As I thought of Master Benedict,
it came to me.

"The Cistercian order," I said, triumphant. "They created it some four hundred years ago." I'd got so hung up on
the fact the symbol looked like a road map, or a stick man,

I'd forgotten all about these old things. "I haven't seen this in ages."

"How is it a number, then?" Tom said.

"You see these little branches off the main line? Each of those represents a digit. The top right is the ones digit, the top left is the tens, bottom right is hundreds, and bottom left is thousands. Like this. You see?"

"I suppose," Tom said uncertainly. "But how do you know which actual number it is?"

"That's what the shape of the branch tells you. Let's see if I can remember."

I racked my brain, trying to think what each one was. I found it easier to picture if I actually imagined Master Benedict sitting beside me, his hands inking the paper with care.

Straight out is one . . . then a little lower is two. Angled down is three . . . and up is four . . .

I think I got it right—or at least I hoped I did. I had no idea where my master's old notes on the Cistercian ciphers were, so it was my memory or nothing.

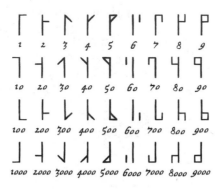

"Now what?" Tom said.

"We put this together with the symbol the Raven gave us." I circled each of the branches, comparing it to the chart I'd drawn.

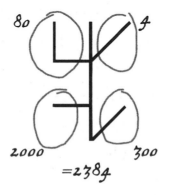

"That's four . . . plus eighty . . . plus three hundred . . . plus two thousand. So all together . . . 2384."

Tom compared it to the numbers on the papers. "There's a match!" he said.

He plucked out the letter with 2384 written on the back. He was all ready to open it, when he hesitated. "Are you sure you got it right?"

As sure as I was ever going to be. There were a few numbers in the chart I wasn't certain about. But I was confident the 1 and 2 were the right marks, which meant the correct number had to be in the two thousands. Since none of the other eight numbers matched that, we had to have the right letter. I hoped.

Tom took the playing card from inside. I could almost read his mind as he stared at it. *Does this really save me?*

It wasn't the only thing to wonder about. Like Sally's card, Tom's also had a single symbol on the back, printed in the center of the oval.

Unlike Sally's, I knew this symbol right away.

THE FOUR ELEMENTS			
▽	earth	cold and dry	melancholic
▽	water	cold and wet	phlegmatic
△	air	hot and wet	sanguine
△	fire	hot and dry	choleric

"A triangle, pointing down," I said. "That's water."

"What does it mean?"

I didn't know yet. *Sally has marcasite. Tom has water.*

"Can you mix them?" Tom said.

"Not really. Pyrite doesn't dissolve in water." Out of curiosity, I peeked at a couple of the other cards for the different letters. They all had different symbols on them—which made me hope even more desperately that we'd chosen the right one.

"I'm guessing there'll be a third symbol on the card for me," I said. "Maybe these will make sense when we have them all."

Either way, we'd made our decision. We needed to move on. The Raven had written another message in the letter with Tom's card. We read it together.

You bend the knee to a fool, failing to see that the fool is a dying piece of meat like you. Visit the place where he will rot. Then rob his ancestors.

Dominator sapientissimus

Rex piissimus

Redemptor optimus

Dominus aeternus

Imperator gloriosus

Rex

Tom found this riddle the most unsettling of all. "The Raven's messages are getting more cruel."

He wasn't wrong; this one practically bled from the page. On the positive side, I thought I understood what the riddle was asking.

"The 'fool' has to be the king," I said. It wasn't just that our Merry Monarch was thought of by some as a buffoon. There was no other man we bent a knee to.

"'Visit the place where he will rot'?" Tom said. "Where's that?"

"Westminster Abbey," I said. "Charles's grandfather was buried there. His father should have been buried there, too, but Oliver Cromwell denied him that."

It had become a rather sore point with our king—especially since Cromwell was buried in the abbey upon his death. But Charles had had his revenge. The year he returned to the throne, on the anniversary of his father's execution, Charles had Cromwell's body dug up, his corpse hung in chains and beheaded, and his skull displayed on a pole outside Westminster Hall.

"Wait a minute," Tom said, reading the last part of the riddle again. "We're supposed to rob *Westminster Abbey*?"

"Actually, I think I might know what that means, too. Or at least where to look."

"Then what are these words at the bottom about?"

It looked a little like a prayer—and sounded like one, too. "It's Latin," I said. "It means 'wisest ruler, most pious king, greatest redeemer, eternal lord, glorious commander,' then 'king' again."

"That's an awkward sort of prayer."

"That's because it's not a prayer. It's another code."

"You know it?"

"Absolutely," I said. "We need to get back to Blackthorn."

CHAPTER
41

IT WAS THE ODDEST FEELING YET,
returning to my shop.

This time, it wasn't because of what had happened in
the past month. It was what had happened before I'd ever
met Master Benedict.

If Peter Hyde really is the Raven, I thought, *then he once
lived in this very room.*

When Peter was Master Benedict's apprentice, he'd
have done everything the same as me. Worked here, in
the shop and at the workbenches. Learned here, spread
out on the floor, nose buried in one of our master's books.
Slept here, on a palliasse under the counter, the same

place I'd rested my head for three years. He'd lived the life I'd loved.

Then he'd thrown it all away.

And seeing the newest puzzle had finally made me certain: The Raven was Peter.

"These codes with the riddles," I said to Tom. "The Polybius square. The Cistercian numbers. Now this third one, Latin words disguised as a prayer. The only reason I know them is because *Master Benedict showed them to me the first year he took me in.* And the only way the Raven could know that is if he learned those same things himself, the same as me.

"Peter Hyde was my master's apprentice. He's the only other one of us still alive. So he's the only person in the world who'd know exactly what I know. That's what these puzzles are, really: A message to me. That's why the Raven chose them; so I'd recognize them. It's why he sent me that pigeon feather as a clue, too. Peter *wants* me to know it's him. He wants me to understand whom I'm facing. He wants to match me. And then beat me."

I sighed. "That's what this is about, Tom. We thought I'd angered the Raven by taking the Templar treasure. But now we know, from the way he uses bribes: He doesn't really care about the money. That's just his way of keeping score. It's not why he hates me so much. And it's not why he'll make me pay.

"It's because Peter thought *he* should be *me*," I said. "He sees how much Master Benedict cared about me. My master left me his home, his shop, his sash, everything—while Peter feels Master Benedict betrayed him. Peter Hyde, the smartest apprentice he ever had, discarded, stabbed in the back. Worthless."

"Master Benedict didn't think Peter was worthless," Tom protested.

"Of course not. But it's what *Peter* thinks that matters. It's what makes him who he is. And that hurts him more than anything else ever will in his whole life. So when the Raven beats me, it won't just be me he's destroying. It'll be his last revenge on Master Benedict, the man who let him down."

And as I realized that, I realized something else about the Raven, too. I didn't share it with Tom. I knew it would scare him. Worse, if Tom knew about it, when the time came to end this, he'd stop me from doing what I now knew I needed to do.

Tom shook his head. "That's madness. It doesn't make any sense."

I smiled sadly. "Not to you. But that's only because you're nothing like him."

That was something Lord Walsingham had taught me, not long after the king had placed me in the spymaster's service.

We always project our own feelings onto others, Walsingham had said. *We imagine they will like what we like. We imagine they will feel what we feel. It is a blind spot in our minds. Most people literally cannot believe that something they have never experienced could actually happen.*

Here is an example, apprentice. Pay attention the next time someone is cruel to you. What they're really showing you is not so much what will hurt you, but what they think *will hurt you—because it's precisely what will hurt* them. *Their choices will tell you more about them than their words ever will.*

And I finally saw it now, in everything Peter was doing. He wanted to show me how badly Master Benedict had made a mistake. Tom would never understand the Raven's cruelty because there wasn't an ounce of cruelty inside him. He might think Peter mad, but Peter was just evil. Full of selfish, prideful evil. As evil always is.

"You'd do anything to save someone you care about,"

I said to Tom, "even if it meant sacrificing your own life."

"So would you," he protested.

When he said that, I couldn't meet his eyes. "I suppose I would."

"You're sure about this, then?" Tom said. "There's no one else the Raven could be?"

"Who else could know what Master Benedict taught me? Who would even know each of these ciphers?"

"Lord Walsingham would. Wouldn't he?"

"It's not Walsingham," I began, but I trailed off.

Tom had made a very good point. The spymaster *would* know these ciphers.

I have spent my lifetime studying codes, he'd told me, the very first day I'd met him. He'd even corresponded with my master. Isaac had told me that.

Which made me wonder: Why hadn't Walsingham mentioned it?

That's just his way, I thought. He was even more private than Master Benedict. An occupational hazard of being a spy.

But the idea was running around now in my head.

Was it possible *Walsingham* was the Raven?

No, I thought. *It's Peter. It has to be.*

Strangely, as I argued with myself, it was the spymaster's voice I heard. Even now, he was making me challenge my assumptions.

Peter does fit the Raven's pattern, he said, *but a pattern is not a guarantee.*

It's not, I agreed. *But it's the most logical assumption.*

And what have I told you about making assumptions? he prodded. *For that matter, how do you know Walsingham isn't Peter?*

That's ridiculous.

Why? Simon told you the Raven had a reputation for playing roles, worming his way into society by pretending to be someone else. Why not Walsingham?

I didn't know what to make of that. Was such a thing actually possible?

It occurred to me that although I'd seen the spymaster nearly every day in the past month, I still knew nothing about the man. I had no idea of his family, his history, how he came to the position of spymaster. Nothing.

That doesn't mean anything, I argued. *Like I said, Walsingham is extremely private.*

So is Lord Ashcombe, the spymaster said. *Yet you know of his grandson. You know of the days he spent at young Charles's*

side, and his years with the king in exile. You know his son died
of the flux, and his father died of old age. That Sir William
Leech was his favorite sword master, and that he likes Dutch
spice cake and hates Spanish wine—

Stop, I said. *Walsingham can't be Peter Hyde. Peter*
would be in his twenties. Walsingham's at least ten years older
than that.

So you believe. And yet. Even if Walsingham isn't Peter . . .
well, the Raven is an expert at turning people into traitors. Who's
to say he hasn't turned the spymaster to his side?

It was a horrifying thought. As spymaster, Walsingham
had access to every piece of intelligence in the kingdom—
and command over dozens of agents, of whom only he
knew their names. There was virtually nothing he couldn't
discover, control—or sabotage.

And now the past few days ran through my head.

Walsingham had had Elinor Bagley's place searched.
He said it was because he'd suspected the Raven was turning people with large bribes. What if he already *knew*
that's how the Raven worked—because he'd been bribed
himself?

The spymaster had disappeared a couple of times when

I'd gone searching for him, too. The night of the ambush at Barnham Wood, he'd supposedly gone to Guildhall. Maybe he'd gone to help the Raven destroy the Templars instead. And the night Dr. Kemp was murdered, Walsingham was nowhere to be found—until he showed up, late, to the theater. That wasn't proof; his job did require him to leave his office from time to time. But maybe he was missing last night because he'd already *been* to the theater—to help eliminate George Gifford and his actors.

Worst of all, when I'd learned about Arthur Pembry, he'd ordered me to keep it quiet. Even from Lord Ashcombe—the one man I knew for certain was no traitor at any price. The spymaster's reasoning had seemed logical. But then that very night, both Gifford and Pembry were murdered. Keeping their secrets forever.

The Raven has turned your head around, Master Benedict said. *It's making you question everything.*

Maybe I needed to. The stark truth that had brushed against my mind earlier now flared, burning bright.

Almost nobody can be trusted anymore.

It left me feeling terribly, terribly alone.

Tom nudged me. "Christopher?"

"Sorry—what?"

"I asked if you were all right. You were just standing there, blank."

At least I'd always have Tom. "Just thinking. Come on, let's get to work."

The first thing I did was refill my vial of ipecac and powdered charcoal. Then I filled two more vials and gave one of them to Tom.

"Will we really need all of that?" he said, worried.

"If there's one thing we can guarantee," I said, "it's that before the Raven's finished this game, somebody's going to get fed arsenic."

Come to think of it, I prepared a fourth vial, just in case. I could give the extra one to Isaac. I'd really wanted to stop by his bookshop to check on Sally before we came here, but it would have taken us too far out of our way, and we were still up against the clock. While I no longer believed Sally had been poisoned, I did want to see that she'd recovered from hitting her head. At any rate, the route to Westminster Abbey would take us that way, so I'd see her soon enough. The thought of it made me work faster.

I filled my coin purse with guineas of my own to replace

the coins I'd given to the priest at the Tower, plus a few extra if I needed more later today. Then I dove into Master Benedict's stack of books.

"What are you looking for?" Tom asked, watching.

"The answer to our prayers." I pulled a heavy tome from the middle and held it up. "Or at least the Raven's."

CHAPTER
42

"WHAT IS THAT?" TOM SAID.

I rubbed dust off the spine. "The first book ever written about how to hide things in plain sight. It's the *Steganographia*, by a Benedictine abbot named Johannes Trithemius—"

The bell rang over the shop door downstairs.

Someone had come in. Tom and I exchanged a glance. Given what had just happened in the street, we drew our weapons.

"Hello?" a deep voice called.

I thought about staying silent. Then I realized it was obvious we were here; our horses were tied up outside.

"Who's there?" I called, guns pointed down the stairs.

"That you, Rowe?"

I didn't recognize the voice. It seemed familiar to Tom, though. He frowned and led the way down, sword ready.

It was two of the King's Men. They'd already entered the workshop at the back, looking curiously at the apparatus. The man who'd spoken nodded toward us. "Oh, it's you, Bailey—what are you doing with that blade?"

Embarrassed, Tom sheathed Eternity. He knew these men; he'd sparred with them many times. I recognized them, too, though I didn't know their names.

Tom did. "Sorry, Wilkins. I guess we're a little jumpy with all that's going on."

"Dark days," Wilkins agreed.

"Is something wrong?" I said. "Why are you here?"

"To fetch you. The Earl Walsingham wants you back at the palace."

I paused. "Why?"

"What, do I question orders?" Wilkins said. "His Lordship said get you, so here I am. Let's go."

Still I hesitated.

As the spymaster's apprentice, I had no right to refuse to go with them. Frankly, I doubted the King's Men would even let me decline. They were under orders, too.

But Walsingham had never sent soldiers for me before. If he'd wanted me, he'd always sent a servant.

That's because you were always in the palace, I told myself. *The soldiers are here for your protection.*

But I couldn't get my previous argument out of my head. *What if he's working with the Raven—or worse, he's the Raven himself?*

What was I supposed to do?

The answer came to me in a flash. And again, in Walsingham's voice.

If I am your enemy, he said, *would you want me to know you've figured that out?*

"Something wrong?" Wilkins said.

"No. Sorry. Just give me a second." I turned to Tom, speaking quietly. "Take this. And this." I handed him the book I'd found and a second vial of the ipecac and powdered charcoal. "Go and check on Sally, make sure she's all right."

"What?" he said, surprised. "I'm coming with you."

I didn't want him with me. If this was a trap, and these men were traitors, having Tom there would only get him killed.

"I'll be safe," I said. "Look, I don't know what Lord Walsingham wants. If he keeps me for a long time . . . we have to be sure Sally's all right."

He couldn't really disagree with that. He also had no reason to think I was in any danger from Wilkins and his companion, either. Tom trusted these men as brothers-in-arms, and I hadn't shared my worry about Walsingham working with the Raven.

He was a little puzzled by the book, though. "What do I do with this?"

"Just hold on to it. This, too." I handed him the Raven's last letter. "After you've checked on Sally, meet me at the main entrance to Westminster Abbey. We'll finish what we need to do there."

Reluctantly, Tom agreed. I turned back to the King's Men. Inside, I wondered if the Raven would consider this breaking the rules. I wasn't allowed to use any of the king's resources to play his game. To be fair, that was the opposite of what was happening right now—the King's Men were actually forcing me to stop playing. I couldn't solve the Raven's riddles until I was free of them. Taking me back to the palace was a hindrance, not a help.

But then there was nothing much fair in the Raven's

heart. If he was watching me, I'd just have to hope he saw things my way. "Ready to go now," I said.

I felt like I was riding to my death.

We left the horses at the stables. The King's Men escorted me all the way to Walsingham's office. I couldn't decide if I wanted to run into Lord Ashcombe or not. While I was still ashamed of how I'd lied to him yesterday, except for the king, Ashcombe was the only man in the palace I knew for sure I could trust.

I rested my hands on the grips of my pistols the whole time. My escorts didn't even notice; they were used to weapons of all kinds. They just accompanied me pleasantly enough, gossiping between themselves—some sergeant named Hobbes had lost all his pay gambling and was digging himself deeper in debt—until we reached our destination and Wilkins knocked on the door.

"Enter," Walsingham said in his quiet baritone.

The spymaster was sitting at the little side table, staring at his chessboard. There appeared to be a game in progress, though he was alone. I wondered if he was playing against himself. It's not like he could find any other opponent to match him.

"Christopher Rowe, as requested, my lord," Wilkins said.

Walsingham nodded, a command for me to enter and for them to shut the door as they left. I actually started to relax a little. If this was a trap, surely the soldiers wouldn't have let me keep my pistols. There was only the spymaster in here, and he was unarmed.

You're forgetting something, Master Benedict said in my head. I didn't know what that meant—until I glanced over at the bookcase behind his desk.

The secret passage. The one I hadn't known about until two days ago. Someone could be hiding inside. In fact, someone could have been hiding in there every single time I'd been here.

That was unlikely, true—unless Walsingham was owned by the Raven.

"It's Thursday," Walsingham said.

I blinked. "Um . . . yes?"

"You missed our appointment."

Oh—I'd forgotten. Every Monday and Thursday afternoon, Walsingham expected me to sit and play chess. "Sorry, my lord. It slipped my mind."

"Has something else occupied your time?"

"Well . . . after yesterday . . ." I searched about for a

believable lie. "I thought I might follow up on some leads."

"Regarding?"

"Well . . . um . . . you know, Dr. Kemp . . . obviously at some point he was taken. By the Raven. So . . . I thought I'd check around Blackthorn to see if anyone had seen anything. Because he was staying at the Missing Finger, across from my home. And with everything else that's happened there, with Mr. Sinclair—"

"Had they?"

I'd lost track of what I'd been saying. I'd been rambling—something that often indicates the speaker is telling a lie, as Walsingham had once pointed out. "Had they what?"

"Seen anything."

"Er . . . no."

"How do you think Kemp was taken, then?"

Walsingham watched me as I spoke. I knew he was scrutinizing me, parsing every word. It was unnerving. How could I imagine I would get away with lying to *him*? It was a good question, though—and one that hadn't occurred to me.

How *had* Kemp been captured?

And where?

"I . . . don't know," I said truthfully. "Dr. Kemp was

always visiting patients. And he wasn't the nervous sort. I don't think he'd have noticed if someone was following him."

I thought about it some more. "He could have been lured to a home under the guise of examining someone who was ill," I said. "It would have been pretty easy to capture him—"

Wait. I'd forgotten something.

And I realized I'd made a huge mistake.

CHAPTER
43

I SLAPPED MY FOREHEAD. "JACK!"

Walsingham regarded me silently.

"Dr. Kemp had an apprentice, Jack," I said, dismayed. So worried about the Raven, I hadn't even thought of the boy. "I forgot all about him. What happened to him?"

"A good question," the spymaster said. "One to which I have obtained no answer."

That surprised me. He hadn't known Kemp before last night. Though of course he would have begun to investigate the doctor after his murder.

Unless Walsingham's working with the Raven, I thought.

In which case, he'd already know everything about him. "You looked for Jack?" I said.

"Of course." Though there was no judgment in Walsingham's voice, I couldn't help but feel rebuked for my error. "According to the agent I assigned, the boy has not been seen since yesterday morning. It is fair to assume that he is either dead and disposed of by the Raven, or was the one who betrayed Kemp to his killer. Possibly both."

That made sense. The murders of Pembry and Gifford showed that the Raven was eliminating every tie back to him. If Jack had been bribed to deliver Kemp, it was doubtful the apprentice would have lived long enough to spend his ill-gotten gains.

But if he hadn't been killed . . . who knows what he might have seen or be able to tell us?

I noticed Walsingham was watching me. "Anything else?" he said.

"No," I said, feeling foolish.

"In that case, let us begin. Sit."

I balked. I'd hoped he was going to let me go without playing. "Um . . . could we do this another day? I'd still like—I mean, I'd like to follow up on Jack."

"As I said, I already have an agent handling that. Unless you have another matter that is pressing?"

I couldn't very well tell him the truth. Whether he was the Raven's puppet or not, I wasn't allowed to make use of the king's resources. And I couldn't think of an immediate lie. "Not exactly."

"So." He motioned to the empty seat across the table.

Resigned, I sat, though I made one last effort to escape. "My lord . . . I don't think I'll be much use today. My mind's too filled with everything that's happened. I can't really concentrate."

"Then this will be an excellent exercise," he said. "It will train your mind to focus, even when you might wish otherwise." He returned the pieces to their starting positions, except for two pawns, which he concealed in his fists. "Choose."

I tapped his right hand. He opened it to reveal the white pawn. "Your move," he said.

So we began. If he'd hoped I'd concentrate—train my mind, as he put it—that wasn't going to happen. I played quickly, moving the pieces without much, if any, thought. I just wanted to get this over with so he'd let me go.

Our sessions had always been long affairs, in which I

was expected to give each move as much careful consideration as he did. He'd usually quiz me at the same time, sometimes about the game, more often about unrelated topics, to try to keep my mind sharp. So I expected him to slow the game down, either by playing slowly himself or by ordering me to stop rushing.

Instead, he stayed quiet and matched my tempo. My early moves, mindless and reckless, were met by his own. When I sped up further, so did he. We began to play so quickly, in fact, that I actually started to pause to contemplate the best move. And as we played like this, something strange happened.

I began to win.

He took a pawn. I took a knight.

He took another pawn. I took his bishop.

He made a careless move with his rook. I took advantage of his error to use my knight in a fork attack on his king—and so I captured his queen.

It continued, a bloodbath in my favor, but he refused to slow down. *He's trying to keep up with me,* I thought, amazed. *And he can't. He's losing.*

Up until now, the game had been utterly silent. So when, after I made my next move, Walsingham spoke, I nearly jumped out of my chair.

"How is my game?" he said.

"Sorry, my lord?"

"My game. How am I playing?"

"Um . . . with respect, my lord, not well."

"Which is the most important piece in chess?"

It was such an easy question, I hesitated, thinking there must be a trick answer. "The king."

"And who has the advantage in our current game?"

"I do."

"Explain."

I looked at the board.

"You've captured one bishop, one knight, and two of my pawns," I said. "I have your queen, one rook, one bishop, both knights, and three pawns. I'm up a pawn and three pieces, two of which are major."

"Such a lead is nearly insurmountable," Walsingham said.

Was he conceding? "It is."

"So explain," he said, "why you're about to lose."

"I . . ." What?

I stared at the board.

Slowly, he reached across and moved his queenside bishop's pawn one space forward.

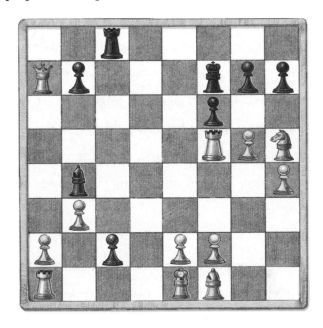

It was checkmate.

Moving his pawn had discovered checkmate when it cleared a path for his bishop to attack my king. The king was blocked, with only two spaces where he could move, one of which was covered by the bishop, the other by his newly advanced pawn. And for all my advantage in pieces, none of them could block his lone bishop in time.

I'd lost.

Walsingham spoke softly. "As you stated: In chess, there is only one piece that matters. The king. You have many more resources than I do. And yet you lose. Because while you are decimating my pieces, I don't care about my pieces. I only care about your king. So all of your resources are useless—will always *be* useless—unless you use them the way they are most needed."

He reached out and placed a finger against my king. Slowly, he tipped it over. It rattled, then lay still.

The spymaster regarded me, speaking even more quietly than before. "Is there something you would like to tell me, apprentice?"

There was.

I didn't know if Walsingham was with the Raven or not. At that moment, I didn't care. There was something I wanted to tell him more than anything.

I'm lost, I wanted to say. *I don't understand the game I'm playing, but I know the Raven's rigged it so I'll lose. Even if I win, I'll lose. I don't know how, but he'll see to that. And my very worst nightmares, the ones I have every single night, will come true.*

I need you. I need you, and Lord Ashcombe, and the king, and the Templars, and Master Benedict, and my friends, and all the things the Raven's rules deny me. Because I don't know what to do. Please help me. I don't know what to do.

That's what I cried in my heart.

Out loud, there was only one answer I could give.

"No," I said.

CHAPTER
44

TOM WAS GOING TO BE ANGRY WITH ME.

Westminster Abbey was just south of the palace, only a few minutes' ride. I doubted anything would happen to me along the way, but I knew Tom would be furious that I'd headed there without an escort.

He probably thought I wouldn't be so foolish as to go alone. That the same soldiers who'd brought me to Whitehall would escort me to Westminster. But being dragged back to the palace was one thing. Having them guard me as I rejoined the Raven's trail would definitely break the rules.

It did leave me feeling terribly exposed. I couldn't help glancing around, my head on a swivel. It was unsettling being by myself—or almost by myself, anyway. I still had my faithful girl, Blossom. I patted her neck, and she chuffed in response.

For all my worry, I made it to Westminster Abbey without incident. After tying up Blossom, I went to the main entrance on the west side of the church, where we were supposed to meet, expecting a scolding.

But Tom wasn't there.

He should have been. The King's Men, enjoying their time in the city, had been in no hurry to return me to the palace. Walsingham's questions and our game of chess had delayed me further.

After our earlier worries, Tom and I had pushed along faster, trying to make up for lost time. Then the soldiers had come and made things worse. Now the bells in the tower were ringing five fifteen p.m.—which left us an hour and a half before sunset, when the Raven's game would end. Tom and Sally had their playing cards with the symbols on the back. If we didn't find mine . . .

Something had to be wrong. Tom should have easily

returned to Isaac's, checked on Sally, then made it here before I arrived. He never would have risked leaving me waiting. Yet there was no sign of him.

Which meant something had delayed him.

Now I worried about what that could be. Did he get waylaid on the way to Isaac's by that skulking man in the mask? Or was there a problem with Sally? Had she been poisoned after all?

Sick with worry, I paced before the main entrance. Five minutes passed. Then another five. Then five more.

Where was he?

I went to Blossom, ready to untie her and ride over to Isaac's. *What if he's on his way here?* was the thought that made me pause. If I missed him on the streets, then by the time I got there and back, our time would be up.

But where *was* he?

Images of him lying in some alley bleeding to death became too much. I hopped on Blossom and pulled away from the church.

"Christopher!"

It was Tom. He was maneuvering Lightning through the crowd, Sally behind him on Beatrice. My relief at seeing him—seeing both of them—almost dispelled my worry at his delay. Almost.

At least Sally was all right; otherwise she wouldn't have come. I slid from my saddle and hugged her with relief. She hugged me back.

I could get used to this, I thought.

Then I remembered where we were and what we were supposed to be doing. I stepped back, flushing a little. Sally's face was just as red.

I cleared my throat and turned to Tom. "Where were you?" I asked in frustration as we hitched our horses.

"Sorry," Tom mumbled. He was flushing, too, but from his own embarrassment. He knew he'd left me exposed. "I was . . . there was . . . I was delayed. I . . . I thought I was being followed."

"What? When? By whom?"

"I don't . . . nobody. There was nobody. I just thought there was. This stupid game is making me jump at shadows."

He was so ashamed, he wouldn't even look at me. Now I felt bad about the way I'd spoken to him. "I'm just glad you're all right. You, too," I said to Sally. "You're sure you're feeling better?"

"I told you," she said. "It wasn't poison. I was just a little dizzy from hitting my head."

In that case, it was time to get to work. After all that waiting, we barely had an hour left before sunset. "Where's the book I gave you?"

Tom pulled it from his saddlebag. He'd tucked the Raven's letter inside the front cover. Sally hadn't seen either one yet. She huddled close to me, reading the prayer as I began leafing through the pages of the *Steganographia*.

"Tom told me you found a new code?" she said.

"That's it, right there," I said. "The prayer *is* the code. It's a substitution code."

"You mean like the Caesar cipher?"

"Not exactly. With Caesar, or Vigenère, you swap one letter for another, which makes the message unreadable. With Trithemius's method, you don't replace each letter with a letter. You replace each letter with a whole *word*."

I showed them the key, written out in the volume.

A	Deus	A	clemens
B	Creator	B	clementiſsimus
C	Conditor	C	pius
D	Opifex	D	piiſsimus
E	Dominus	E	magnus
F	Dominator	F	excelſus
G	Conſolator	G	maximus
H	Arbiter	H	optimus
I	Iudex	I	ſapientiſsimus
K	Illuminator	K	inuiſibilis
L	Illuſtrator	L	immortalis
M	Rector	M	æternus
N	Rex	N	ſempiternus
O	Imperator	O	glorioſus
P	Gubernator	P	fortiſsimus
Q	Factor	Q	ſanctiſsimus
R	Fabricator	R	incompræhenſibilis
S	Conſeruator	S	omnipotens
T	Redemptor	T	pacificus
V	Auctor	V	miſericors
X	Princeps	X	miſericordiſsimus
Y	Paſtor	Y	cunctipotens
Z	Moderator	Z	magnificus
W	Saluator	W	excellentiſsimus

"It's actually a pretty clever system," I said. "With something like Vigenère, when you see it, it's obvious you have a code. An enemy might not be able to break it, but they know from the start that you're hiding something. Even if they can't read the message, that still might cause you all kinds of problems."

"They could torture you to give them the key," Tom said.

"Exactly. The best kind of secret, then, is when no one knows you have a secret at all. That's what steganography is: hiding something in plain sight."

I tapped the book. "That's what Trithemius came up with. Instead of one letter replacing another, each letter is replaced by an entire word. The words he chose were words of worship, so the code would look like a prayer. And with this book, we can solve it."

I copied the code the Raven had given us onto the back of the paper. Then, above each word, I used the key in the book to match it to the correct letter.

F	*I*
Dominator	*sapientissimus*
N	*D*
Rex	*piissimus*

T	*H*
Redemptor	*optimus*
E	*M*
Dominus	*aeternus*
O	*O*
Imperator	*gloriosus*
N	
Rex	

"And when we put that together," I said, "we get . . ."

FIND THE MOON

"Find the moon?" Tom said. "What does that mean?"

"I don't know." I nodded toward Westminster Abbey. "I guess we'll find the answer in there."

CHAPTER 45

WESTMINSTER ABBEY WAS SOME-thing special.

In a very real way, the Collegiate Church of Saint Peter, Westminster—the abbey's official name—was the heart of our nation. Every one of our kings and queens had been crowned here since William the Conqueror in 1066. In fact, a pope had once ruled that one *couldn't* be crowned king of England unless it was done at Westminster's High Altar.

The church had been built to reflect the majesty of its importance. Though the main entrance was plain compared to the magnificence of Notre-Dame Cathedral in Paris, the interior was awe inspiring, with its massive pillars, gilded ornaments, and intricate stonework. The way it stretched above us, combined with the narrowness of the nave, made it seem like the tallest building in the world. As if, if the arches reached a few feet higher, they might break through the sky and gaze upon heaven.

But the church itself was not where we needed to go. Passing through the nave, we turned right before the transept and went into the Cloisters. When this place was still an abbey, before King Henry VIII broke from the Catholic Church and confiscated all the monasteries, this was where the monks would have spent most of their time. From the covered walkway, with its vaulted ceiling and old medieval flagstones, we could look out through the colonnade at the garth—the grassy square with a fountain in the center.

"It's so pretty here," Sally said.

It was, but we hadn't come for a picnic. "Where are we going?" Tom said.

"The Pyx Chamber," I said.

"The what?"

"Pyx. It's a wooden box where newly minted coins are tested to make sure the silver is pure."

"How do you know this?" Sally said curiously.

"Master Benedict told me. He brought me here once." I

remembered it, in part, because it was so unusual. My master had never had any interest in politics or coronations or things like that. He'd brought me here instead to talk about architecture—and to teach me a little something about how to melt metals in our workshop.

Tom recalled the Raven's last riddle. "Visit the house where the king will rot . . . and rob his ancestors." He looked surprised. "That's what you think it means? Find the Pyx? We really won't have to steal anything?"

I nodded. "If the Raven is Peter, then Master Benedict brought him here, too. He knows this place for the same reason I do. That's why he chose it." At least I hoped that's what the riddle meant. Because if I'd got it wrong, we really would need to start looting some tombs.

The Pyx Chamber was in the southeast corner of the Cloisters. It was one of the few parts left of the original abbey, constructed six hundred years ago. A pair of steps led down into a dark, damp stone chapel. The vaulted ceiling here was lower, with rounded arches of worn stone, supported by thick, round pillars. The floor was paved with medieval tiles, small, uneven squares of red and black.

A stone table had been built into the far wall. Master Benedict had said that was where they tested the silver.

At the moment, the chamber was being used for storage. Trunks and chests lay everywhere, some piled on top of each other. To our right was a cope chest, a curved bureau designed to allow the priest's vestments to lie flat. When open, it would look like a semicircle—

Find the moon, I thought.

That was what the riddle told us to do. And that cope chest, when open . . . it would look like a half-moon.

Heart thumping, I slid out the drawers and searched them, hoping to find a third playing card. But all I found was the expected priestly garb. I examined the chest more carefully, feeling under the drawers and in the dark corners. I even tapped the wood, listening for echoes, in case there was a hidden compartment.

Nothing.

"Did we get the riddle wrong?" Sally said.

If we had, we were finished. We were already almost out of time. "There are a lot of chests in here," I said, trying to keep my spirits up. "I guess we search them all."

Tom looked around in dismay. "Where do we start?"

"With whatever's in front of you."

While I'd searched the cope chest, Sally had kept watch for anyone coming. We didn't have that luxury anymore.

All of us now flipped open lids, dug through the contents of the chests—mostly clothes and linens—then moved on. I was just beginning to panic when Sally cried out.

"Oh! Look! A message."

We hurried to the far corner, where Sally, half-hidden behind a pillar, knelt before an open trunk. She reached in and pulled out a bar of what looked like silver. It was heavy; her arm strained to hold it.

She showed it to us, excited. "Did I just rob the king's ancestors?"

Tom and I peered inside the trunk. The message Sally had mentioned was painted in white on the underside of the lid.

You still need my twin.

"What does that mean?" Tom said.

I didn't know. But inside the trunk were seven more bars of metal, all different sizes and shapes: some long and narrow, some wide and fat, and one cube. All had a silvery sort of color, though; even with the dim light of our two lanterns, I could tell they weren't all the same metal. We both reached down to pull out an ingot.

Then I spotted what lay below them. Under each was a paper, folded upon itself like an envelope. Just like we'd seen in the Temple Church.

Tom and I froze at the same time.

"What are these?" Sally said. She reached in to pull out another bar.

"NO!" Tom and I shouted simultaneously. Now Sally froze with us.

"What did I do?" she squeaked.

"Just . . . where was that bar sitting in the trunk?" I said.

She pointed—and there lay a folded piece of paper.

"Put it back exactly where you found it," I said.

She did as asked, then backed away. "I don't understand. What did I do wrong?"

"It's a trap," Tom said, and he explained how we'd found multiple TOM cards in the Temple Church. "We have to work out which one is the right one."

"But what is it we're actually looking for?"

The hint was in the last letter we'd received. "'Find the moon,'" I said. "That has to be the clue."

"You mean like a moon shape? On one of the bars?"

"Did you see anything on the one you picked up?" Tom said.

"No. It was smooth."

"I don't think it'll be that simple," I said. "If this is the last puzzle, the Raven will want to challenge me. And it'll be with something Master Benedict taught me; I'm sure of it."

"What did Master Benedict teach you about the Moon, then?" Tom said.

Actually, I couldn't remember him ever talking about the Moon at all. Had he?

"But we *are* trying to choose the right metal?" Sally said.

"Yes."

She peered back into the box. "They all sort of look like silver to me."

"They aren't," I said. "This one's too dull. I bet it's—" I drew my knife and dug it into the bar. It was soft and gave way. "Yes, that's lead. The one in the corner isn't shiny enough, either; that's probably iron . . ."

I trailed off.

The *Moon*. Find the *Moon*.

"Sally," I said. "That's the answer."

CHAPTER
46

"WHAT IS?" SHE SAID.

"Silver," I said. "The Moon. The Moon is silver."

"The color of it, you mean?" Tom said.

"No. The *metal*."

I pulled out the key of alchemical symbols.

PLANETARY METALS

⊙ *gold / Sun*

☽ *silver / Moon*   ♃ *tin / Jupiter*

♂ *iron / Mars*   ♀ *lead / Venus*

☿ *mercury / Mercury*   ♄ *copper / Saturn*

"Each of these metals," I said, "is matched to a heavenly body. The Moon is *silver*. See?" I pointed to the symbol on the chart. "That's what we're looking for. We have to work out which of these bars is silver."

"How?" Sally said.

I wasn't entirely sure. I'd already eliminated two of them, so I took the lead and the iron out of the trunk, with the folded papers underneath, and set them aside. That left six to go.

"What are the rest of made of?" Tom said.

"Things that look more like silver," I said. "That would be . . . tin. Polished steel."

"Pewter," Sally said.

"Antimony, too. And then there's paktong."

"What's that?" Tom said.

"A false silver. It's made in the Orient. I can't remember what it's made of. But it looks just like the real metal."

"How do you distinguish them, then?"

I wasn't sure. In daylight, with a rag and a little polish, it would have been easy to eliminate at least a few of them. Steel would never shine as nicely as silver, and I could probably distinguish tin, pewter, and antimony in the same way if I looked closely enough.

The Raven wants to test me, I thought, *with what we learned from Master Benedict.*

My master had taught me about Archimedes's experiments. The ancient Greek had worked out how to determine if a metal was pure or mixed with something else by measuring how much water it displaced. But I didn't have the tools for that, and the irregular shapes would make that impossible to calculate here. Which was almost certainly the point.

What else had Master Benedict taught me about silver? I thought of my sash, and what was in there, if I could find something of any use.

Oil of vitriol, maybe?

The vitriol dissolved metals. But not *all* metals. When cold, it wouldn't dissolve silver. You had to heat it up first. That might be a good test.

Except antimony behaved the same way. And I had no idea how paktong would react to oil of vitriol. Maybe it behaved like silver, too.

So then what? What did the Raven expect me to do?

"Maybe this message is a clue," Sally said.

She pointed to the words painted under the lid. *You still need my twin.*

I didn't see how that was relevant. Twin what? Each metal bar was a different size and shape from the others.

Did it mean "more silver"? I had coins in my purse. But what would that do? Silver finds silver? How?

I closed my eyes, trying to remember anything else my master had taught me about silver. *It's shinier than most metals,* I heard him saying. *It's soft, but harder than gold. It's fairly easy to shape. It conducts heat quicker than any other metal.*

Heat—maybe that was the answer. If I placed each bar in the flame of the lamps and timed how long to feel the heat . . . no. Again, the different shapes would affect the results.

"Hey," Tom said.

I looked up at him. He was staring across to the other side of the chamber.

"What is it?" I said.

"This trunk," he said thoughtfully. "The Raven probably put it here for us to find, right?"

"I'd imagine so."

"So look at that." He walked over to a trunk near the stone table and nudged it with his foot.

Sally looked from one trunk to the other. "They're the same."

The message. *You still need my twin,* it said. A twin trunk?

"Open it," I told Tom.

"I can't. It's locked." He rattled a padlock on it.

Sally peered into the open trunk. "Maybe there's a key in here?"

"We don't need a key," I said suddenly.

"Why not?"

"Because we have *this.*"

I pulled the oil of vitriol from my sash and got to work. Slowly, I dripped oil of vitriol on the lock's arm, watched it bubble, then wiped it off and poured another few drops. The familiar acrid stink of the smoke made me cough, so I stepped back and let the vitriol do its job.

Once it was more than halfway done, Tom took the lock and bent it. The arm snapped off, and he opened the chest.

"Odd's fish," he said. "It's full of *ice.*"

I frowned, thinking he'd made a mistake. But when I stepped forward, I saw he was right. This was an ice chest. I didn't know how long it had been sitting here, but it had to be at least several hours. The ice inside had already begun to—

Melt, I thought.

That was the answer.

CHAPTER
47

"THIS IS IT," I SAID. "THIS IS WHAT
we've been looking for."

Sally stared into the trunk. It was April, too warm for
ice anywhere near London. "Where on Earth did this come
from?"

"Norway, probably. Or the Scottish highlands. They
ship it down in giant boulders, so it won't all melt." Master
Benedict used to buy ice all the time, except for a month in
the summer when the price got too high. We used it to give
certain remedies a chilled bath. He'd even built an ice vault
right in our workshop to store it.

Now I had to be looking at several pounds worth of the

331

stuff, just melting away. Which I supposed was nothing for a man who handed out five-hundred-pound bribes.

The point was I knew what to do with it. "We need some chips," I said. "An inch square, half an inch thick."

Tom hacked away pieces with his knife. Ice freezing my fingers, we went back to the trunk with the metal bars in it. Carefully, I placed a piece on each one.

"Now watch," I said.

The ice began to melt. Slowly, water started to pool on each of the bars.

Except for one of them. On the widest, the ice melted the instant it touched the surface. Water pooled and ran over the side, a thin, twisting rivulet.

"There," I said. "That's the silver."

"How do you know?" Sally said.

"Because silver conducts heat better than any other metal. So when you place ice on it, it melts right away."

And that was my final proof. The Raven *was* Peter Hyde. Who else but Master Benedict would know something this obscure—and guarantee the Raven knew that *I* knew it?

I took the folded paper from under the silver, shaking off the drips of water. Then I opened it.

The first thing I saw was the playing card.

Like the others, it was oval in shape. Mine was the king, with CHRISTOPHER printed in bold letters.

I stared at it for quite a while, finally understanding the full depth of what Tom and Sally had felt when we'd found theirs. This was supposed to be the warrant that saved me. Yet at the same time, it felt like a threat. A reminder that there was someone out there capable of great evil—who'd set his sights on *me*.

But I felt something a little different inside, too. Unlike the others, I didn't really think this would spare my life.

Sally interrupted my thoughts. "What symbol did you get?"

I turned the card over. As with their cards, my symbol was printed in black ink.

A circle, with an upside-down triangle on top.

I frowned. "I don't recognize this."

I studied the key my master had made.

THE THREE PRINCIPLES		THE FOUR ELEMENTS	
salt — the contractive force	crystallization, contraction	earth — cold and dry	melancholic
sulphur — the expansive force	dissolution, evaporation	water — cold and wet	phlegmatic
mercury — the integrative force	balancing salt and sulphur	air — hot and wet	sanguine
		fire — hot and dry	choleric

PLANETARY METALS		TERRESTRIAL MINERALS	
gold / Sun		saltpeter	realgar
silver / Moon	tin / Jupiter	quicklime	cinnabar
iron / Mars	lead / Venus	sal ammoniac	tartar
mercury / Mercury	copper / Saturn	litharge	marcasite

CORROSIVES		WEIGHTS & MINERALS	
aqua fortis	aqua regia	one pound	one scruple
vinegar	distilled vinegar	one ounce	one pinch
		one dram	one pint
oil of vitriol		ANA equal amounts	

INSTRUCTIONS/PROCESSES			
calcination	sublimation	sugar	honey
congestion	separation	spirit	wax
fixation	ceration	essence	powder
solution	fermentation	still	distill
digestion	multiplication	take	mix
precipitation	caput mortuum	alcohol	compose
purify	oil	retort	receiver
digest	filter	night	boil
		day	

None of them fit. In fact, none of them were even close.

"Are we missing any symbols?" Sally said.

Not as far as I knew. Isaac had said these were the only pages Master Benedict had given him for safekeeping. And I'd been through pretty much every book at Blackthorn. I'd never seen any other list.

So what did it mean?

What do you do when you can't find the answer? Master Benedict said.

I remembered what he'd told me. *I step out of the way and let my mind find the answer for me.*

So that's what I did. I put the card away with Tom's and Sally's for the moment. I'd let my mind work on that problem and come back to it later. In the meantime, as at the Temple Church, the folded paper also contained a letter, sealed with a circle in red wax. I opened it.

The decisions are made. The game has ended.

Go to the stables in the morning. And all your questions will be answered.

"I don't understand," Tom said.

I should have felt relieved. Instead, I just felt exhausted. "The Raven's saying we've chosen our cards. And tomorrow, we'll face the consequences of those choices."

"I thought the warrants were supposed to spare us," Sally said.

I didn't tell them what I really thought. "I guess we'll find out."

"What do we do until then?" Tom asked.

"I don't want to go back to Berkshire House," Sally said, nervous.

"Why not?"

She hugged her arms to her chest. "I don't want to be alone. After today, I just . . . I don't know who's on our side anymore. We can't trust anyone at the palace."

I didn't think it was a good idea to go to Whitehall, either. While I didn't believe the Raven would harm us tonight—I was convinced he wanted to end things by facing me down in person, like his note said—if Walsingham was in league with the Raven, I didn't want to be around him. Even if he wasn't, I dreaded seeing him again, or worse, Lord Ashcombe, and having them grind me down trying to find out what I'd been doing all day.

And there was still the possibility of others at the palace

having been bribed. Though I was surprised to hear Sally felt the same way. "We'll take you back to Isaac's," I said. "You'll be safe there, at least."

"No," she said, her voice hard. "I don't want to keep drawing attention to him. Maybe the Raven already knows how important Isaac is, and maybe I might not really matter to the Raven. None of us might, except as a way to hurt you. But this"—she plucked the SALLY card out of my hand—"means I'm a target either way. I'm not putting Isaac at risk just to save my own skin."

I understood exactly how she felt. "All right. But we can't stay at Blackthorn." If the spymaster wanted to bring me in, that would be the first place he'd send the King's Men to look. "So where do we go?"

Sally had what she thought was the perfect answer. "Simon's."

"How is that a good idea?" I said. "We'll be putting him in danger, too."

"Not really. The Raven already sent a Covenanter to try to kill him last month; it's not like he doesn't know he's our friend. If he wants to punish Simon again, he'll do it whether we're around or not. What's in our favor is that Simon has guards he's known for years."

"That doesn't mean anything," I cautioned her. "We've seen how easily the Raven turns people, even against the king. And two of his guards are young—for all we know, one of them could *be* Peter Hyde."

Sally made a face. "I doubt the Raven's spent the last ten years living in Nottinghamshire."

That was a good point, but still. "Whether Simon trusts them or not, to us, they're still strangers."

"I know," Sally said, frustrated. "But where won't that be the case? Everywhere we go, we'll be surrounded by strangers. There's nowhere else left to turn."

It was true. Trust was what the Raven had stolen from us all. "What do you think?" I asked Tom.

"Actually, I was going say Simon, too," he said, downcast. "Everywhere else is too dangerous."

Simon's it was, then. "But look," I said, "we can't tell him *anything* about what's going on."

"Why not?" Sally said. "He wasn't included in the Raven's rules. Doesn't he deserve to know?"

"Yes, but . . ." I reminded them what Dr. Kemp had said about Simon's injury. "You know what a hothead he is. If he finds out what's been happening to us, that we're supposed to go to the stables tomorrow, we won't be able to stop him from dragging himself along. He can't really help us against the Raven, and regardless, we can't do that to him. No matter what."

They couldn't really argue with that. Still, Tom was even more dismayed. He hung his head, ashamed. "I hate all this lying."

"So do I," I said. "But, as Lord Walsingham told me, sometimes lying is part of the job. Even to friends."

That really made Tom's spirits sink low. "What's become of us?" he said quietly, more to himself than anyone else.

It was a good question. All this lying, the secrecy . . . it was one thing when I was serving the king in Paris. Now the Raven had us lying to friends—and the spymaster telling me that was my job.

Just as Tom said, I hated it. There was no other way to put it. I hated it.

But I'd stay quiet nonetheless. For one more day, I'd keep my mouth shut.

Because now Simon's life depended on it, too.

CHAPTER
48

SIMON WAS DELIGHTED TO SEE US.

I wasn't nearly so happy to be here—and not just because I worried we might bring the Raven's wrath to Simon's home. I couldn't help but wonder about the six servants the vicomte had brought down from his family's estate.

Of the four men, two were too old to be Peter. Daniel, the steward, was in his fifties, and Patrick, the cook, had to be near that age. The other two men, Michael and Taft, were young and strong—playing the role of servants, but really here as guards, as Dr. Kemp had realized. I watched them carefully as Daniel let us in, but all they did was greet me with politeness, relaxing as soon as they saw who was at the door. I detected nothing in either of them that would indicate they knew more about me than they should.

The same was true for the two women. Neither could be Peter, of course, but that didn't mean they couldn't be bribed. The older, Marjorie, was married to Daniel, and about the same age. Mary was seventeen. Both of them were as pleasant as the men, and apart from a respectful greeting, neither paid the slightest bit of attention to us.

Then there was Henri.

Simon had told us he'd found Henri on his way to England, in a hamlet near Calais. He'd been carrying a bale of hay all by himself, which impressed Simon enough to hire the man as a bodyguard. More important, Henri had no connection to Paris, so Simon was as certain as could be that he was free of the Raven's influence.

But was he?

It seemed unlikely that Henri himself could be Peter. Not because he spoke no English, or because he clearly wasn't all that bright; both of those could be an act. I just didn't think the Raven could have positioned himself in Simon's path to London on the off chance the vicomte would be impressed with his strength and hire him on as a bodyguard.

But . . . Henri was a man like any other. Which meant he *could* be bribed.

I eyed him carefully as we went upstairs. He ignored us as usual, scratching at his backside. I simply didn't know what to make of him anymore.

Or anything else, I thought glumly.

Simon welcomed us into his room with the enthusiasm of a man utterly desperate for company. He was lying on his stomach, looking miserable. "I told you, I am *dying* of boredom," he complained. "I can barely get out of this bed to relieve myself. Which is its own personal hell—ah. My apologies for the language, Sally."

She laughed. "I've heard worse. How are you feeling?"

"Other than the agony of tedium? My back is on fire. Just a small conflagration, you understand. It's when I move that it turns into an inferno."

"At least someone still has their sense of humor," I said.

He made a rude noise. "It's about all that's left to me. Other than my brandy. Speaking of which, would you like a glass? It's nearly time for dinner."

"Actually," I said, "we were hoping to spend the night, if that's all right."

"Really? Of course! Stay the night. Stay forever." He gestured to a drawer in the side table. "There's a deck of cards in there. Have you ever played All Fours? Michael taught it to me; he says everyone's mad about it back home."

Honestly, after what the Raven had left for us today, a game of cards was the last thing I wanted. But Sally dutifully opened the drawer to take out the deck.

Then she stopped, staring into the nightstand.

Tom and I looked at her, puzzled. Slowly, she reached in and brought out the cards. When she did, both of us stared with her.

They were oval—*exactly* the same type of cards as the ones the Raven had left for us.

Simon, facedown in his pillow, hadn't noticed we'd all frozen. "The rules of All Fours are a little complicated," he said, "but I'll explain. Everyone gets three cards—"

"Where did you get those?" I said, voice trembling.

"Get what?" He rolled, grimacing, to spy the deck in Sally's hand. "Oh, the cards? Mary bought them this morning. Elegant, aren't they? The design is all the rage in Paris this year. I'm rather fond of it myself. It's easier for me to hold them lying like this."

I took the deck from Sally and rifled through it. The

cards weren't the same in every way as the ones we'd found. Simon's deck had a crisscross pattern on the back instead of alchemical symbols. And, of course, there was no SALLY, TOM, or CHRISTOPHER marked on any of them. Still, this couldn't be a coincidence.

Could it?

"Where did she get them?" I said, still breathless.

"I have no idea. Ask her; I'm sure the shop will have more." He seemed to think I wanted a deck of my own. "Mary!"

We heard her come up the stairs. When she entered, she was holding a duster. "Yes, my lord?"

"Christopher wants to know where you bought these."

"At the market, my lord."

"Which market?" I said.

"Just down the way, north of the Strand."

"Covent Garden?"

"That's the one."

That didn't make sense. "Covent Garden Market sells produce."

"That's right." She seemed puzzled by my confusion.

"So some farmer was selling cards?" I said.

"Oh, it weren't no farmer," Mary said. "Was a cart by

the exit. I'd all loaded up my basket with the day's greens, but when I saw a man selling knickknacks and gewgaws from Paris, I think to myself, maybe my lord wants something from there. So I goes over, and the man shows me these cards. A right pretty set, I thought, so I buys them."

She looked from me to Simon. "Did I do something wrong?"

"No, of course not," I said. "I just thought it was strange. Covent Garden being a farmer's market and all."

"Always a sharp deal to be found if you keep your eyes open, my lord," she said with some pride.

Simon dismissed her as I stood there, mind racing.

What Mary had described wasn't unusual. Traveling merchants, who couldn't afford a stall, frequently set up carts near popular markets. They'd hawk their goods cheaply, undercutting the regular sellers, until the market sent toughs to move them along. And like Simon said, these cards were popular in Paris, so why not in London? We often copied what was fashionable across the Channel.

Just a coincidence, I thought.

I could hear the spymaster's suspicions in my mind. *Is it? Or are you trying to convince yourself?*

I didn't know. Could the Raven have arranged something like this? If he'd been watching Simon's household, he'd recognize servants like Mary, who did the shopping every morning. It would be the easiest thing in the world to position a cart along the way, then persuade her to buy a pretty set of French cards for her master—who he well knew had recently arrived from Paris.

It really could just be a coincidence. The thing was, it *felt* like a taunt. Like the Raven was throwing the cards in my face. *I can go anywhere,* they said. *There's no place you'll be safe from me.*

And that was assuming Mary's story was true. She could have been bribed by the Raven to give Simon the cards, so I'd see them and not know what to do.

But how would the Raven know I'd come here? I argued. *Mary bought the cards this morning. And I hadn't planned on visiting Simon again until all this was over.*

She claims she bought the cards this morning, Walsingham said. *She may be lying. Also: Do you believe the Raven couldn't manipulate where you'd go? His threat—and his rules—cut off nearly all other avenues of escape.*

Of everything the Raven had done—if, in fact, he'd done it at all—this was, in its way, the most chilling. To think that he could be so inside our heads that he'd be able to predict our coming here . . . I'd never felt so powerless.

Master Benedict tried to calm me. *You don't know if any of that's true,* he said. *Mary might have bought the cards innocently. And Simon's is the safest place to be tonight.*

I'm so lost, I said to him. *Please help me.*

You'll find a way, he said. *I believe in you.*

If only I believed the same.

With Simon bedridden, dinner was served in his room. Daniel and Patrick brought in a narrow table, placing it beside the bed so Tom, Sally, and I could sit facing the vicomte. He remained lying down, plucking roasted pork from his plate with his fingers and drinking copious amounts of wine. Our visit had really lifted his spirits.

"You picked an excellent night to stay," he said, dipping his bread in the oil. "I've had nothing to do all day. Kemp promised he'd visit at lunch, but he never showed, the quack. . . . What's wrong?"

A pit sank in my stomach.

He doesn't know, I thought. *No one's told him about Dr. Kemp.*

I felt like such a fool. Of course he didn't know. If I hadn't been so wrapped up in my own troubles, I'd have realized Simon would never have been so cheerful if he'd known the doctor was dead. He'd have been absolutely mad with rage.

I was horrified—and even more horrified about what I did next. Because I couldn't tell Simon what had happened. He'd be uncontrollable.

"It's nothing," I said quickly.

Simon paused, his hand in the bowl, bread soaking up the oil. His eyes narrowed, and he looked from me to Sally to Tom, who was too ashamed to even meet Simon's gaze.

"Why *are* you here?" Simon said, his humor gone. "You have rooms at the palace; I know this. I also know you're working on something secret, and have been for weeks. So why *do* you want to spend the night with me?"

I couldn't tell him the truth. And yet, I couldn't give him a complete lie. He'd never believe me unless it was something I wouldn't have been willing to share.

So I gave him both truth and lie. "Three days ago," I said, as if embarrassed I hadn't told him, "I was arrested. For murder."

"*What?*"

"I was framed," I said hastily. "By the Raven. He murdered my neighbor, and . . . and an old apprentice I once knew. He left the bodies in the alley behind my home. And he bribed some woman to lie and say she saw me do it."

Simon let out a blistering string of French curses. Grunting at the pain, he tried to rise. Sally scrambled around the table to hold him down, as did Tom. He struggled, but with his back in agony, he couldn't push them off.

"Stop, you'll tear the muscle," I said, alarmed.

"I don't care," Simon said, outraged. "You must call me to the court immediately. I may be French, but I am a vicomte, and I hold a great deal of land in England. I will speak on your behalf."

That actually would have carried a lot of weight. Lord Ashcombe, no doubt, would have done the same thing—although now that I'd lied to him, I wasn't so sure he'd ever speak to me again.

"There's no need," I said. "There won't be any trial. Lord Ashcombe has already sorted it out. It's just . . . the constables took me from my home. And I'm worried that, after foiling the Raven's plans, he might target me more . . . directly."

That seemed to make sense to him. He relaxed a little. I pushed it a bit more, to get him off the trail. "I just thought it best," I said, "if I didn't always keep the same routine. But I understand if you don't want us to stay anymore."

"Arrête tes bêtistes," he said, disgusted. "You think I'll let

you go now?" He glared at me. "You lied to me yesterday so I'd remain in my bed. Rotting like a dead fish."

"I wouldn't have put it *that* way."

Simon sighed, his anger cooling somewhat. "I suppose this is justice after how I treated Uncle Marin."

"You were wonderful to your uncle," Sally said firmly. "You kept him calm because you loved him. We care about you, too."

"Yes, yes. No need to lay it on so thick." He gave us all one final glare. "Deal the cards. We'll play for money. And as punishment for keeping me in the dark, I expect you to lose."

I forced myself to smile. Because I was pretty sure this was the last time Simon would ever be cheerful back. When he found out I'd lied about Dr. Kemp . . . I knew he'd never forgive me.

CHAPTER
49

IT WAS A JOYLESS EVENING.

We stayed with Simon until late. We finished our dinner; then he taught us All Fours, which we played as he told us stories of Nottinghamshire and Paris. We even drank a little of that brandy that he and Dr. Kemp loved so much.

And I hated every minute of it.

How many friends had I lost by keeping all these secrets? How many had I come to not trust?

My life has become nothing but lies, I said in my head.

You're being too hard on yourself, Master Benedict said. *Sometimes a lie can be a kindness.*

Nothing about this seemed kind. I felt so wretched, I had to leave the room for a few minutes so Simon didn't see how miserable I was. As an excuse, I told everyone I was tired of these pistols hanging from my belt and wanted to put them away before we continued. He had Mary show me where I'd be staying.

I'd been given a giant room on the top floor of the house, with what would have been a lovely view of the field across the street if it hadn't already been dark—and if such things mattered to me just then. All I wanted was a few minutes alone. "I can find my way back," I said.

"Very good, sir," Mary said, and she began to go.

"Wait."

She paused. "Yes, my lord?"

I knew I should ask her a question before she left. At that moment, I didn't really care enough to do it. And yet, as Walsingham had once said to me, *Sometimes a job must be done, whether you feel like doing it or not.*

Both Master Benedict and the spymaster had taught me to do my duty. They'd be disappointed in me if I didn't. That was the only reason I bothered to ask.

"I think I'd like a deck of those playing cards you bought this morning," I said.

"Course, my lord," Mary said. "I'll run down there first thing tomorrow."

"Oh, I'll do it. I've been meaning to go to Covent Garden, anyway. Just . . . the man who sold them to you. What did he look like? So I'll know whose cart to check."

"Young fellow. Nice looking. Had all his goods under a blue tarpaulin."

Young, I thought. Could be Peter. Or . . . "By any chance, did he have short brown hair?"

"Yeah, I'd say."

The priest? The one from Saint Peter's? "Did he have a French accent?"

"Sounded like a Londoner to me."

So not the priest I'd been looking for. Unless the accent was fake. Which Peter could easily do.

"One last thing," I said. "Do you know who printed the cards? Were they printed here, I mean, or in France?"

She blinked. "Wouldn't have thought to ask, my lord."

It was a strange question; there wouldn't have been any reason for an honest servant to care. But the Raven had obviously had his own deck prepared. If I could find the printer, maybe I could discover who'd placed that order.

It was a pretty good clue, actually—but I'd come upon

it too late. Both market and printer would be closed at this hour, and we had to get to the stables in the morning as the Raven had instructed us. I'd never get to pursue this lead before it was finished.

But maybe someone else would.

"Could you bring some ink and paper to my room, please, before we retire for the night?" I said.

"Course, sir. I'll arrange it straightaway."

I left my pistols and apothecary sash on the desk. Then I returned to the others.

After another hour of cards and storytelling, Sally was the first to collapse. Worn out by a rough day, she nodded off in her chair a couple of times before she finally jerked her head up, bleary-eyed, and said, "Please tell me my bed has soft pillows."

Simon laughed. "The softest. Sleep well."

She headed out, half swaying with drowsiness toward her room. Her departure gave me the perfect opportunity to head out, too. A few minutes later, I made a big show of yawning. "I think Sally had the right idea."

Simon sighed, a little disappointed. This was the most entertainment he'd had in a month. "Of course, you must all be exhausted," he said as Tom collected the cards and set the table to the side. "Sleep in as long as you like. I'll see you all for breakfast."

"Sure," I said, even though I knew otherwise. What was one more untruth added to a mountain of lies? I shook my head, hating what the Raven had turned me into.

Sally's room was on the way to mine. I passed it, then stopped, lingering just beyond her closed door.

I won't be having breakfast with her, either, I thought.

I stood there, wishing to see her face. It was strange. I mean, it wasn't like I hadn't seen her a thousand times before. And yet . . . this time was different.

Just tell her, I said to myself. *Tell her how you feel.*

I hesitated, debating. Then I went back and knocked lightly on her door.

"Sally?" I said softly.

No answer. She'd probably already drifted off to sleep.

I shouldn't wake her, I thought.

But another part of me said, *Yes, you should.*

I knocked again, a little louder.

"Something wrong?"

It was Tom. On his way back to his own room, he'd caught me in the hallway at Sally's door.

My face grew warm. "I was just going to say good night," I said.

Tom grinned at me.

"Oh, stop," I grumbled.

I could feel his grin on my back all the way to my room.

As exhausted as I was, I didn't go to sleep right away. It wasn't just Sally I had something to tell. There was another person with whom I needed to make things right.

So I sat at the desk and wrote a pair of letters. One was for Sally. The other was for Lord Ashcombe. I sealed them by dripping the burning candle on the fold, then using the cork from one of the vials in my apothecary sash to press down the wax. The candle was beige, not red, but the vial made the exact same plain circle as on the Raven's letters.

I didn't want to leave it like that. So I scratched a *C* in the circle and held it up to the light.

"I'm coming, Peter," I said.

Then I put the letters aside and crawled into bed.

I still wasn't finished for the night. Keeping one candle burning, I took the playing cards with our names on them and spread them out on the covers. Then I stared at the symbols on their backs. I had my master's key beside me, and I stared at that, too.

Marcasite.

Water.

And . . .

Nothing. There was nothing that fit that third symbol. I tried to twist it around, find something, but there was nothing I could match.

THE THREE PRINCIPLES		THE FOUR ELEMENTS		
⊖ salt *the contractive force*	*crystallization, contraction*	▽ earth	*cold and dry*	*melancholic*
⌬ sulphur *the expansive force*	*dissolution, evaporation*	▽ water	*cold and wet*	*phlegmatic*
☿ mercury *the integrative force*	*balancing salt and sulphur*	△ air	*hot and wet*	*sanguine*
		△ fire	*hot and dry*	*choleric*

PLANETARY METALS		TERRESTRIAL MINERALS	
☉ *gold / Sun*		◐ *saltpeter*	⚼ *realgar*
☽ *silver / Moon*	♃ *tin / Jupiter*	Ψ *quicklime*	⚵ *cinnabar*
♂ *iron / Mars*	♀ *lead / Venus*	✳○✳ *sal ammoniac*	*tartar*
☿ *mercury / Mercury*	♄ *copper / Saturn*	♌ *litharge*	♉ *marcasite*

CORROSIVES		WEIGHTS & MINERALS	
▽͞ *aqua fortis*	℞ *aqua regia*	M℔ *one pound*	Э℈ *one scruple*
✝ *vinegar*	✛ *distilled vinegar*	℥ *one ounce*	P℔ *one pinch*
⊕₂ *oil of vitriol*		ℨ *one dram*	O℔ *one pint*
		ANA	*equal amounts*

INSTRUCTIONS/PROCESSES			
⊤ calcination	◡ sublimation	Σ sugar	honey
♉ congestion	♏ separation	⊶ spirit	⌽ wax
♊ fixation	↗ ceration	♆ essence	℞ powder
♋ solution	♅ fermentation	♏ still	♏ distill
♌ digestion	〰 multiplication	℞ take	♄ mix
⊽ precipitation	☉ caput mortuum	⛰ alcohol	compose
♍ purify	oil	♋ retort	receiver
8 digest	◇ filter	♋ night	boil
		6♂ day	

If I combine two of them, I thought, then I get close. The triangle on top was water. But what would the circle be?

On the card, the circle symbol was empty. But none of the circles in the key were. Salt had a horizontal line through it. Saltpeter had a vertical one. Gold had a dot in the center. Oil of vitriol had a cross and a little tail. Even the actions at the bottom of the key weren't pure circles: Congestion had horns, and *caput mortuum*—meaning "worthless remains," the leftover residue of an experiment—was a death's head, with dots for eyes and mouth.

And even if I could have made the symbols fit, none of those combinations meant anything. Salt water—or saltpeter water—might be something, but gold did nothing in water, and oil of vitriol just got diluted. And none of these did anything with marcasite. I wasn't even sure marcasite was right in the first place.

A soft knock on the door made me sit up. Tom poked his head in. "I saw your light," he said. "Everything all right?"

"Just trying to work out this last problem," I said.

"I'm sure you'll get it."

I sighed. He had such faith in me.

"You should get some sleep," he said.

I made a face. "Don't think that's going to happen tonight."

"Well, you'll be safe. I'll keep watch over you and Sally."

I nodded, grateful. He closed the door.

I didn't expect his words to mean so much. Of course Tom would keep me safe; he always did. I just didn't think it would let me relax enough to sleep. Regardless of what kind of tricks I thought the Raven might play tonight, or whether he'd leave me alone to stew in my own fear, I still had this problem I couldn't figure out.

But Tom's care did mean something. It made me understand exactly what I had to do.

So, for the first night in a month, I lay down, closed my eyes, and drifted off straightaway.

FRIDAY, APRIL 9, 1666

Abandon all hope, ye who enter here.

CHAPTER 50

I FELT STRANGE IN THE MORNING.

I'd slept. My nightmares had still tormented me, but instead of keeping me awake, I'd drifted back to sleep every time. So when I finally got up, I didn't feel as muddled as I had these last few weeks.

I couldn't describe the feeling. Though it wasn't quite right, the closest I could come was a sense of . . . clarity. Not because I'd solved the problem of the Raven. Because I'd finally realized something deeper.

I *couldn't* solve the problem of the Raven.

Back in Paris, the first time I was pitted against him—before I even knew he existed—Tom and I had set a trap for our enemies. We'd worked out who they were and what they wanted. Then we'd lured them to a place of our choosing, so we could surprise them. They'd been ahead of us for so long, they never realized the tables had turned.

This time was the exact opposite.

We didn't know who our enemies were. We knew the Raven, of course—Peter—but who else was on his side? Simon's servants? Walsingham? The stranger passing by on the street?

We knew what the Raven wanted, too. Me, humiliated, defeated—and then dead. But beyond that? We had no place to lure the Raven, no trap we could spring. And no allies. The king and his friends were denied us, the Knights Templar had been destroyed. It was the Raven choosing the place this time, the Raven setting the trap. We would walk into it as clueless as the day we started.

And we would lose.

So the clarity that the morning brought was not about me winning. It was me losing.

And that means I have to lose alone.

It was still dark when I got out of bed. Quietly as I could, I wrote a third letter, this one to Tom. I placed it with the letter for Sally on my pillow, where they'd be sure to be found. Then I dressed, donned my sash and my pistols, and crept down the stairs.

I slipped out the back, making my way to the horses; we'd stabled them here last night. Since it was so early, I wasn't expecting anyone else to be up. So I jumped when a figure loomed in the twilight.

"Going somewhere?" Tom said.

I cursed, trying to calm my thumping heart. "You scared me."

Tom stood in front of Blossom, arms folded. "I should do a lot worse. You were going to sneak off without me, weren't you?"

I almost denied it. But I was tired of the lies.

"It's me the Raven wants, Tom," I said. "Once he has me, he won't—"

"Stop," Tom said. "Just stop. Don't you remember what I said to you in Devonshire? What you said to me as the pirates were closing in? Whatever happens, wherever we go, we'll face it together. We're friends forever."

He lifted himself into Lightning's saddle. Then he waited.

I suppose I should have known better. I belted Blossom's saddle on and mounted her. She chuffed into the cool air.

Tom glanced over at Beatrice, resting peacefully in her stall. "What about Sally?" he said.

"I left her a letter."

He grinned. "I *bet* you did."

This time, he almost made me laugh.

With the streets empty, it was a quick ride back to the palace. We dismounted at the stables but didn't put our horses away. I handed my reins to Tom and said, "Wait here."

"Oh, no," he said. "I'm not falling for that twice."

"I'm not going to sneak off without you," I promised. "I have a letter I have to get to Lord Ashcombe." I told Tom how I'd written down everything that had happened, including the playing cards, and that if the King's Warden could find the printer that made them, it might lead back to the Raven. "I'm going to leave it on my bed. The servants will find it and give it to him. Just in case."

Tom understood what I meant. *Just in case we didn't make it back.* Still, he made me swear on Master Benedict's soul I wouldn't leave him behind at the palace. I did, even as I pointed out that I *couldn't* leave. We wouldn't know where to go until the Raven's message was delivered.

When I returned from my room, the answer was waiting. Tom held a letter between two fingers, like it would poison him if he touched it any more.

"Courier brought this to the palace gate," he said nervously.

"Did you see the man who left it?" I asked.

He shook his head. "A rider in a cloak, moving at speed, tossed it to the guards without stopping."

I suppose I hadn't expected any less. As the letter was addressed to me, Tom hadn't opened it yet. So I broke the familiar red seal, and we read it together.

Go to the center of Clerkenwell Green.

It's time we meet.

CHAPTER
51

DAWN BROKE AS WE REACHED THE fields.

A deep, vivid sunrise painted the grass, growing taller with the marching of spring. Dew sparkled in the light, turning the green red, a strange sea viewed from alien shores.

Tom and I had met here, when I accidentally bonked him on the head with rotten fruit from my very first catapult. Now a stranger stood in the distance, silhouetted against the horizon. He was wearing a cloak, pacing in the center of the grass.

"What do we do?" Tom whispered.

"Talk to the man," I said.

"That's it? Just go say, *Good morning, Mr. Raven. How are you?*"

"That's not the Raven."

Tom squinted across the green. "How do you know?"

"That man's too impatient. And too exposed. The Raven will want to meet us somewhere private."

"So who is it?"

"Another courier, I'm guessing." I dismounted. "Wait here."

I stamped across the green, the dew wetting my boots. The man on the hill watched me as I approached, drawing a letter from beneath his cloak.

He was young, with a scar on his nose. "You Christopher Rowe?" he said.

When I nodded, he stuffed the letter in my hands like he was glad to be rid of it. Then he began to hurry away.

"Wait," I said. "Who gave this to you?"

"Some fellow in a mask," the courier said, unhappy I'd stopped him. "Paid me a pound last night to wait for you here in the morning."

"The mask was golden, I assume? With a smile?"

"That's the one. Look 'ere, I don't want no more part of this, all right? I just want to go home."

"Don't."

"'Scuse me?"

"Don't go home," I said. "Do you travel to other cities, or do you only work here in London?"

"I go wherever you want, if you got a message and the coin."

I fished around in my purse. "Do you know Seaton? It's a village in Devonshire."

"Naw, but I can find it."

"Good." I handed him four pounds, a huge overpayment. "Head there immediately and ask for directions to Robert Dryden's farm. When you reach it, tell Robert that Christopher wishes him and Wise well, and thanks them again for saving his life."

"That's it?"

"That's it."

Though he clearly thought I was strange, he shrugged and said, "I'll set off now."

"Make sure you do."

He left. I read the letter, then took it back to Tom, who watched the courier ride away.

"What was all that about?" he said.

"I sent him out of the city."

"Why?"

"Because the Raven's getting rid of every trace that

could lead back to him," I said. "If that courier doesn't leave London, he'll end up dead."

Tom nodded soberly. "What did the letter say, then?"

I let him read it for himself.

Go to the fountain at Winford Street and Gravel Lane, near Aldgate.

We'd actually seen that fountain before. Though outside the city walls, it was a reasonable walk from Tom's house. "Will the Raven be there, do you think?" he asked.

I got on Blossom. "No. We'll probably get another message sending us somewhere else."

Tom frowned. "What's the point of that? Why run us all over town?"

"To make sure we aren't being followed. In case we broke the rules. The Raven wouldn't appreciate being swarmed by the King's Men."

He was clearly taking every precaution before springing his trap. I suppose I should have expected nothing less.

I was right about the meeting at the fountain. It was another courier with another message to another destination. This man I sent off with orders to go to the market and buy the nicest bottle of rum anyone was selling. Then he should head out to sea to find Roger Haddock, captain of the *Manticore*, give him the rum, and tell him to enjoy it with Christopher's compliments.

Tom caught me smiling at the departing courier. I told him about the message I'd sent. "I wish we could be there to see it," I said. "Captain Haddock's going to be so confused."

Tom looked puzzled. "You're having fun with this."

"Why not? Most of the time, we deal with people who've already been murdered. Feels good to be able to spare a life, for once."

He couldn't argue with that.

As for the message, it sent us to the main doors of Saint Paul's Cathedral—a spot we knew very well. There we found another courier, this one a boy a couple of years older than me. I sent him east to Ipswich, with orders to find the best baker in that city, buy a Dutch-style spice cake, and bring it back to Lord Ashcombe at the Palace of Whitehall.

Even saying it made it hard to keep a straight face. The odd look the boy gave me made me laugh outright.

Tom stared at me like I'd lost my mind, too. "Did you just send Lord Ashcombe a spice cake?"

"Yes."

"Why?"

"He likes them."

"Yes, but . . . *why?*"

"I've run out of friends in other cities to send messages to. This should keep that courier out of London for a week." Hopefully, that would be enough time for the Raven to give up tracking him down and move on.

"Should I be worried about you?" Tom said.

"I thought you'd find it funny," I objected. "But no. There won't be any more couriers, anyway. This is the real message."

I showed it to him.

A warehouse of red brick stands among others on Old Swan Lane, south of Thames Street. Go inside. And your journey will come to an end.

CHAPTER
52

THE WAREHOUSE THE RAVEN SENT
us to was as out of the way as a place could possibly be. Old
Swan Lane, near the docks south of Thames Street, was a
narrow path barely large enough for a cart to get through.
While the city had started to show some life as it recovered
from the plague, the buildings along this lane looked abandoned.

There had been someone here recently, however. And
it wasn't ordinary traffic; the lane ended at a gate barring
travelers from reaching the river this way. Judging from the
rust on the padlock, the gate hadn't been opened since the
sickness shut everything down.

No, it was the warehouse itself that had been worked on. There was only one made of red brick, as the Raven's letter had indicated. All its windows were boarded up, but the wood covering them was unweathered and undamaged. Warehouses abandoned during the plague would have been looted, the boards torn away, the windows beneath shattered.

A side door opened off the alley. There was a shiny new padlock hanging from it, unsecured. Someone had left the way open for us.

Tom drew his sword. Using the point of the blade, he pushed the door ajar. There was no squeak; I could smell the oil on the hinges. Inside was a fresh sort of smell, too: sawdust and mortar. Builders had been here sometime in the last few weeks.

The side door opened into a corridor with offices. They were all empty except for one, which had a single desk shoved against the back wall, a chair on its side atop it. The storeroom at the end of the passage was just as empty.

But as we entered the open space, I could see a path had been cleared through the dust and dirt, leading from a shuttered loading gate on the dock side to what looked like a larger office along the far wall. Except when we opened that door, we discovered it wasn't an office at all.

Behind the door were stairs, going down. They'd been built very recently. The walls still smelled of limewash, and the stairs were newly laid stone. Every five steps, a candle burned, the wax hardly melted. Someone had arrived just before us.

Tom grabbed my arm. "Do you think the Raven's down there?" he whispered.

"Yes."

"So he's trapped!"

I shook my head. "He wouldn't leave himself without another way out. He's probably built an escape passage from whatever's below."

"Maybe he hasn't, though. Why don't we go get the King's Men?"

"How long do you think that would take?" I said. "The Raven's deliberately chosen this place to be as far away from help as possible. Whitehall's a long ride to the west. The Tower's closer, but by the time we got there and back, he'd certainly be gone."

"Then you go," Tom insisted. "I'll stay here and keep watch."

I sighed. "Tom . . . there's no way he hasn't planned for that. We were probably spotted the second we arrived. If we leave now, I guarantee it won't end well for either of us."

"So what do we do?"

"We came here to finish this," I said. "So let's finish it."

We went down.

The stairs changed direction. After fifteen steps, the passage opened into a small, U-shaped landing, turning back upon itself. And here we found the strangest thing yet.

It was a door—but not like one I'd ever seen before. This door was made of steel, rivets hammered into it in a pentagon pattern. Yet the oddest part was the mechanism in its center.

There were three levers, painted blue, in a row across the middle. A fourth lever, painted red, was directly above them. Each lever was a foot long. Beside each of the three blue levers was a sort of wheel, the numbers from 0 to 9 engraved around the edge of a circle. An arrow was notched into the door beside each wheel, pointing to a number. At the moment, all three wheels were set at 0.

The red lever had no wheel beside it. Instead, on its left, was a mirror, six inches wide, three inches high. It had been placed at eye height—my eye height, anyway; Tom was a foot taller than me. To the right of the lever was a note, pinned under one of the rivets in the door.

Choose your fate.

Use the blue levers to turn the dials and make a three-digit number. When you are ready, pull the red lever. If you do not know the number, then reflect on the path you have chosen, and the answer will reveal itself.

Choose carefully. If you choose the correct number, you will earn the right to meet me. If you choose the wrong number, then one of you will die.

CHAPTER
53

TOM STARED AT THE NOTE.

"I'm beginning to think," he said, dejected, "the Raven's just toying with us."

I was pretty sure that was the point. He kept making us feel like we were accomplishing something—solving each puzzle—then he pulled the rug out from under us every time. It was a reminder that he was in control, and it filled us both with despair. Which was likely also the point.

It's more than that, Master Benedict said.

What do you mean? I said.

The Raven's game has a pattern. Do you recognize it?

A pattern?

I wasn't sure what my master was getting at. Thinking on what he'd said, I pulled tentatively on the first of the blue levers. As it moved, the dial to its left turned.

Chunk.

The numbers on the dial shifted clockwise. The arrow now pointed to the *1*.

Tom, surprised, pulled down on the next lever. The dial beside that lever shifted—*chunk-chunk-chunk-chunk*—and now the arrow beside that dial pointed to *4*. He pushed it all the way back up, and it chunked back to *0*.

"Have you ever seen anything like this?" Tom said, amazed.

"Never." But I understood the mechanism now. Pull the levers, change the numbers. It was a fascinating piece of engineering.

Tom cranked two of the blue levers some more, spinning both dials beside them. I stopped him. I didn't know how fragile the mechanism was. The last thing we needed was to break it.

"So," I said. "We use each blue lever to set each of the three numbers. Then pull the red lever to open the door."

"What are the right numbers?" Tom said.

"I don't know."

"Wait," Tom said, alarmed. "This says if we choose the *wrong* number, one of us will die. How can we just pick one out of a thousand and not lose? And how will we die, anyway?" Suddenly, he stepped back, dragging me with him. "Is the door going to explode?"

That didn't seem likely. I suppose the red lever could be attached to some kind of sparker with a fuse that lit some gunpowder. My mind tumbled, trying to work out how such a mechanism might work.

That's not important, Master Benedict said. *Think of the Raven's pattern.*

His pattern?

He's modeled his game on our time in Paris, I said.

Yes, Master Benedict said.

There we had the Templars' riddles to follow. Here we have his.

Yes.

Then at the end, we set up a trap. But he's the one setting the trap now.

Yes, Master Benedict said. *But what happened at the end?*

We beat Aphrodite and the Minotaur.

No. Before that. What did you face?

We had to get through the Templars' secret—

Door, I thought.

I stared at the steel door in front of us.

That's what he's doing, I said. *Even after we'd solved the Templars' riddle; even after we'd worked out all the clues . . . we still had to figure out how to get past the secret door.*

And how did you do that? Master Benedict said.

I used what I'd learned while I was solving the previous puzzles.

My master smiled.

That was the answer.

"We *know* the number," I said to Tom, excited.

"We do?"

"We have to. That's the point. The Raven wouldn't make us guess. Somewhere along the way, he gave it to us."

Tom frowned, thinking. "There were numbers on the papers in the Temple Church."

That was my first thought, too. But those were all four digits, and this door needed three.

Three digits, I thought.

And three places we went to. The Tower. The Temple. The Abbey.

Would that mean . . . a number for each location?

But what would they be? I'd never heard of such a

thing. And I was pretty sure we hadn't seen one while we were there.

Tom was getting frustrated. "This isn't fair," he grumbled. "The game promised we'd be saved if we found those stupid playing cards. We're not supposed to get blown up by a door."

I stared at him.

"What?" he said. "What did I say?"

"The cards," I said. "The *playing cards*. That's it."

CHAPTER
54

"WHAT'S IT?" TOM SAID.

"Look at what the note says." I pointed to the middle paragraph. "'If you do not know the number, then *reflect on the path you have chosen*, and the answer will reveal itself.' The *cards*. The cards are supposed to save us. And they're what we chose along the way."

"So . . . the cards give us the numbers?" he said. "I didn't see any numbers."

I hadn't, either. And peering at the images on the cards showed nothing hidden.

Except for one thing.

"The symbols!" I said. "The symbols on the back!"

Kneeling on the stone, I flipped the cards over so all their symbols were showing. I placed them in the order we'd found them: SALLY, TOM, CHRISTOPHER.

"These must give us our numbers," I said.

"But how?" Tom said uncertainly. "Did you work out what the symbols mean?"

"No," I said, frustrated. I pointed from left to right. "Marcasite. Water. And . . ."

What?

I still had no idea. I'd exhausted all the possibilities on Master Benedict's key.

Don't concentrate on what you don't know, Master Benedict said. *Start with what you do know.*

He was right, as usual. If I could figure out the numbers for what I did know, then maybe it would help me solve the ones I didn't.

"The middle symbol," I said to Tom, "the triangle, is water. We know that for sure."

"Is there a number assigned to water?" he said.

Not as far as I knew. Although . . . "What if it's the points?" I said. "The points of the triangle, I mean. Three points . . . the number three."

"Makes sense," Tom said. "Though couldn't it just be the sides instead?"

That was a possibility, too. But in this case . . . "That's the same number," I said, heart thumping a little faster. "There are three sides to a triangle. The number three, again."

Excited, I picked up the first symbol, the one that looked like marcasite.

"All right," I said. "This has . . . one, two . . . um . . ."

I wasn't sure how to calculate points on this one. I'd count the two end points of the T on top of the circle for sure. But what about where the lines crossed? And what about where the T met the circle in the center?

"And the sides," Tom said. "How many sides does a circle have? One?"

I thought back to my geometry. "Technically, it's zero."

"The dials have a zero."

"Right, but you'd have to include the lines in that. So that would be two." Or three, if you considered the top line as two pieces instead of one.

I shook my head. "This can't be it," I said. "The only way to get an answer is by guessing. And I'm sure the Raven doesn't want me to guess. He expects me to work it out."

Tom threw his hands up. "So what, then?"

"We're still missing something." I stood and looked at the instructions again.

Choose your fate.

Use the blue levers to turn the dials and make a three-digit number. When you are ready, pull the red lever. If you do not know the number, then reflect on the path you have chosen, and the answer will reveal itself.

Choose carefully. If you choose the correct number, you will earn the right to meet me. If you choose the wrong number, then one of you will die.

What had I missed?

My master returned. *Remember the pattern,* he said.

Which—oh. The Raven's modeled his game on what we've done before.

Right. And what did you learn from the Templars?

We'd learned a lot of things from the Templars. They were masters of misdirection. Their answers were literal; it seemed like they meant one thing, but if you looked at what their riddles actually said—

Literal, I thought. *Their answers were literal.*

"There," I said. "*There.* That's the clue!"

"Where?" Tom said.

"Right there," I said. "The mirror. Look at what the note says. '*Reflect* on the path you have chosen.' Reflect— *like a mirror.* The mirror is the key."

"I . . ." Tom blinked. "All right. But how?"

I held the TOM card up to the mirror. In it, I saw my reflection. I was holding the card with my left hand. Mirror-me was holding it with his right. But the symbol . . .

"The symbol's the same," I said.

It was just a triangle, pointed down. Its reflection was identical to the original.

In fact . . .

"All of them are," I said.

Tom shook his head. "I don't have the faintest idea what you're telling me."

"The symbols. They're all symmetric. They're the same whether you reflect them in the mirror or not."

"I see that. But what's that got to do with finding a number?"

And then I understood.

CHAPTER
55

"THE REFLECTION," I SAID. "THE reflection *is* the number."

Tom stared at the mirror. "It's a triangle," he said. "Exactly the same as before."

"Yes. That's the key. It's symmetric. I mean, it's *already* symmetric."

"Will you please just give me the answer?"

"Look," I said. "The clue says to *reflect* on the path. So look at the symbols. The reason they look the same in the mirror as on the card is because *they're already reflections of themselves.*"

I'd arranged the cards in a row. Now I rearranged them so that they were in a column, in the order we'd found them: SALLY on the top, CHRISTOPHER on the bottom.

"Each side is a mirror image of the other," Tom repeated. "I still don't see any numbers."

"Because you're looking at the whole symbol. *You have to remove the reflection.*"

And I covered the left half of the symbols with my arm.

$$\begin{aligned} &5 \\ &7 \\ &3 \end{aligned}$$

Tom stared in amazement as the numbers suddenly appeared. "Five . . . seven . . . three. You found it! So . . . 573? That's the number we use?"

"It has to be."

"But how do we know the numbers are in the right order? Couldn't it be 375 instead? Or some other combination?"

Good question. I bit my lip. "Well . . . the clue said the path we chose. Five, seven, three was our path: Tower, then Temple, then Abbey. The order we got the cards should be the order we arrange the numbers."

At least I hoped so. Either way, there was no point in waiting. I shifted the blue levers so the dials chunked to the right numbers, the arrows pointing at *5-7-3*. Then I took hold of the red lever above them with a quick prayer.

"Here goes nothing," I said.

I pulled it.

CHAPTER
56

CHUNK.

The sound came from deep within the door.

I let out a breath. "Well, we didn't explode."

"The day's still early," Tom grumbled.

But we'd got it right. With both Tom and me shoulder-ing it, the steel portal swung open. The passage led deeper, like before.

And there was a body on the stairs below us.

The corpse of a man lay sprawled four steps down. Blood had dried in the center of his shirt, an even bigger dried bloodstain on the back. He'd been stabbed from behind.

His scarred, callused hands and the tools in his belt

around his waist marked him as a craftsman; almost certainly the man who'd built the door. I wondered what he'd thought he was working on when this lock had been commissioned. A vault, to hold the warehouse owner's wealth? Either way, with his usefulness ended, the Raven had silenced him for good. We shook our heads in dismay and moved on.

As before, the steps went down to another landing. This time, we found not a door, but a portcullis blocking our way. A heavy, steel-spoked wheel was set into the wall, the kind one would find at a drawbridge. Through the bars I could see an identical wheel on the other side.

"Another trap," Tom said. "Of course."

Was it? I didn't see a trap, or anything that indicated a riddle. "This wheel must open the gate," I said, and I tried turning it. I couldn't get it to budge. "Is it locked?"

"Let me try," Tom said, and he threw all his weight against the wheel.

It turned. Tom grunted, his muscles straining. The portcullis lifted slowly, the sound of chains rattling behind the wall.

The iron clanged at the top. "Does it lock on its own?" Tom said, voice tight. "It's not holding in place."

"Try it," I said.

Tom let go. The wheel spun round, and the gate came down with a terrible crash.

My ears rang. "That was a bad idea," Tom said.

But I was beginning to understand the mechanism. "I think we need to lock it with the wheel on the other side. It's designed for two to operate."

And that's not a coincidence, I thought. If the Raven knew anything about me, he'd know Tom would never allow me to leave him behind. He'd clearly planned for it; I could never have lifted this portcullis on my own.

"Do it again," I said.

"Easy for you to say," Tom grumbled. But he cranked the wheel once more, until the gate was fully raised.

"Don't let go," I warned him. If the gate fell, I'd be skewered.

Maybe that's the point, I thought.

I paused. I looked all around, seeing if I could spot anything—a shifting stone in the floor, or the like—that might trigger a trap to drop the gate as I passed beneath it.

Tom was turning red. "Could you hurry up? I'm not holding a box of feathers here."

I didn't tell him my suspicions, because he'd probably

forbid me from crossing under. But I couldn't see anything obvious, so, with a deep breath, I leaped through.

I landed just fine.

"Turn the other wheel," Tom wheezed.

I did as he asked. As he'd already done the heavy lifting, this one spun easily. My only worry was when I reached the end. I wasn't strong enough to lift the gate; would I be able to hold it there, at least, until Tom could get through?

There was only one way to know. I cranked the wheel until I felt something strange at the end. "Was yours spongy at the top—?" I began.

Then I heard a crack.

Something snapped beneath the wheel in my hands. Behind the wall came the rattle of tumbling chains.

And the portcullis came crashing down.

CHAPTER 57

TOM LEAPED AWAY IN ALARM. THE iron slammed into the stone, the noise deafening inside the passage, like being trapped inside a ringing bell.

Confused, Tom sprang forward to turn the wheel on his side again. It spun freely now, without any resistance at all.

"This wheel doesn't work anymore," Tom said. He stared in horror through the bars. "But . . . I didn't let go! Why did the gate fall?"

It took me a moment, but I understood. "It *was* a trap," I said.

"What?"

"That's what the second wheel was for. The first one was

too heavy for me to move; it took your strength to turn it. That guaranteed you'd be on that side when I crossed. This wheel . . ." I spun the spokes on my side. "It wasn't meant to lift the gate at all. It was designed to break something inside the wall, so your wheel would slip its chain. The gate comes down. And the Raven traps me on this side, all alone."

Tom listened, his horror returning as he realized how we'd been duped. This was the Raven's final trap. And we'd sprung it.

He smacked the now-useless wheel beside him in frustration. Then he bent to grab the portcullis near the bottom. He tried to lift it.

It wouldn't budge.

Tom strained harder. His face turned purple, veins bulging along his temples. He groaned, throwing all his strength at it, his muscles stretching his shirt so much it tore at the shoulders.

I wouldn't have thought it possible, but he actually succeeded in lifting the gate—half an inch. Then it crashed back down.

He paused, panting. "I almost got it," he said between breaths. "You grab on that side. I think we might be able to lift it together."

I stood there a moment. "No."

"No, really, come on. We can do it—I'm sure we can."

"No, Tom. We can't."

"What are you talking about? You saw it move. I just need a little help—"

He broke off as he looked up at me.

"Christopher," he said in alarm.

"This is what the Raven wanted," I said quietly. "His grudge is with me. Like I said back at Blackthorn, it's nothing to do with Paris, or the Templars, or stolen treasure. It's about Master Benedict. It's about what I got, and the Raven—Peter—didn't."

Tom stood. "Stop it—"

"I'm right; you know I am. The Raven never thought of you as anything other than a tool to hurt me. Well, now he's fulfilled his promise. He's taken away the things I love, one by one, until there's only him and me."

"No." Tom strained against the gate. "No!"

"This is a good thing, Tom," I said. "It means you don't have to die. Not you, nor Sally, nor anyone else. I'm glad for it. Too many people have died because of me already."

"Rubbish," Tom said. "None of this is your fault. Everything that's happened is the Raven's doing. No one else's."

He's right, Master Benedict said.

I know, I said. *But now that I also know the truth about the Raven . . . he's given me this chance to go on alone. From here on, anyone else who dies* is *my fault.*

"Christopher. Listen to me," Tom said. "Just listen. We can get this open. Even if we can't, you have oil of vitriol. You can burn through the bars."

"I don't have enough vitriol for that."

"Listen—"

"Do you know why I don't sleep anymore?" I said.

"I . . . what?"

"I don't sleep. You know that, right? Before last night, I hadn't slept properly for a month. Do you know why?"

He was silent for a moment. Then, quietly, he said, "You have nightmares."

"Do you know of what?"

"I always assumed it was the Raven."

"Sort of," I said. "They're *because* of the Raven, but they're not about him. They're about you."

"Me?"

I nodded. "Do you remember what you said to me a month ago? You said if the Raven wanted to get me, he'd have to step over your dead body to do it."

Tom stared at me.

"That's what I see," I said. "You dead. Poisoned, actually. I see every bit of good times we had. Then I see every time you saved my life. And then I see you choke and die. And every time, the Raven whispers in my ear, *You did this.*"

"It's just a dream," Tom said.

"But he's right. You say all this is the Raven's fault, and I suppose, up until now, that's been true. Not anymore. I got you into this. Now I have the chance to keep you out."

"No!" Tom thrust his hand through the bars, straining to catch my jerkin. He almost got me, too. I stumbled, dodging backward, and nearly fell down the steps.

"Please," Tom said. "Don't do this."

"I wouldn't," I said, "if I had a plan. Some way to get us out of this. But I don't. The Raven beat me. I know it was never a fair game: He knew who I was, while I didn't figure out he was Peter until too late. And he took away everyone else who could help. The king, Lord Ashcombe, Lord Walsingham. The Templars most of all. If we could have joined forces with the Templars, if we'd had them on our side, I think maybe we could have caught the Raven. He knew that. It's why, before he made any move against me, he took the Templars away. So I'd be helpless.

"The spymaster tried to tell me that yesterday," I said. "Maybe he's working with the Raven, maybe not. Either way, he understood: To beat the man, I needed *all* my friends. So he took them away, one by one. And now it's just me."

"He'll kill you," Tom said in anguish.

"I know." I pulled both my pistols. "But if I'm going to die, I promise you this: I'm going to die behind a cloud of gun smoke."

I turned to go.

"Wait," Tom said, desperate. "It's not . . . it's not over. I can still help you. I can." He seemed to be struggling to say something. "You just have to get me through here."

I stared down the steps. "You know," I said, "I owe Master Benedict so much. He gave me a whole new life, one I never imagined I could have. Just as I never imagined he'd ever be gone. And because of that, because I never imagined that future, he died before I could tell him how much I loved him. I wish I could have seen it coming. I wish I'd told him how grateful I am. I wish I'd had the chance to say thank you."

I turned back. "Thank you, Tom," I said.

Then I went down.

CHAPTER 58

THERE WAS ONE MORE LANDING.
But this one held no barrier, no gate, no trap. It just
turned around, and at the bottom of those steps was an
open door.

Tom's howls echoed after me. I heard the clanging of the
portcullis as he kept trying to lift it, never able to get it high
enough. "Wait! Christopher! We're not finished yet! You're
not alone! Just bring me with you! CHRISTOPHER!"

I gripped both my pistols, fingers on the triggers, as I
descended the final stair.

Then I stepped through the door.

There was a room on the other side, freshly limewashed, the walls spotless. Unlike the warehouse above, however, this room wasn't empty.

A leather pack rested in the far corner. There was a table in the center, with a chair on either side, one facing the door, the other facing away. On the table was a silver tray, with two crystal goblets and a matching decanter. The decanter contained a clear liquid, though whether it was water or some spirit, I couldn't tell.

Next to it was a small black leather pouch, tied tight with purse strings. And beside the tray, strangely, was an hourglass. It was the same kind Master Benedict and I used in our workshop as timers. In fact—

This was *my* hourglass, stolen from Blackthorn. I recognized the burn on the wooden base. I'd scorched it years ago, when I'd knocked a candle over.

The hourglass measured fifteen minutes. From what little sand had run down, it had been turned over no more than a couple of minutes ago.

And the man who'd turned it over stood behind it.

He was dressed in a heavy cloak, boots, and gloves. The cloak had a hood, drawn forward to shadow the man's face. But I wouldn't have seen his face even without it. He was wearing a smiling golden mask: Thalia, Muse of Comedy.

One hand rested on one of the chairs. The other held a pistol. It was aimed directly at me.

"Welcome," the masked man said.

His voice was muffled, but I could tell he spoke with an accent. Somewhere from the north of England, I thought, though it was a little hard to make out.

Was this the Raven? It was impossible to tell. The accent sounded real, but something told me it wasn't—just like the voice he was putting on. It was a disguise, designed to fool me. I was sure of it.

I also wondered: Would the Raven serve himself up so easily? He had a pistol, but I had two. And mine were pointed straight back at him.

There was a trick here. I was certain of it. I just didn't know what it was.

"I know what you're thinking," the masked man said. "You're thinking, *He can't possibly be the Raven. The Raven wouldn't leave himself so exposed.* Correct?"

It was unnerving to hear my own thoughts as if plucked from my head. *Which is why he said it,* Master Benedict said.

"So let me assure you," the man continued. "I *am* the Raven. This I promise."

"Then why don't you show me your face?" I said.

"Time enough for that later. For now—"

"No." Keeping one gun trained on him, I tucked the other into my belt, just long enough to draw the three playing cards from my pocket. I threw them toward him. They fluttered and fell at his feet.

"I played your game," I said, redrawing my second pistol. "'One day to find the warrants that grant salvation.' Well, I found them. So I won. By *your* rules. Now do what you promised. Leave us alone."

"You did indeed pass the trials," he said. "And you found the warrants that grant salvation. So: I grant it. I will not kill Sally. I will not kill Tom. In fact, as you'll soon discover, I'm not even going to kill you."

I didn't believe a word of it. "Then why did you bring me here? The game is over."

"Oh, no, Christopher. The game is never over. That's what makes it so much fun. You see, I made you a *different* promise, a long time ago, and it still needs to be fulfilled. There's one thing left to teach you."

The hourglass continued to run down. A third of the

sand was gone. Five minutes passed, ten minutes left.

"I don't intend to let you teach me anything," I said.

"I respect the sentiment," he said, "but I'm not offering you a choice."

"You'll find it's not your choice to make." I pointed both muzzles at his chest. "What's to stop me from just killing you now?"

"I don't know? What is?"

The only reason I hadn't shot him yet was because I didn't know for sure he was the Raven. I needed him to take off that mask.

"Not going to say?" the man said. "Well, then, I'll tell you. You won't kill me, Christopher, because you're not the type. You're not a cold-blooded murderer. Not in your heart. And not by anything Master Benedict taught you."

And he lowered his gun.

That was when I knew: This *was* the Raven. He was too clever, too intuitive, too knowing. It really was the Raven, standing before me.

I stared at him for a moment.

Then I lowered my pistols, too.

"You're right," I said. "Killing you—killing anyone—is something I never wanted. I wanted to be an apothecary.

I wanted to help people. To heal them, to make them feel better. And nothing Master Benedict taught me ever went against that."

I sighed. "I'd have been so happy, just being his apprentice forever. But that wasn't to be. So I ended up with new teachers. There's Lord Walsingham, who taught me to be a spy. To lie when needed, even to my friends, even when it tore me apart.

"But there's another man. A man who stepped into my life and cared for me, no matter how aggravating I was. His name is Richard Ashcombe," I said to the Raven. "And he taught me a few tricks of his own."

I raised my pistols and shot him.

CHAPTER
59

CLACK.

The triggers pulled; the hammers fell. The flints struck the frizzens, sending up sparks. They ignited the powder, which flared with a violent hiss.

But my guns didn't go off.

I stood there, staring dumbly at my pistols.

And the Raven laughed.

He sabotaged me, I thought. Somehow, he'd managed to sabotage my guns. How had he done this?

He didn't tell me. He just laughed and raised his own pistol once more.

"Come now, Christopher," he said. "After all the trouble

I went to, setting this whole place, this whole *game*, up for you." He waved at the room around us. "Surely you didn't think I'd leave anything to chance? That I'd fall to something as vulgar as Ashcombe's guns?"

I stood there, uncomprehending. Blood rushed in my ears: panic, humiliation, complete and utter bewilderment. Behind me, upstairs, I could still hear Tom. He'd stopped shouting for me some time ago. Now he just worked on lifting the gate. *Clang.* Pause. *Clang.* Pause. *Clang.*

Once again, the Raven seemed to read my mind. "Tom's so noisy, isn't he? Why don't you shut the door? Give us some peace and quiet."

Head still buzzing, I did as he said. Not because I wanted to follow his commands, but because anything I could put between me and Tom might keep my friend alive.

"Now sit," the Raven said.

I moved to the chair closest to me. The Raven waved me past it. "The other one, please. Facing the door."

I wasn't sure why it mattered until I approached the second chair. Then I saw: There were shackles on the arms and legs, placed to clamp my wrists and ankles.

For a moment, I balked. I thought about lunging at him. But as I'd moved, he'd moved, too, keeping the table between us. I'd never get him before he shot me. He really was taking no chances.

So I sat.

"Lock yourself in," he said. "Legs first, then your right wrist."

The clamps were cold. I thought about trying to trick him by not closing the padlocks, but he'd planned for that, too. The padlock wouldn't shut until it made an audible click. He waited until he'd heard all three.

"Now your left," he said.

I placed my left wrist in the clamp. Again he gave me no chance to fight him; he approached from the right, his gun pointed at my head the whole time. He locked me in completely, testing the padlocks, just to be sure. He needn't have bothered. They held me tight, enough to make my hands and feet start to tingle.

Then he grabbed my neck, bending me forward in the chair. Surprised, I struggled, but he wasn't trying to hurt me. Instead, he yanked up my shirt at the back and undid my apothecary sash.

"Just in case," he said.

He placed it in the corner near the small pack, but not carelessly. He folded it carefully, laying it down with reverence.

By the time he was finished, half of the sand had slipped through the hourglass. Seven, maybe eight minutes left. Until whatever he was expecting would happen.

"What now?" I said.

The Raven placed his pistol on the table—so close, and yet impossibly far out of reach. Which was, again, the point.

"Now?" he said. He pushed his hood back. "Now we finally, truly, meet."

And he removed his golden mask and showed me his face.

CHAPTER
60

I STARED INTO INTENSE BLUE EYES.

And my guts twisted with the wrenching pain of betrayal.

I'd hoped to see a stranger. Instead, I saw—what I'd thought—was a friend.

"Simon?" I said.

Simon Chastellain grinned down at me. He dropped the false accent, just like he'd dropped the cloak and mask. No more disguises. And yet his face now seemed more a mask than the one made of gold.

Because it *was* a stranger behind those eyes. The true self he'd kept hidden from all of us. A man alien and cruel.

But . . . it didn't make any sense. "How?" I said. "How can you . . . ?"

"What?" Simon said. "How can I be out of bed, with my terribly injured back?"

Before I could say yes, he turned and lifted his shirt.

I stared at perfect skin. Not a wound. Not a scar. Not a mark.

He was never stabbed, I realized. "But . . . I saw it," I said, confused. "I saw the dagger in your back."

"Did you?" He let his shirt fall back down. "Did you see the knife in my flesh? Did you see my wound leaking blood? What did you see, Christopher? What did you *really* see?"

"I . . ."

He went over to the small pack in the corner and drew something out. He tossed it on the table in front of me.

It was a dagger—or at least *part* of a dagger—with a large, conical pommel and a smooth, cylindrical grip. The blade, long and flat, ended abruptly where it attached to a piece of curved leather. The hilt was the exact same type of dagger the Covenanter assassins had used, the one Dr. Kemp had shown me after saving Simon's life.

Except there was no blade beyond the curved leather. This wasn't a real dagger at all. It was a piece of stagecraft, a prop, meant for an actor to wear under his shirt, to make it *look* like he'd been stabbed.

And as I stared at it, I realized so much more.

I never *had* seen the actual wound. After we'd helped Simon up to my bedroom, Dr. Kemp had sent me from the room to collect things he needed for the surgery. When I went back up again, Dr. Kemp's body had blocked my view. I hadn't seen Simon again until he was wrapped in bandages, "blood" leaking through.

Not real blood, not a real dagger. Not even a real surgery. Everything had been a fake.

Including . . . "Dr. Kemp," I said.

Simon smiled.

"He was in on it," I said, heart sinking. "He was working with you the whole time. *That's* why you killed him. You're getting rid of anyone who can trace the Raven back to you."

Simon nodded. "Kemp had outlived his usefulness, except as an example to be made in front of you. His apprentice, Jack, was also in on it, if you're wondering. Sadly, now rotting in a ditch near Bethnal Green."

"But . . . *why?*" I said, beyond confused. "Why be the Raven? What's all this about? What could Master Benedict have ever done to you?"

"Well, who did you think the Raven was?"

"Peter," I said. "Peter Hyde. He was Master Benedict's old apprentice. . . ."

Simon's grin widened as I trailed off, his eyes shining with amusement.

And then I understood.

"You," I said in shock. "You're not Simon Chastellain at all. *You're Peter Hyde.*"

Simon—no, not Simon, Peter—gave a little bow. "It's so nice to finally, properly meet another apprentice of our master's."

My mind was spinning. I actually thought I might pass out. "But how . . . I don't . . . After you ran away, how did you . . . ?"

"An interesting story, I think you'll find."

And he sat on the table and told it.

CHAPTER
61

"**WHEN MASTER BENEDICT BETRAYED**
me," Peter said, "I didn't know where to go. I couldn't stay
in London; the constables were searching for me. And even
if they were lazy, our master wasn't. He'd have chased me to
the ends of the Earth to make me pay for humiliating him."

"He wasn't punishing you," I said, still reeling. "He
cared about you. He wanted to make sure you'd be all
right."

Peter sneered. "Of course he did. Well, after fleeing
from Master Benedict's *kindness*, I made it all the way to
Birmingham. I tried to find work up there, but all I could get
were odd jobs that went nowhere. To get an apprenticeship,

I'd have to expose my background. And that would just put me back where I started.

"Fortunately, I ended up on a different path. One of the things I'd always been good at was imitating other people. Accents, mannerisms, even their handwriting—as you've seen with my forgeries. So I used these skills to join a troupe of traveling actors.

"I say 'actors,' but they were little more than thieves. They would stage impromptu street performances to distract the crowd while two of them cut purses in the audience. They were small and petty. But the lessons I learned from them became my *new* education."

Peter looked proud of himself. "I was an exceptional thief," he said. "Perhaps even a better cheat than I'd been an apothecary. But the *smallness* of what I was doing chafed at me. So as my stature in our company grew, I pushed us in a new direction.

"Instead of picking pockets, I told them, why not try for greater things? One of my best roles was an earnest young noble—so why not become that man permanently? We could travel from town to town, and instead of snatching pennies from the crowd, we could worm our way into higher society—and the higher prizes they promised.

"My new friends thought this was an excellent idea. So instead of Peter Hyde, actor, I became Peter Wallis, son of a baron, with holdings in some far-flung town near Scotland, somewhere no one we'd meet would ever have been.

"The first place we tried it was Coventry. And everyone, absolutely everyone, was taken in. I hobnobbed with the best of that city, and not one of them ever knew I wasn't the real thing."

A fire burned in Peter's eyes. "It was *exhilarating*," he said. "The others were delighted because we made more money than they'd ever dreamed. But I didn't care about that. It was the *role* I loved. Being a new person, living a new life.

"And that became an education beyond price. I learned how to manipulate people, how to guide them in any direction while making them think it was their idea all along. I learned the value of a bribe, how to make it so large that none but the most sanctimonious would refuse.

"My companions objected to the waste. Why pay a pound, they said, when you could pay a penny? They couldn't understand. It wasn't the coin I cared for. It was the *victory*. The sheer pleasure of taking another man and bending him to my will." He made a fist, like he was crushing someone's soul in his grasp.

"I played that role for years," he said. "But it grew boring. The thrill I'd once got from our little deceptions dulled to nothing. I began to wonder: Was this really all that was meant for me? I wanted something even greater. And then it happened."

He stared off into the distance. "There were two men, Christopher, who changed my life. The first was Master Benedict. The second was Simon Chastellain. The *real* Simon Chastellain."

CHAPTER
62

"WE WERE IN NOTTINGHAM WHEN
I first saw him," Peter said. "My troupe had just arrived.
Simon had come to town to attend some party. And when I
saw him, I knew instantly who he was.

"You see, not long after Master Benedict took me in,
I asked him why he'd chosen me as an apprentice. He said
he'd been impressed with my answers at the testing. But the
real reason he stopped to watch me was because I reminded
him of someone."

"Simon Chastellain," I said, suddenly understanding.

Peter nodded. "Master Benedict had grown very fond of
the boy while in Paris. And Hugh Coggshall had graduated

to journeyman some years ago. Our master missed having a child running about Blackthorn—and I think, by this time, he was starting to regret not having a family of his own. So when he saw me, he said I looked so much like this Simon Chastellain that he took me in.

"I didn't think anything of it at the time. Someone else looked like me; who cares? It's not that uncommon. But when I saw the real Simon riding by in Nottingham . . . well, it was uncanny. I won't say we were twins; we weren't identical. But we could have easily passed for brothers.

"I confess: I was fascinated, and not just because we looked alike. That connection to Master Benedict still lingered. I suppose . . . I suppose, on some level, I'd missed it."

"But you threw it away," I said.

Peter's eyes went hard. "*He* threw it away. He should have—"

Peter cut himself off. He sat there a moment, just fuming. By the time he returned to his story, he spoke calmly again, as if it didn't matter.

"As I told you," Peter said, "I was fascinated. I abandoned my earlier plans. I sent the troupe off on a different piece of trickery and contrived to be introduced to Simon instead.

"Well. He was just as fascinated as I to meet his lookalike. I never told him who I really was, of course, or mentioned Master Benedict. But I used what our master had taught me about Simon to create a common sentiment. We soon became fast friends, and he invited me to stay with him on his estate."

Peter smirked. "It wasn't much of a holding. Some cattle and lumber; it hardly compared to Maison Chastellain in Paris. But it was a decent life, and an easy one, and I fit into it like I really was Simon's brother. And he treated me as nothing less.

"It was Simon who named me, by the way," Peter said, sounding wistful. "I've always loved birds. Such beautiful creatures. How wondrous it would be to fly." He drifted off for a moment. "I used to feed them, every morning. They'd come from everywhere, spend time around me. One of them was a raven. She was so clever, Christopher, you'd hardly believe it. I used to give her walnuts, still in the shell. She couldn't crack them herself, but she understood—I swear this is the truth—she realized that at noon every day, the farmers would drag the carts from the barn. She'd place the walnuts under the wheels, so when the cart moved, the weight of it would crack the shells for her."

He smiled at the memory. It was the only time his eyes showed any humanity.

"We were friends, she and I," Peter said. "I gave her food, and she would bring me little gifts: beads, a piece of glass, a coin she found in the dirt. Simon said it was as if she thought I was a raven, too. And when he said that, it just felt . . . right. I didn't have to be Peter Wallis, or Peter Hyde. I could be whomever I wanted. I could be the Raven.

"And thinking about that was what changed my whole path. Because as I spent time with Simon, I began to wonder: Why *couldn't* this be my life? Why did I have to *pretend* to be a peer, when I fit so easily among them?

"That very night, Simon and I got to drinking. We went up an old watchtower to shoot arrows into the darkness of the forest, just to amuse ourselves. But when he stood by the edge, mind addled with drink, swaying with the pull of the bow, I thought: It would be so easy. Just push him over the wall. I could steal his life, make it my own.

"That was the wine talking, of course. As I said, we looked like brothers, but not twins. No one on his estate would ever think I was him. But the thought had dug its way into my mind. I began to wonder: Could I do such a thing? Could I become Simon Chastellain? Could I not merely invent a new life, but actually *steal* one? At first, I dismissed the idea as folly. But it wouldn't go away. And then I finally saw how to make it happen."

Peter looked at me. "Though Simon had never returned to Paris, he'd kept a correspondence with his uncle Marin. But in the fall of 1664, Simon grew worried. The letters from Marin became confused. Often his uncle wrote as if he were living in the past. The affliction you saw in Paris had begun.

"That was when it hit me. In Paris, Simon would still be Simon Chastellain, vicomte d'Aviron. He'd live in luxury, in the court of Louis XIV, as an equal. *But no one there had seen Simon since he was eight years old.* No one would know I wasn't him.

"So I began to encourage him to move to Paris, to care for Marin. We'd go together, I said, just the two of us, a grand adventure.

"Simon fell for it. Eagerly, he arranged our trip, writing to Paris that he was coming. We gathered our supplies, mounted our horses, and rode for Hull, where a ship had been commissioned to carry us to Calais."

Peter paused for a moment. The look in his eyes told me what happened next.

"You killed him," I said.

Peter regarded me calmly. "Yes. Once we were away from Nottingham, I made us camp in the woods for a night, rather than take rooms at an inn. Part of the adventure, I said. Simon thought it a lark, living in the trees like old Robin Hood. He agreed. That was the night I poisoned him."

Peter's voice grew soft, remembering. "Simon Chastellain was the first man I ever killed," he said. "I watched him grow ill. The sweat on his brow. The cramps. He begged me, once he began to vomit. He begged me to help him. He never understood that I was the one who'd done this to him. He begged me, like I was his only friend."

This was the worst thing I'd ever heard. I could never have imagined anything so cruel.

"I left him there, in the woods," Peter said. "I took his clothes and buried him among the trees. Then I rode away, no longer Peter Wallis. I was Simon Chastellain. And much deeper, I truly became the Raven.

"The old thrill returned, fluttering in my guts, as I approached the docks in Hull. Yet when I told them I was Simon, no one questioned the truth of it, even for a second. I boarded and made for France.

"Paris, I thought," Peter said. "In Paris, they'll see through me. My skin was alive with the possibility. Marin, at least, would surely see, even thirteen years later, that I was not his beloved nephew. *Les grands luminaires de Paris*— they would have to see through my disguise. Recognize I wasn't truly one of them."

He shook his head. "None of them, Christopher. Not one. So I set in motion my plans. I dismissed all of Marin's old servants and replaced them with those who would work for me. Rémi and Colette I knew from years before. They were actor-thieves, like I'd once been, whom I met one time we worked in Dover. With them in place, I began to loot what remained of Marin's wealth.

"But my disguise required me to spend inordinate amounts of time with him. At first, it was beyond tedious. He wouldn't stop going on about the Templars and their treasure. The ravings of a crumbling old man. And yet . . . as I listened, I began to recognize certain truths. The old fool was actually right. The Templars *did* still exist. And their treasure was out there, somewhere. The only reason he hadn't found it was because he hadn't followed the right instructions. He never tried to eliminate le Bel's descendants.

"So I set about doing just that. And . . . well, you know the rest."

I thought back to the first time I'd met Simon—or who I'd

thought was Simon. He'd caught me holding a trap designed to kill Minette, King Charles's sister. He'd accused me of setting that trap, threatened to slice my guts open with his sword.

At the time, I'd thought it was genuine outrage. Now I realized it was all a lie. He'd known perfectly well I wasn't the assassin—because *he* was. He'd known I was a spy from the very beginning. He'd even screamed at me. *Who sent you?* For a moment, I'd seen not Simon Chastellain, but Peter Hyde. The Raven.

And his reaction had been greatest when I'd mentioned . . . "Master Benedict," I said.

Peter nodded. "I couldn't believe it when you spoke his name. I thought I'd finally been caught. I would have killed you there and then. Until I saw *that*."

He waved his pistol at my apothecary sash in the corner. I remembered how he'd changed when he'd laid eyes on it. How shaken he'd been when I told him Master Benedict had died.

"You weren't acting," I said, understanding. "You really were upset to hear he was gone."

Peter sneered. "I'd promised him a reckoning. His death denied me that."

That was a lie—at least partially. Yes, Peter would

have liked to get even with our master. But back in that study in the Palais, I remembered: He'd been hurt by the news. On some level, as old as he was, he was still that wounded child.

And then I remembered, too, him lying in my bed, the bed that had once been Master Benedict's. I'd brought him a copy of the *Odyssey*, and he'd gone quiet. *Dream of Odysseus, child,* he'd whispered. *Dream of coming home.*

Simon had told me Master Benedict had said that to him in Paris. Now I knew the truth. Master Benedict had said it to *Peter*, one cold night, when the boy had been scared and lonely.

What Peter had thrown away was staggering. And I knew I'd never understand it, not for the rest of my days. "Was anything you told me true?" I said.

He shrugged. "Not really. When I told you I had to leave Paris, I didn't. Instead, I disguised myself and hid from you in the city, tracking you as well as I could. Not well enough, clearly."

"And Rémi? I suppose you were the one who actually killed him?"

"Colette, too," he said matter-of-factly. "After you foiled my plans in Paris, I sent them to hide in a farmhouse south of the city. I got rid of them once you left for England. They knew far too much. And new allies are always a bribe away.

"I did have an agent following you on the way back. But the man I'd placed on your boat died in the shipwreck. I'm glad you survived, at least." He regarded me with respect. "Other than Master Benedict, you were the only person who ever thwarted me, Christopher. I couldn't let that go unanswered. So when you sent me that first letter from Southampton, I was overjoyed. I'd already dreamed up myriad ways to challenge you again. Once I knew you were alive, I put them into motion.

"My contacts in London told me there was a plot brewing among Covenanters against the king. I supported them with funds stolen from Marin's coffers and planned a new theft of my own. I bought a few people in Whitehall and arranged for Covenanters to be placed there as well. And this time, I set *you* back. That just left the deciding game, to see who would win." He smiled.

"But how did you find out who the London Templars were?" I said.

"The same way I learn everything else: with bribes. The Templars have been exceptional at keeping their secrets, but once you realize they still exist, it's not as hard as you'd think to identify a member or two. Do you remember the marquis de Nogent-sur-Seine?"

I shook my head.

"You met him, briefly, in Paris," Peter said. "At breakfast, after watching the king rise."

Oh—right. "He asked me if I was of the gown or the sword."

"He's a Templar."

I blinked. "He is?"

Peter nodded. "He's also a man who's grown unhappy with his failure to advance among the knights. An appallingly large bribe was sufficient to turn him—along with a promise to help him become the next grand master. He knows where the current grand master keeps the records of the various chapters, and was able to provide me with Domhnall Ardrey's name here in London. Once I knew about Ardrey, it was easy enough to discover who his compatriots were and eliminate them."

A traitorous Templar. Though I'd suspected it, I could still barely believe it. Such a thing could be enough to corrupt their organization forever.

I had another question. I wasn't sure if he'd answer, but I needed to know. "The men you turned at Whitehall . . . was one of them Lord Walsingham?"

The Raven laughed, delighted. "Why, Christopher. Did I really confuse you enough to suspect the spymaster? How wonderful."

He chuckled. "No, of course not. Everyone thinks Ashcombe is the most dangerous man in the palace, but they're so wrong. Ashcombe is predictable. The kind of man who, if you tried to bribe him, would stick a sword in your guts before you'd finished making the offer. Walsingham is much slipperier. He'd *take* your bribe—then only *pretend* to serve you, while still working secretly for the king. I wouldn't even go near him."

His answer made me ashamed that I'd suspected the spymaster of treason. I'd made such a mess of everything.

"I killed Wat for you, at least," Peter said. "You should thank me for that."

"You killed him to frame me," I said.

"Not at all. I *used* him to frame you, true. But I killed him because he murdered Master Benedict. I told you, Christopher, our master's life was mine to decide. After you told me the whole story of the Cult of the Archangel, I had my contacts in London track Wat down. Easy enough to do when one's a thief—which is exactly what Wat had become, up in Newcastle.

"Allies of mine kept an eye on him until I was prepared to deal with him personally. When the time was right, I lured him to Oxford with the promise of a big job. I made sure Wat knew why he was dying as I thrust in the knife."

Peter said it with complete satisfaction. "I'd planned to frame you with Wat's body alone," he continued, "but I was sloppy. While checking the alley was clear, I was spotted by that idiot Sinclair. I had no choice but to get rid of him, too."

Peter glanced at the hourglass on the table. The sands had almost run down. "Our time together is up, it appears."

"Wait," I said. "At least tell me: How did you sabotage my pistols?"

"The powder in the barrels," he said. "Originally, I'd planned to make you leave your guns behind before I told you where this warehouse was. You staying at my home took care of that. Mary replaced your powder with pure charcoal after you left your guns in your room. Completely unnoticeable. Until you try to fire them, that is."

Of course. I'd been worried about one of the servants working for the Raven. The truth was worse. "They were *all* in on it," I realized in dismay. "They couldn't be your old servants from Nottinghamshire. They'd have recognized right away you weren't Simon Chastellain."

"Indeed. They are, in fact, my old acting troupe."

"Are you going to kill them, too?"

"I haven't decided." He stood and picked up his pistol.

"You're going to shoot me, then?" I said bitterly. "I figured you'd use poison." Just like on the real Simon.

The Raven sighed and drew a second pistol from his leather pack in the corner. "How many times do I have to tell you? I'm not going to kill you, Christopher. I've brought someone else here to do that."

I frowned. "The gate upstairs is down. No one can get through it."

"For the moment. The wheel you turned slipped the chain from the pulley, which is why the first wheel broke. But that's not the only part of the mechanism. When the gate slammed shut, a blade sliced some sandbags holding up a counterweight behind the wall. It should take about fifteen minutes"—he tapped the nearly empty hourglass—"before enough sand runs out and the counterweight drops, lifting the gate once more. I'm rather proud of the design, if I do say so myself."

The last few grains fell in the hourglass. Then it was empty.

"Any minute now," Peter said.

All I could think was: *Tom. He's still up there, I'm sure of it. What happens when the Raven's allies come down? They'll kill him.*

I listened for the rising gate. It was hard to hear through the door, but when I heard faint rattling, I knew it was going up.

Run, Tom, I thought. *Please run.*

Footsteps thundered down the stairs.

Peter put his golden mask back on. Then he stepped behind me, his pistol against my head.

"Here comes your executioner now," the Raven said.

Then Tom burst through the door.

CHAPTER
63

HE LOOKED FURIOUS.

Tom had drawn his sword. He held it in both hands, gripping the hilt so hard, his knuckles were white. He saw me sitting at the table. And he saw the Raven behind me, once again wearing his golden mask, one muzzle pressed to my skull, the other pointed at him.

"You see?" the Raven said to me. His false northern accent was back. "What did I tell you?"

Tom? My *executioner*?

Ridiculous.

It was true that Tom looked murderous. His three-foot

holy blade gleamed in the light. Any enemy would by terrified by it.

But Tom? Come to kill me? I'd never, ever believe it. Not for anything in the world.

"Have a seat," the Raven said.

If Tom was surprised to see the mask, he didn't show it. If anything, he looked a little on edge. He glanced about the room: at my pistols and sash in the corner with the Raven's pack, at the table, at the tray. His eyes fell on the leather pouch; then he quickly looked at me.

Tom still hadn't seen the Raven's face. "Get out of here," I said, desperate.

"You won't be needing that," the Raven said, indicating Tom's sword.

Tom didn't budge. "Let Christopher go."

"Come now; you know I'm not going to do that. If you want a chance to save his life, put your weapon down."

"No," I said. "Tom, go. Just go."

The Raven pressed the barrel hard into my temple. "A bit late for that. Either you sit, Tom, or I shoot Christopher. And then I shoot you."

"Tom," I said.

But he wasn't going to listen to me. Resigned, he laid Eternity on the floor.

"Kick it to the corner," the Raven said. "The knife on your belt as well."

The blade rattled over the stone, bumping until it stopped against the pack. Tom tossed his knife after it, still in its sheath.

"What now?" Tom said.

"Sit," the Raven said. "And please: Keep your hands where I can see them."

Tom took his place across from me, resting his palms on the table. The Raven tucked his second pistol back into his belt, keeping the first aimed at me.

"Let Tom go," I said. "This is between you and me. I'm the one who crossed you. Tom was just following orders."

"*You* brought him into this," the Raven said as an edge crept into his voice. "You're smug, Christopher. Do you know that? You're smug with the love of our precious Master Benedict. With the love of your so-called friends. *That's* why he's here. To show you the truth of what happens when his life is on the line."

"If you don't understand Tom," I spat, "it's because

every time someone cared about you, you threw it away. You rejected Master Benedict. And you murdered the best friend you'd ever had."

"Ah, but I *learned* something then," Peter said. "As I watched my 'friend' die, I saw inside him. He was so scared. He'd have done anything—*anything*—to stay alive. Even if it meant poisoning me in return."

I knew I'd never convince him. Peter's heart had been twisted a long time ago. But if he thought he'd make me doubt *my* best friend, he really was mad. "Tom's already risked his life for me more times than I can remember."

"Not the same," Peter said. "Not the same at all. *Risk* isn't a *promise*. The fact that both of you are still alive proves it. So I'm going to show you the difference. Because only one of you is walking out of here today."

"You promised not to kill either of us."

"And once again, I tell you: I won't."

The Raven took the two goblets from the tray and placed them in front of Tom, side by side.

"Pour the water," he ordered Tom.

Tom hesitated only long enough for the Raven to swing the pistol back in my direction. He poured two glasses from the crystal decanter beside them.

"That pouch on the tray," the Raven said. "Can either of you guess what's in it?"

Tom's eyes flicked to the pouch, then quickly looked down. He didn't answer, but I could guess only too well.

"Arsenic," I said.

"Correct. Pour the entire pouch into one glass, Tom—one glass only. And no tricks."

Tom untied the pouch and tipped it over the goblet on his right. A fine white powder spilled out, sinking into the water.

If Walsingham's instruction in poisons hadn't been enough, Master Benedict's notes would have been. That much arsenic could kill all three of us many times over. Anyone who drank from that glass would die—and painfully.

"Mix it well," the Raven said. "We don't want it all clumping at the bottom."

Tom used the silver stick on the tray to stir the poison in. He wouldn't look at me.

"Excellent," the Raven said once the water was cloudy. "Now the final game begins. There are two goblets before you. One of you will drink from one. The other will drink from the other."

He smiled. "And Tom will decide who gets which glass."

CHAPTER 64

I STARED AT THE GOBLETS IN HOR-
ror. But it was Tom who gave voice to my thoughts.

"You're a monster," he said, head bowed.

The Raven scoffed. "I am the same as everyone else. I look after myself. I'm just more honest about it than you are.

"You see," he said, "I've *studied* death. Watched it up close. Stared into the eyes of a man who finally understands that all he was, all he is, and all he'll ever be, is about to end. It is then, boys—and *only* then—that you really reveal the truth." He leaned in and whispered in my ear. "That's what you're about to discover."

But I knew better. Peter was so far gone, he couldn't understand someone like Tom. "Tom? Tom. Look at me."

He wouldn't.

"Look at me, Tom."

"Whoever drinks the poison," Tom said to the Raven, head still bowed. "You promise you'll let the other one live?"

"You have my word," Peter said.

"Don't listen to him, Tom." I strained against the shackles. "What could his word possibly be worth?"

"What choice do I have?" Tom said.

"Give me the poison," I said. "I promise, I won't blame you. Just give it to me."

He sighed. "You know I can't do that."

He pushed the clear water goblet toward me. Then he picked up the poisoned one, staring at it.

The Raven watched intently. He was still wearing the mask, but I could tell he was smiling.

"Tom. Listen to me. *Tom.*"

Tom took a deep breath.

"Tom," I said. "*Look* at me. *Give me the poison.*"

He raised the goblet to his lips.

"Stop."

Tom stopped, goblet hovering at his mouth.

But it wasn't me who'd commanded him. It was the Raven.

Behind the mask, Peter chuckled. "Very good. Very good. Well played."

Tom looked at him sharply.

"Truly," the Raven said. "Impressive. Totally believable, your performance. You both could have been part of my troupe. Could have robbed the whole world, we three."

Slowly, Tom placed the goblet on the table in front of him. His face was flushed.

"What are you talking about?" I said. "What's going on? Tom?"

"Oh, come now, Christopher," Peter said. "I caught your trick last night. I already know this is just an act. A little scene the two of you cooked up to catch me off guard."

I had no idea what he was talking about. But from Tom's reddening face . . . Tom *did*. "Tom?" I said. "What . . . ?"

"Wait," Peter said. He turned my head to face him and stared through his mask into my eyes. "You didn't know. You really *didn't* know."

Then he laughed.

His whole body shook with laughter. It was a sound of pure delight. Of victory.

And Tom looked devastated.

Peter took off his mask and threw it away. But when Tom saw Peter's face—the face of the man we thought was Simon Chastellain—Tom didn't look surprised. Just disappointed.

Still laughing at me, Peter wiped his eyes. "The ox," he said, back to his regular voice. "The big dumb ox kept the truth from you. I was right. I was right. How wonderful."

"Tom . . . what's he talking about?"

"Tell him," Peter said.

Tom just shook his head.

I didn't understand. Peter was talking like Tom had betrayed me. But he wouldn't betray me. He just wouldn't. My voice trembled. "Somebody tell me what's going on."

"Tom doesn't think it's poison," Peter said.

"What?"

"In the goblet. Tom doesn't think it's poison. He doesn't think it was arsenic in that pouch."

That didn't make any sense. "What was it supposed to be?"

The Raven waited for Tom to answer. This time, he did. "Powdered sugar," Tom mumbled.

I don't think I'd ever been so confused. Was this some sort of cruel joke? "Why would you think it's powdered sugar?"

"Because Tom switched the pouches last night," Peter said. "While you were sleeping, while he was supposedly 'patrolling' my house to keep you safe, he snuck down to the cellar. He found the pouch of arsenic I'd placed behind the wine bottles and switched it with an identical pouch he'd brought with him. Then he hid the arsenic behind some old paintings leaning against the wall."

I stared at Tom. He still wouldn't meet my eyes. But I could tell by the way he was squirming that Peter was telling the truth.

"What Tom didn't know," Peter continued, "was that I already knew he'd try something like that. So I had Michael hide in the shadows behind the water barrel. He saw the whole thing. Then he came and told me, and I switched the pouches back."

But . . . "Why would you . . . How did you know?" I said to Tom.

He was too devastated to answer. Once again, Peter spoke for him. "Isn't it obvious? The Templars told him."

The *Templars*?

My head was spinning. "The Templars are gone," I said. "You killed them."

"I destroyed the *London* chapter of Templars," Peter

said. "As you might imagine, that made them quite angry with me. The marquis de Nogent-sur-Seine told me the grand master ordered one of their knights from France to track me down. The same man revealed my plans to Tom. An old priest of your acquaintance, I believe."

An old priest . . . from France? "Father *Bernard*?" I stared at Tom. "When did you speak to Father Bernard?"

"Yesterday," Peter said. "My troupe was following you in disguise the whole time. When the King's Men took you from Blackthorn to Whitehall, Tom went to your friend Isaac's place." Peter grinned. "When Tom was late meeting you at Westminster Abbey, he claimed it was because he thought he was being followed. That was a lie. It was your priest friend who intercepted him.

"Tom was quite shocked to see the man, to say the least. So I knew this was the first time Father Bernard had spoken to you in London. My man couldn't get close enough to hear what they discussed, but when Tom left him, holding a pouch like that"—he motioned to the pouch on the table—"it was clear he intended to swap it.

"If you're wondering where Father Bernard is now," Peter said, "he's at an inn just north of the city. I've already instructed my men to make sure he disappears.

As for you . . ." Peter couldn't stop grinning. "It seems the priest didn't trust you to keep that secret. So much for your friends, the Templars.

"You see, Christopher?" he said. "I am always ahead of you, no matter who tries to help. And you, Tom"—Tom raised his head, his face ashen—"now you know the truth, too. Your plan has failed. That *is* arsenic in your glass.

"So," Peter said. "We play our final game once more. Tom drinks from one goblet, Christopher gets the other. And this time, Tom, understand: There are no tricks left. That goblet *is* poisoned. So one of you *will* die."

CHAPTER
65

TOM SAT SLUMPED IN HIS CHAIR.

He'd begun to sweat, and he mopped his brow repeatedly. He stared at the ground in a daze. When he finally spoke, I could barely hear him.

"I'm sorry," he said.

"It's all right," I said.

Tom lifted his head. He looked absolutely stricken. Sweat cast a sheen over his skin. He'd turned deathly pale, and his eyes were pleading.

"I tried," he said.

"I know," I said. "It was very brave, what you did."

Tom's voice broke. "I'm sorry I lied to you. I thought, if

you didn't know . . . maybe it would be easier to fool him."

"Don't," I said. "I'm not . . . you have nothing to apologize for. *I'm* sorry. It's my fault you're in this. Just give me the poison, all right?"

Tom buried his face in his hands. He was shaking. "Nothing's changed, Christopher. Not really."

"It has," I said desperately. "*I'm* to blame. This is my fault, it really is. So just give it to me— no!"

He'd picked up the poisoned goblet.

"Tom," I said. "Stop. Stop it."

Peter's eyes narrowed. "What are you doing?"

Tom looked at him. "You said I get to decide. I choose me."

"Nonsense," Peter said. "Nonsense. This is another trick."

Tom regarded him sadly. "You really can't understand, can you? You really did think I'd poison Christopher to save myself."

Peter stared, as if trying to understand the game Tom was playing. But the longer he stared, the more he began to realize Tom wasn't lying. His expression shifted from sneering incredulity to confusion—and then to outright anger.

His face grew red. His teeth clenched. "Why would

you . . . Look at him." He motioned toward me. "Christopher's nothing special. I tricked him, and I beat him, and then I beat him again. But you, Tom . . . you could have a future. Ashcombe respects you. The king adores you. You could rise to become his highest general. He'd make you a *duke*. Do you not understand? You could carve a legacy that would last *forever*. Everyone—*everyone*—would remember your name."

Tom just looked back, puzzled. "Why would I want any of that?"

Peter was flabbergasted. "Why . . . why would you . . . ? You could have more power than any commoner in our nation's history . . . and you'd throw it *away*? For *what*? What *do* you want?"

Tom bowed his head. For a moment, he didn't answer. Then he spoke.

"You know what I want?" he said quietly. "I want to be a baker. I want to buy a house next to Christopher, and build a big kitchen, and have my own shop in the front, where I can smile at all the customers who come in. I want to get married. I want to find a nice girl and have a big family. I want ten children. And Christopher could marry Sally and have children of their own. And of course my kids will have to look after his, because you know with those two, anyone they create will be an absolute disaster. So I'll teach my sons to watch over them, and I'll pray every night that they get to have even a small part of what we've shared. And we'll grow old together, and we'll die together, surrounded by people who love us, in friendship and peace. That's what I want."

The tears in my eyes made Tom just a blur. I blinked; they ran hot down my cheeks. "Please don't do this," I said to him.

The Raven was glowing now with fury. "You're pathetic," he said, half confusion, half rage.

Tom shook his head. "I feel so sad for you. You had Master Benedict. And you could have had Christopher— could have had all of us—on your side forever. Instead, you threw it away. For what?"

"When I'm done," Peter said, voice dripping with contempt, "I'll own half this world."

"That's *why* I feel sad for you," Tom said. "You could own every inch of it, and you'd still never truly be happy. Whatever *I'll* never have, at least, for a while, I had that."

And he drank the poison down.

CHAPTER
66

I SCREAMED. "NO! *NO!*"

Tom shuddered. He buried his face in one hand, shaking.

"Tom," I said. "Listen to me. Go to my sash. I have ipecac. Take it. Tom!"

"It's too late for that," Peter said, voice tight.

He was right. Ipecac took several minutes to work. With that much arsenic, Tom was already dead. His body just didn't know it yet.

My heart was tearing apart. "I'm here," I said. My words caught in my throat. "I'm here, Tom. I'm right here with you."

The goblet slipped from his fingers. It rolled across the table, then fell to shatter on the stone.

"I'm here," I said. "I'm right here. I'll always be here. Tom?"

Shakily, he stood. Peter stepped back, alarmed, and raised his pistol. It had just occurred to the Raven that a dying Tom had nothing left to lose.

Get him, Tom, I thought. *Get him. Make him pay for what he's done.*

But Tom wasn't looking for revenge. He stared about the room in confusion and pain. He staggered a step, then another, not seeing where he was going. Peter circled the table opposite him, keeping it between them the whole time.

"I'm here, Tom." I could barely get the words out anymore. My heart was in such pain. "I'm over here. Come sit with me. I'll stay with you."

I didn't know if he could hear me anymore, or if the pain had gotten too great. He staggered another step, then bent over, crying out in agony. The cramps had started.

The poppy, I thought. *In my sash. The poppy would quiet the pain. He could take it all and slip into sleep instead.*

But even if I could make him understand, it was too late for that, too. Tom staggered a few more steps, hands out, as if reaching for something.

"Here," I pleaded with him. "I'm here."

He vomited. He fell to his knees, gushing a great torrent of water.

Please, Lord, I prayed. *Please let him get rid of enough of the arsenic.*

Yet even as I said it, I knew it was futile. Throwing up was the body's way of trying to rid itself of the poison. By that point, too much had already been taken.

Tom crawled toward the open door. He vomited again, this time nothing but a string of bile. Peter watched, face red, as the best friend I'd ever have reached the doorway.

Before Tom was halfway through, his arms, once so strong, finally failed him. He collapsed, facedown on the stairs, his legs still in the room.

"No," I said.

Tom gasped for air. One, two, three strained breaths.

Then he was gone.

CHAPTER
67

THE ROOM WAS STILL.

There was no sound, no nothing—except from me. My ragged weeping broke the silence.

I screamed and thrashed against my shackles. The metal tore the skin from my wrists, smearing blood.

I didn't feel it. I didn't feel anything but my torn-up heart.

Peter stood in front of the table, his back to me, staring at Tom's lifeless body. I couldn't see Peter's face, but his fists were clenched, one around the grip of his pistol, the other digging his nails into his skin. He gripped the gun so hard he accidentally pulled the trigger. It fired, the boom deafening, the bullet smashing chips from the stone at his feet. He leaped in shocked surprise, then let loose a string of curses more foul than I'd ever heard.

I drew juddering breaths until I found my voice. When I spoke, it was low, raw, and it hurt.

"I'm going to kill you," I said. "I'm going to kill you with my bare hands."

Peter's voice was tight. "You won't get the chance."

Even through my grief, my own rage, I could tell Peter was furious. I didn't think I'd ever seen anyone so livid.

Why?

He'd killed Tom. And in doing that, he'd hurt me with a wound so deep it would never heal. I was broken. So why was he so angry? He won.

No, Tom said in my heart. *He lost.*

You're gone, I cried. *He took you away. How could he have lost?*

Because it wasn't about killing you or me, Tom said. *Peter made you a promise. When he failed, he lost. And now he'll never, ever get to win.*

I didn't understand. A promise? What promise?

Then it came to me.

I am going to make you suffer, the Raven had once told

me. *I will do this by taking away the things you love, one by one, until there is only you and me. And then, once I have stripped your life bare, you will understand.*

When I'd read those words, I'd thought the Raven meant he was going to kill them all. Take the life of everyone I cared about. But now I finally understood what he really wanted.

He wanted me to be as alone as he was.

Peter had arranged everything so I'd come here with Tom—because he needed Tom to play his twisted game of poisons. But what Peter wanted most wasn't my death. He wanted me to be murdered by *Tom.*

If he could have made Tom give me the poison, then Peter would have shown me that even my best friend—the very best friend anyone could ever have had—even he would abandon me when it came time to decide. Peter wanted me to die knowing Tom had betrayed me, just as Peter believed Master Benedict had betrayed him. Then I really *would* have died alone, with everything I loved taken away.

But Tom had saved me.

Now he lived in my heart. Just like Master Benedict. And nothing Peter ever did could take Tom's victory away.

I threw it back at the Raven, as hard as I could. "You

lost," I said, nothing but contempt in my words. "Tom defeated you. *Tom* did. And that will eat you inside for the rest of your miserable days."

Peter bashed me in the head.

He whipped around, swinging across the table to crack the butt of his smoking pistol into my cheek. The barrel, hot, lashed my ear. I tasted the metallic tang of blood, felt it trickle through my hair down to my neck.

I laughed at him.

He hit me again, the other side this time. The pain was so intense, it blinded me. I had to close my eyes and grit my teeth until it subsided.

When I could see again, Peter stood in front of me, face taut, knuckles white, his glare daring me to speak. I obliged him. "Are you going to beat me to death, then?"

The hatred in his eyes said he was considering it. But he managed to master his rage. "I told you I wouldn't kill you."

"Enough lies." I was so tired. "I know you can't let me live."

"Why not?"

A ridiculous question. "I know who you are."

"Oh?" Peter leaned across the table. "And who, exactly, is that? Am I Peter Hyde? Peter Wallis? Simon Chastellain? Or am I someone else entirely?

"My time as Simon is done, yes. But what next? I can become anyone, anywhere." He switched languages: Spanish, then Italian. "Perhaps I'm a *vizconde* now, living on a coastal estate in Valencia. Or maybe I'm a journeyman apothecary, traveling north from Genoa. Where will you look for me? Who will I be?"

Peter sneered at me. "Offer whatever threats you like, Christopher. I've shown you you're no match for me. Neither is the king and all his men. And neither are the Templars. Your friend, Father Bernard, is dying as we speak. As for me, I have only one task before I disappear. I intend to achieve what even Philippe le Bel and Pope Clement the Fifth could not. I will destroy the Templars for good."

I spat blood at my feet. "They'll kill you before you even get close," I said, defiant. "One traitor won't be enough to take them down."

"Ha." He'd regained some of his smugness. "You of all people should understand by now: One traitor is all I've ever needed. Nogent-sur-Seine didn't just sneak in and read the grand master's records. He told me who the grand master of the Knights Templar *is*. Would you like to know?"

I didn't answer.

"You met him in Paris, as well," Peter said. "But this

man you'll remember. It's Jean-Baptiste Colbert, Louis XIV's closest advisor."

It was shocking to hear it—yet at the same time, it made sense. Who better to direct the course of events than the man with Louis's ear?

"Why would you tell me that," I said, "if you're going to let me live?"

"You misunderstand the situation. I *did* say I would let you live. I just didn't say *how*." Peter smiled without humor. "You'll stay here, in that chair for now. At least until I've taken care of Grand Master Colbert."

I stared at him in horror. "That will take weeks. Months. I'll die long before then."

"Perhaps. One can live a long time without food. And you can't say I'm not generous; I'm leaving you plenty of water." He plunked the decanter in front of me. "And if you *do* die, well, like I said: I won't be the one who kills you, will I?"

He tucked his pistol into his belt. "Goodbye, Christopher. I've really enjoyed our time together. It's just a shame Blackthorn chose the wrong apprentice. Because, unfortunately for you, *invictus maneo*. I. Remain. *Undefeated*—"

A blade pierced his chest.

Peter gaped in shock. He stared down at the metal point, his blood dripping from the tip to stain his shirt below. His hand grasped for the pistol in his belt, but he had no strength to pull it. He looked up to stare at me, uncomprehending.

"Master?" he said.

Then he collapsed.

His body crumpled to the floor. Peter Hyde—the Raven—died.

And standing behind him was Tom, with a long, thin dagger—a real dagger, this time—in his hand.

CHAPTER
68

I WAS DREAMING. I HAD TO BE.

Except this was the exact opposite of my nightmares. Here, the Raven lay dead. And Tom was standing over him instead.

"Tom?" I croaked.

Tom looked at the body at his feet. His face was lined with deep sadness, hurt by the life he'd had to take. Still, he knelt and used his dagger to ensure the Raven was dead, as Sir William Leech had taught him.

"Tom."

He glanced up at me, embarrassed. He searched through the Raven's pockets as I stared at him in confusion.

"I can't find the key to your shackles," he said.

I continued to stare as he came around the table. Since he couldn't unlock my restraints, he just tore the chair apart instead. Taking two of its legs in his giant hands, he strained, until the base splintered and I tumbled to the floor. It wasn't until he stripped the wood from my manacles and slipped my limbs from their bonds that I truly understood he was real.

Pins and needles stabbed my fingers, a moment of agony as blood rushed back in. I could barely stand, both feet fallen asleep. But I tackled him with all the strength I could muster.

We sprawled on the stone. *"You're alive you're alive you're alive!"* I shouted. Then I thumped him in the chest. I think it hurt my tingling fist more than him.

"Ow!" he said. "Why'd you hit me?"

"Why'd you make me think you were dead?" I felt the strangest combination of sheer joy and total outrage. "I don't understand—you had the cramps; you threw up. Why . . . ?"

"Oh. That was the ipecac."

"Ip . . . what? Where did you get ipecac?"

"You gave it to me yesterday. Remember?" He fished the two empty vials from his pocket.

"But . . . when did you drink that?" I said.

"Before I entered the room," he said. "That was Father Bernard's plan. The ipecac would make me sick, so when I drank powdered sugar instead of arsenic, I'd still get ill. So the Raven would believe I'd actually been poisoned."

"But . . ." I was more confused than ever. "That doesn't make sense. That much arsenic you had . . . the instant you swallowed it, it was over." I started to panic again. "Throwing it up isn't enough to save you. Your body's taken too much."

"I didn't drink poison," Tom said, and now he looked puzzled, too. "It wasn't arsenic in that pouch."

"Then what was it?"

"Powdered sugar. I tasted it the instant it hit my tongue. It was so sweet, honestly, it was all I could do not to throw up right at the table."

None of this was making sense. "Didn't you switch the original pouch in the cellar, like Peter said?"

"Yes."

"So . . . when he switched it back, it *should* have been arsenic."

Tom spread his hands, lost. "I can't explain it."

My mind raced, trying to understand. There was only

one possibility I could think of. "That has to mean . . . someone *else* in Simon's—Peter's—house must have switched the pouch *again*."

Tom frowned. "Who would do that?"

A small voice answered from the doorway. "Me."

CHAPTER
69

WE TURNED.

Sally stood there, staring, as if unable to believe we could be alive.

Then she flung herself at me. At first she hugged me fiercely. Then she drew back and looked into my eyes, before burying her head against my chest again.

I was so stunned, I could barely react. *"You?"* I said. "You switched the pouches?"

She looked up at Tom. "Are you all right?"

"My tongue tastes like I licked a goat," he said.

She laughed, a wild peal of relief. She drew his head down and kissed him on the cheek.

And I *still* had no idea what had happened. "Everybody *stop*," I said. "Sally—when did you switch the Raven's pouch? And how did *you* know about this?"

"I switched it last night," she said. "After we left Simon's—er . . . Peter's room, I didn't go to mine. I snuck downstairs and hid in the linen closet by the cellar, peeking through the door, watching."

I blinked. *That* was why she hadn't answered when I'd knocked. She hadn't been asleep—*she hadn't been in her room at all.*

"I waited until I saw Tom go down, then sneak back upstairs. When I saw Michael creep up after him, I hurried into the cellar. There I swapped the Raven's original pouch— the one Tom hid behind the oil paintings—with one I had, *also* filled with powdered sugar. Then I took the Raven's pouch up to my room and dumped it out the window."

"So . . . wait a minute," I said, trying to follow what they'd done. "Tom swapped the Raven's pouch with sugar. Then you *took* the Raven's pouch and replaced it with your *own* pouch of sugar. So when Peter had the pouches switched back . . ."

"He never had any arsenic anymore," Sally said. "He was only swapping sugar for sugar."

My mind was spinning. I looked at Tom, but he seemed just as puzzled as I was.

"How did you know what was happening?" Tom said to her. "How did you know what to do?"

"And how did you even get here?" I said. "You couldn't possibly have followed us."

"We didn't," she said. "We followed him." She motioned to Peter's body. "The Raven was so focused on you, so sure he had the upper hand, he never realized we'd already turned the tables."

"Wait a minute—We? Who's 'we'?"

She bit her lip. "Maybe they should explain that."

She turned toward the door, waiting. A moment later, five more people entered the room. And at the head of them was a most familiar face.

"Father Bernard!" I said.

Father Bernard smiled at me. Behind him were four men. One I didn't recognize—but I was shocked to see I knew the other three.

Two were the Frenchmen we'd met yesterday on Fleet Street, shooting their guns and shouting about assassins following them. The third familiar face was the priest—the young priest from Saint Paul's, the man I'd been searching for for a month.

"It is good to see you again, *mon fils*," Father Bernard said, speaking in his thickly accented English. "Though I suspect you are a little cross with me."

I stared at them. "Templars," I said. "You're all Templars."

Father Bernard nodded. "You have met most of us already. I shall introduce you properly." He indicated the two we'd seen yesterday. "Raymond and Guillaume." The priest: "Father Hugo. The gentleman you do not know is Marc-Antoine."

They all offered greetings, smiling broadly.

I didn't smile back. Lips tight, I said, "I think you owe me an explanation."

"*Bien sûr.*" Father Bernard walked over to the remaining chair, then sat with a sigh, feeling his age. "Always there must be stairs," he said. Then he began his tale.

"After you left Paris," Father Bernard said, "the Templars wished to keep eyes on you. Partially because we planned to invite you to join our order, but also because you had done us a great service, and we knew you were still in danger from the man calling himself the Raven. We sent Hugo, one of our more junior members, to England to watch over you, and also to inform Domhnall Ardrey and the London chapter of the situation.

"When you did not arrive, we feared you were dead, until we received word that you were in Devonshire. Once you finally returned to London, we were prepared to watch for danger. We were not, sadly, prepared for the Raven's assault on our order.

"We learned the Covenanters were planning to attack your king. We did not realize the Raven was scheming with them. It caught us off guard—with tragic consequences. Ardrey and the others were murdered. Hugo only survived because he was not of the London chapter, and so was not known to the Raven.

"That terrible night of the explosion, something became clear to us. Domhnall Ardrey was a most cautious knight. Only someone with inside knowledge of the Templars could have discovered his chapter so easily. We knew then we had a traitor in our midst. Our problem now became not only discovering who the Raven was, but who had betrayed us from within."

"You didn't know the Raven was Peter Hyde?" I said.

Father Bernard shook his head. "It was Sally who told

us this. We *had* managed to discover the Raven was associated with Simon's house here in London. We suspected the vicomte was the Raven, but we had no idea he wasn't the real Simon Chastellain. Nor could we be certain the Raven wasn't one of the servants. He was always cloaked when he left the house, so we never saw Peter's face. If we had, we'd have known his back injury was fake, and thus known for sure he was the Raven.

"In any case, it was clear the contest between you two was coming to a head. A week ago, we watched Mary buy a large quantity of arsenic, purchased in a pouch like that." He gestured at the pouch on the table. "It was also clear, therefore, that poison was the tool he intended to use to kill you. We knew we needed to swap the arsenic for a powder that would look the same. But they had become more careful in the past few days. We couldn't get inside the Raven's house to do this."

"So you enlisted someone who could," I said. "Us."

Father Bernard nodded. "The question then became: How could we perform the actual swap? You see, while Hugo was originally able to follow the Raven's servants, suddenly, they began to elude him. Somehow, the Raven had managed to discover we Templars were still in London."

"The traitor again," Tom said.

"No doubt. This could have been a terrible setback. But Hugo"—he smiled at the younger priest—"realized we could use this to our advantage.

"The last time Hugo was able to slip inside the Raven's house was five days ago. He found where the Raven kept the arsenic in the cellar. So after the King's Men escorted you to the palace yesterday, I took the risk to make contact with Tom personally. I told him someone in Simon's house was the Raven, and what the Raven's plans for you were. I asked him to convince you to stay at Simon's home that evening. Then, when everyone was asleep, he should creep down and replace the pouch behind the wine bottles with one I gave him. Then he should hide the real pouch behind the old paintings in the cellar. And I knew, since both Tom and you were being followed, *that the Raven would learn of my plans, too.* So he would be alerted to Tom's plot, and foil it.

"A trap like that was something the Raven expected from us," Father Bernard said. "And from you. So we gave him exactly that. He turned our scheme against us. Or so he thought."

I was amazed. I'd used the exact same kind of trap

against Oswyn, to put an end to the Cult of the Archangel. I'd even said it to Lord Ashcombe. *He needed to think he'd beaten me. He needed to believe he'd won.*

Apparently the Templars lived by the same rules. Masters of misdirection to the last.

"But if we were all being followed," I said, "how did you contact Sally without the Raven finding out?"

"Ah. That was where Raymond and Guillaume came in." Grinning, the two Frenchmen we'd seen yesterday gave a little bow as Father Bernard continued the story. "These gentlemen produced a distraction—which, I think you will agree, was quite effective. They shot at the man who was following you, then caused an even bigger disturbance. While the Raven's agent was distracted, Marc-Antoine met Sally in the alleyway and gave her instructions."

"That's impossible," I said. "He couldn't have convinced Sally he was a Templar *and* told her everything about the Raven, the arsenic, and the pouch. He didn't have enough time."

"He didn't," Sally said, looking guilty. "He told me he was with a friend of ours from Paris—the friend who'd returned my Saint Christopher medallion. I believed him, because only the Templars could have known about that.

Marc-Antoine told me to pretend I was sick, so you'd put me somewhere safe—the only place Father Bernard could talk to me in secret."

It took me a moment to realize where that was. "You mean . . . *Isaac's*? But . . . that doesn't make sense. We were being followed. Someone would have watched Isaac's place and seen Father Bernard going in."

"No," Father Bernard said. "I can get in and out of the bookshop without anyone seeing me."

"How? There's only one entrance."

"Incorrect, *mon ami*. There are two."

I stared at him. "Where's the second?"

"You are aware the library below was once a Templar vault?"

"Yes."

"So you have forgotten what I told you the last time we spoke?"

I frowned. He'd told me a lot of things. We'd talked about them hiding the treasure and about Jacques de Molay sacrificing himself to conceal that the Knights Templar still existed. And how Father Bernard had suspected the treasure was still beneath Paris, because—

I looked up in shock. "The Templars always leave themselves an escape route," I said. *"There's a secret passage in and out of the old vault!"*

Father Bernard smiled. "And that is what I used. Sally was told to wait downstairs for me to arrive. She was quite surprised to see me emerge."

I looked down at her. She still had her arms around me. "Does Isaac know?" I said.

She shook her head. "I'll tell him when all this is over."

He'd be amazed. In the meantime, Father Bernard said, "That is how I could tell her the plan in secret. Just as I convinced Tom not to tell you, I convinced her not to tell *either* of you."

It was an incredible plan—and, most important, it had worked. But it didn't mean I was pleased about what they'd done. "You could have trusted me," I said, voice tight.

"Of course we could have," he said. "But it was not about trust. The Raven was watching—you, closest of all. It was personal for him; Tom and Sally were only incidental. He expected Tom to try to defend you, so we played upon that. We wagered he wouldn't suspect Sally at all, especially since he never saw me speak to her. So he never really considered her a threat. That was our best chance of defeating him."

Secrets under secrets, I thought. *And traps within traps.* "And I was the bait."

Father Bernard spread his hands in apology. "Yes."

"But why do this to me? You knew they had the poison. If one of them was the Raven, why not capture the whole crew? Why use me like that when there was a good chance I could have died?"

Contrite, Father Bernard answered. "As I told you, we were last able to sneak into Peter's house last week, after Mary purchased the arsenic. We were fortunate enough to discover the pouch in the cellar, but we didn't exchange it then because there was a chance the swap might be discovered. We had to leave it until the last possible moment. Which meant only one of you three could have done it, last night.

"As for capturing them all beforehand . . ." He sighed. "The Raven was a cruel and spiteful man. It was very likely that, even if we had taken and interrogated him, he would never have told us who the traitor inside the Templars was. Knowing we'd been betrayed without knowing who'd betrayed us . . . it would have destroyed our brotherhood for good."

"Better to risk *my* life," I said, somewhat bitter. "And

the lives of my friends. How did you know Peter wouldn't just poison us all and be done with it?"

"Because it wasn't his way," Father Bernard said. "The Raven could have killed you any time he chose. In the guise of Simon Chastellain, he had your complete trust. But that wasn't what he wanted. He wanted to defeat you at his own game and for you to know he'd done it. Not just how—but *who* did it, and *why*. If there was one thing we could be certain of, it was that the Raven wouldn't harm you until he was face-to-face. And he'd tell you everything—absolutely *everything*—that he'd done."

"It was still a risk," I protested.

"A great risk. I apologize. *We* apologize. But in three and a half centuries, only you ever solved our clues and found our treasure. We believed in you."

So many feelings swirled inside. Joy that Tom had survived. Relief that it was all over. Anger and hurt that everyone—including my friends—had lied to me.

But there was gratitude, too. I might be angry about it, but in the end, even though they'd suffered a terrible loss, the Templars hadn't abandoned me.

"Your traitor," I said grudgingly, "is the marquis de Nogent-sur-Seine."

The others looked shocked at the news. Father Bernard closed his eyes. "I have always considered him a great friend," he said sadly.

"What will happen to him?" Tom asked.

One of the Frenchmen from yesterday spoke in heavily accented English. I wasn't sure if it was Raymond or Guillaume. "He will be . . . retired."

That reminded me. "Peter said his troupe was coming to eliminate you this morning."

"They already tried," the other Frenchman said. "They, too, have been retired."

"Though we may no longer be a military order," Father Bernard said, "some of us remain more martial than others."

Raymond and Guillaume bowed with a flourish.

"So it's over," I said, barely able to believe it. "The Raven . . . his allies . . . they're all gone. It's finally over."

Father Bernard nodded. "Which brings me to my final reason for coming here. You have once again done us a great service. Greater, even, than the last time, for revealing our treasure would not have destroyed us, while a traitor in our ranks would have. So we would like to officially invite you to join us. Christopher and Tom as brother knights, Sally as a special ally."

Tom and Sally looked as startled as I was. When we were in Paris, Father Bernard had suggested the Templars might make such an offer in the future. I hadn't really spent a lot of time thinking about it. As for now . . .

"I don't know," I said. "Tom and Sally can make their own decisions. But I'm not feeling all that friendly toward you at the moment."

"I understand," Father Bernard said. "So we will leave the offer open." He reached into his pocket, pulled out three Templar florins, and handed one to each of us. "If you decide to become one of us, or simply ever need our help again, it will be given freely, for the rest of your lives. Just drop your florin in the collection box at the Temple Church, and we will answer your call."

I blinked. "So you *do* still keep a presence there!"

Father Bernard smiled. "It's a beautiful church," he said. "It seemed a shame to just give it away."

APRIL 9–12, 1666

My guide and I came upon that hidden road
to make our way back into the bright world;
and with no care for any rest,
we climbed, he first, I following,
until I saw through a round opening some of those
things of beauty Heaven holds. It was from there
that we emerged, to see—once more—the stars.

CHAPTER
70

WE TOOK THEM TO SEE THE END OF

it all.

Upon returning to the palace, I went to Walsingham and told him about the Raven. I insisted we tell Lord Ashcombe, too.

"I understand that sometimes we need to keep secrets," I said, "but Lord Ashcombe's always been there for me. I don't want to lie to him anymore."

Walsingham regarded me calmly, then agreed. So all of us, Walsingham and Ashcombe, Tom and Sally, too, plus a company of King's Men, went back to the warehouse together, to the place the Raven had meant to be my tomb.

The Templars were long gone. Only Peter remained, his lifeless body in a pool of blood on the floor. There I told them everything—well, almost. I told them about what had really happened the night Dr. Kemp was murdered. I gave them the letter the Raven had left for me and explained the game he'd made me play. I showed them the puzzles we'd solved, and the places we'd gone, and described how we'd spent the night at the home of the man I'd thought was Simon Chastellain, the man I'd believed was my friend. I'd never think of him that way again.

What had happened in this room under the warehouse was the only thing I lied about, and that was only because I'd already made a promise to the Templars. I kept them out of the telling, and the business with the poisons, too. Instead, I said that Peter-as-Simon lured me here and ambushed me when my back was turned. I told them he shackled me and taunted me, and was going to kill me with poison when Tom arrived.

Like a true, loyal friend, he'd been watching over me. And when he'd seen what was going to happen, he hadn't hesitated. He'd drawn the long dagger he kept hidden beneath his doublet, as Sir William had taught him. Then he'd crept up with stealth and killed the Raven before Peter even knew he was there. And so the Raven was gone.

They were almost as surprised as I'd been when I revealed the Raven was my master's old apprentice, and why he'd come after me. "What about Peter's old troupe?" Lord Ashcombe said. "They may come looking for revenge."

Again, I kept the Templars out of it. I said that Peter told me he'd killed them. That, like Dr. Kemp, they'd outlived their usefulness, so he'd eliminated them along with anyone else who might lead us back to him.

It was a perfectly believable story, because it fit exactly what we'd seen from the Raven. Lord Ashcombe accepted it without question. If Walsingham suspected I hadn't told the whole truth, he gave no indication of it. *Everyone thinks Ashcombe is the most dangerous man at the palace,* Peter had said, *but they're so wrong.* Well, in this case, I'd be the one keeping secrets. And the spymaster seemed perfectly fine with that.

I did, however, still owe a few apologies. When Walsingham went upstairs to inspect the door with the number dials, I spoke to Lord Ashcombe in private.

"I'm really sorry," I said.

"For what?"

"For not telling you about this earlier. Any of it. All of

it. I never wanted to not tell you. I just didn't think I could. You've been so good to me since my master died. I just . . . thank you. For everything. I hope you can forgive me."

The King's Warden regarded me for a long while. Then he spoke.

"When His Majesty gave you to Walsingham," he said, "he placed you under the spymaster's command. The order to remain silent came from him, not you. Which makes it between him and me. As for keeping the Raven's letters secret, Peter said he'd kill Tom and Sally if you came to me or anyone else associated with the king. Yes?"

I nodded.

"Then here's what I have to say about it. If a soldier under my command disobeyed my orders, he'd be digging dung holes for a week. And if he chose to protect his own life by endangering the lives of his friends . . . well, he wouldn't *be* under my command. Or anyone else's. Do you understand?"

"Yes, my lord."

"Then carry on, apprentice."

As he turned away, I almost thought—did I just see him smile?

Nah.

. . .

Walsingham required no apology, either. He cut me off practically before I'd started.

"Your decisions were entirely correct," he said, still staring at the door with the number dials.

I stood there, wondering if I should confess something else. The spymaster read me easily, even though he still hadn't taken his eyes off the door.

"There is something you wish to say?"

"Yes," I said. "I *do* owe you an apology. Yesterday, when I was trying to work out who the Raven might be, it occurred to me that . . . well . . ."

"*I* might be the Raven," Walsingham said quietly.

"Yes," I said, squirming. "Or working with him."

"Because I am one of the few people who could know the ciphers the Raven used."

"Yes."

"And because, among Whitehall's inhabitants, I alone know all His Majesty's secrets. Which means I alone am in a perfect position to betray the king."

I sighed. "Yes."

"Then well done."

"I . . . my lord?"

"Your logic was sound," Walsingham said. "I was an

excellent suspect. I would not have trusted me, either. Your willingness to not only consider the possibility I was a traitor but to treat me as if I were—despite my authority as your master—does you credit. Once more, I find your performance satisfactory."

"Um . . . thank you."

"I hope you are convinced otherwise now?"

"Absolutely," I said. "I even asked Peter about it. He said he wouldn't have trusted you with the biggest bribe in the world. That you'd have strung him along the whole time, regardless."

The spymaster raised an eyebrow. "Such high praise. I may blush."

Did he just make a joke? "I understood, too," I said, "what you were trying to tell me. During our chess game yesterday, I mean."

He finally turned to regard me. "Then our time at the board is well spent. Monday, as usual?"

"Yes, my lord."

I walked away smiling.

We were called to see the king that very evening. Ash-combe and Walsingham had informed him of the Raven's demise; he insisted on hearing the story from our own mouths.

We met him in the parlor with all the spaniels. While Tom and Sally became playgrounds for the younger dogs, Barbara, my favorite, crawled into my lap. I scratched her ears as I told His Majesty what had happened. Charles listened, fascinated, asking me questions that somehow made the whole thing feel even more dramatic. When I finished, he sat back in his chair.

"Odd's fish," he said. "The old apprentice of your master. What an amazing thing." Suddenly, he had a thought. "I say: You didn't happen to find more of my jewelry along the way, did you?"

"Er . . . no, sire. Sorry."

"There might be some hidden in the house Peter rented," Sally suggested.

Walsingham had already had the place thoroughly searched. "I'm afraid not, sire."

"Ah, well," the king said. "Easy come, easy go. Though I've noticed 'go' is a lot easier of late."

The steward, Dobson, entered with a polite knock. "Pardon me, Your Majesty," he said. "You wished to be informed when it was time to leave for the theater."

"Oh, I don't feel like going anymore," Charles said. "Tell them I won't be coming."

"They shall be most disappointed, sire."

"Well, they can go hang. Not literally, you understand."

Dobson bowed. "I shall inform them their necks are safe."

"For the moment," Lord Ashcombe muttered.

"I know what we'll do," Charles said. "We'll have a party to celebrate this great victory. Gather the usual rogues, will you, Dobson?"

"If I may remind Your Majesty," he said, "you are already attending a party tonight at Arundel House."

"Oh—yes. I forgot about that. Tomorrow, then."

"Again, sire—"

"Odd's fish. What's the first day I don't have a party?"

"Monday, sire."

"There it is, then."

"Very good. Will you be taking dinner early tonight?"

"Yes. In fact, let's eat in here, all of us," the king said suddenly. "I wish to hear more stories. And I have quite a few of my own. Have I ever told you how I escaped from Cromwell's clutches?"

"No, sire," Tom said.

"Ah!" Charles scratched the belly of the puppy squirming in his lap. "Well, it starts at the Battle of Worcester . . ."

The next morning we went to visit Isaac.

It felt so good to ride there openly. To not wonder if we were being followed, to not worry that I was putting everyone in danger. Even though I'd seen Peter die yesterday, in a very real way, that morning was the moment I truly knew I'd never be troubled by the Raven again.

Isaac, of course, was overjoyed. The weariness melted from his face as he, too, realized the evil was finally gone. I hadn't seen him so happy since I'd met him.

We had an even bigger surprise waiting for him. His arthritis was bad that day, so Tom carried him down those hundred-plus stairs to the alchemists' library. First confused, then astonished, he watched in amazement as Sally went to one of the side rooms and, standing on her toes, pressed a small stone in the wall. He gaped as the secret door ground open.

"I . . . I don't . . ." He suddenly laughed in absolute delight.

"I should have realized this earlier," I said, by way of apology. "Father Bernard even told me so in Paris. The

Templars always leave themselves another way out."

The tunnel beyond the secret door was pitch-black and smelled heavily of mildew. Other than Father Bernard, I doubted anyone had used this passage in three hundred years.

"Where does it lead?" Isaac said.

"I don't know." I looked over at the others. "We didn't think to ask."

"Even better," Isaac said, and he clasped our hands. "What do you say we find out?"

We grabbed a lantern. Isaac led the way.

The bookseller wasn't the only one thrilled to see us that day. When we returned to Isaac's, Bridget came down, landing on me and flapping her wings, full of joy. I held her close, feeling exactly the same.

Best of all, I could finally take her with me again. I carried her out in my hands. As soon as we left the bookshop, she flapped up into the air. Stretching her wings, she soared overhead, free, as she was meant to be.

We rode back toward Whitehall. Though she ducked in and out behind the buildings as we went, she never let me leave her sight. Then, just before we got to the palace, I wheeled Blossom toward Saint James's Park. There, beside the canal, I kicked my horse into a gallop. And Bridget, Blossom, and I all flew together, with nothing but the wind in our ears.

Walsingham had given me some days' leave, which left me with a lot of time to think. Early the next morning, Bridget and I went down to the bank of the Thames. I stood next to it, gazing across the water.

There's something I still don't understand, I said.

My master came to me. *What's that, child?*

How could Peter be what he became? I asked. *Your house was a place of love, of warmth, of understanding. It was a home, in every way a home is supposed to be. How could Peter reject that? How could he live there and still not see?*

Master Benedict's answer was sad. *I tried what I could. I wished I could have done more. And yet . . . sometimes people are simply born with the darkness in their heart.*

Hugh tried to tell you that, I remembered.

He did. But I couldn't hear it. Not then. I didn't understand until I had you.

I'm sorry that Peter hurt you, I said. *I know how hard you must have tried. And I'm sorry for what he did to Simon. I wish I'd met him; Simon, I mean. The real Simon.*

You would have liked him. He was a kind boy.

I thought of what I'd said to Tom back in that warehouse. I said the same thing to my master now. *You gave me everything I could ever have hoped for. I wish you were still here, to share the rest of your life with me.*

I am, he said gently. *I am with you always.*

And we sat there together, he and I, and watched the waves go by.

CHAPTER
71

I STAYED BY THE THAMES THAT
whole morning. I was still sitting on the bank, Bridget
splashing in the river, when footsteps rustled lightly through
the grass.

"May I join you?" Sally said.

I stood. "Of course."

She stared out over the water. "It's pretty here."

"It is."

She hesitated. "Are you angry with me?"

"Why would I be?"

She sighed. "You *are* angry."

"I'm not," I said. "I'm really not. I just . . . I don't know.

I guess I'm just tired. Tired of all the secrets, you know? We've always shared everything before. You, me, Tom. But in come the Templars, and suddenly that's changed. I don't blame anyone for it. I know it's not your fault, and I'm grateful for what the Templars did, but suddenly . . . there are secrets. Between us. I'd hoped . . ."

I broke off, not knowing what to say.

"I so wanted to tell you," she said. "About the Templars, and the poison. I wanted to tell you more than anything. But I kept quiet . . . well, because of something you once said."

"Me?"

She nodded. "Do you remember what you told me about Oswyn and the Archangel's Fire? About the trap you set? And what you said to Lord Ashcombe afterward?"

I'd been thinking of that just the other day. "He needed to think he'd beaten me," I said. "He needed to believe he'd won."

"That was true here, too," she said. "But this time, the stakes were even higher."

Sally took my hand.

"For Father Bernard's plan to work," she said, "Tom had to die. I know how much it must have hurt you to watch that happen. And *that's* why I lied. The Raven needed to see it. He needed to see your grief to believe Tom was really gone. It was the only way to keep you both alive."

She shook her head. "I tried to tell myself that you could pretend," she said. "That you could fake it, just long enough, for Tom to spring the trap. But I didn't believe it. Tom's the truest thing you have left as family. You couldn't fake such terrible grief. You're just not that much of a liar.

"That's why I did it," she said. "And if you hate me, I'll understand—"

"I don't hate you," I said. "I could never hate you. I want . . ." I trailed off.

She held my hand for a while, in silence.

Then she said, "You left me a letter."

Oh. Right. "Um . . ."

She reached into her pocket and handed the letter back to me. The seal was unbroken. "I didn't read it," she said.

I couldn't tell if I was relieved or disappointed. Maybe I was both. "Why not?"

"I couldn't," she said. "Reading that letter would have meant I was never going to see you again. Reading it would have meant you'd gone there to die. And I couldn't take that. I just couldn't bear it."

Her eyes shone wetly. "That's why I lied," she said. "If it gave you even the slightest better chance of coming back alive, I would have lied to God Himself. Because I don't want to be without you. I haven't wanted anything else since that day in Cripplegate, when you sat beside my bed and made me soup. I love you, Christopher. And I want to spend the rest of my life—"

I kissed her.

Monday night was to be the party the king threw in our honor. On Walsingham's advice, the reason for the celebration was kept secret, so as not to expose what had happened. In any case, the king had so many parties, no one really cared why.

After spending all Sunday with Sally, Tom and I both got to sleep in. Monday morning we lazed about our room, only getting up because Tom was starving. In the afternoon, I played chess with Walsingham, as promised. But today I took my time to enjoy the game.

Afterward, I made a quick trip into the city—alone, which was the first time I'd been able to do that in a while.

When I finally returned to the palace, I put on my best clothes and waited for the party to start at the Banqueting House.

As Tom was training with Sir William Leech, his return to our room was delayed. Not wanting to head down without him, I left a note on his bed and went out to the balcony above the Stone Gallery. There I gazed out over the Privy Garden, watching the stars.

They sparkled with extraordinary beauty tonight. In fact, everything seemed to glow. I hadn't felt so happy in so long. Not since my master had left us.

"Christopher?"

Tom stepped onto the balcony. Freshly washed and dressed, he looked very smart. Though his long hair and beard still made him look like a Viking.

"Over here," I said.

He joined me. "What are you doing?"

"Just watching the stars."

"Hey," he said. "Did you hear Lord Ashcombe's grandson will be there tonight?"

I nodded. "Lord Ashcombe told me. He said Christopher wanted to meet the boy who'd pretended to be him in Paris."

"I wonder what he's like?"

"If he's anything like his grandfather, he'll grow up to be a great man."

We stood together in silence a while longer. Eventually, Tom said, "Shouldn't we go?"

"Soon," I said. "It's . . . I don't know. There's something amazing about tonight. I just want it to last forever."

After a pause, Tom said, "You know . . . we haven't really talked about what happened with the Raven. I wanted to ask . . . are you . . ."

"Are you going to ask me if I'm cross with you for lying?"

He blew out a breath. "Well . . . yes."

"Tom. You *drank poison* for me."

"It wasn't actually poison," he said.

"No, but you thought it was. And you drank it without hesitation. Even when I tried to get you to leave, even after I'd left you at the gate, you still sacrificed your life for mine without a second thought. So, no, Tom. I'm not cross with you. You don't ever have to worry about that."

Tom looked like I'd taken a huge weight from his shoulders. "How much leave did Lord Walsingham give you from spy duties, then?"

"One more day," I said.

We'd never had such an extended holiday. "What should we do with it?" Tom asked.

"Actually, I've already made us plans. We're going back to the Tower of London."

"The Tower?" he said, surprised. "Why would we go—oh no."

"Oh yes," I said. "They have thirty-foot cannons, and King Charles said I could—"

"Oh *no*."

I laughed. "I'm joking. We're not going to the Tower. I mean, we *are* going to the Tower, and we *are* going to shoot those cannons. Just not tomorrow. We're going to the Missing Finger instead."

Tom looked at me suspiciously. "Why?"

"Well, I went by there today and talked to Dorothy—"

"Oh *no*."

"I actually think you should give her a chance," I said. "She's very sweet. But that's not what tomorrow's about. It's about Mr. Sinclair's confectionery. Apparently, his son died during the plague, so his home will go to his grandson instead. But according to Dorothy, the grandson doesn't want to be a confectioner. He's already a journeyman cabinetmaker, living in Oxford."

"All right," Tom said, confused.

"So the grandson wants to sell the confection-ery. And I thought, well . . . that's the home next to Blackthorn up for sale. And you, with your pension . . . I think the place would make a really nice bakery. So I set up a meeting with him tomorrow. He'll sell you the house, if you want it."

Tom's jaw dropped. "You mean . . . I could actually have . . . you mean . . . AAAAHHHH!"

He wrapped me in a giant bear hug and jumped around, ecstatic.

It rattled my brain. "Put me down!"

He let me go. "Sorry. Sorry." But he couldn't stop grin-ning. Now he gazed up at the stars, too, and I think he finally saw just how magnificent they really were.

"My own bakery," he said dreamily. "Have you seen inside? What's it like?"

"It's fantastic." I knelt to sketch a layout on the stone. Tom followed my finger eagerly as I traced out the rooms. "It's bigger than Blackthorn, by quite a bit, actually. You'll need to get new ovens, but I figure you could have your kitchen in the back, and there's a lot of storage over here, too. Then you could have your shop with a display in the front, like I do. And the upstairs has tons of rooms for a family—"

"Pardon me, sirs."

We looked up. Dobson stood at the entrance to the stairs.

"Forgive the interruption," he said. "His Majesty, plus Lords Ashcombe and Walsingham, require your presence."

"Right. Sorry," I said, and we stood, smoothing out our clothes. "We'll head to the Banqueting House right away."

"His Majesty is not at the party yet, sir. You should attend them in the parlor, please."

Tom groaned. "Oh *no*. What is it *now*?"

I laughed and slung my arm around him. "I don't know," I said. "But let's go find out together."

ACKNOWLEDGMENTS

It's been my privilege to have so many talented folks helping put these books together. I'd like to say thank you to the following:

To Kara Sargent and Suri Rosen, both of whom offered insights that made this story immeasurably better.

To Liesa Abrams, who shepherded this world from the start, and whose spirit remains in its heart.

To Dan Lazar, who took a shot on an aspiring writer and helped these adventures become all they could have been.

To Valerie Garfield, Jon Anderson, Anna Jarzab, Christina Solazzo, Julie Doebler, Karin Paprocki, Hilary

Zarycky, Michael Rosamilia, Christina Pecorale, Brian Luster, Daphne Tagg, Michelle Leo, Caitlyn Sweeny, Nicole Russo, Kathleen Smith, Lauren Forte, Leslie Tran, Jeannie Ng, Victor Iannone, Gary Urda, and Emily Hutton at Aladdin.

To Kevin Hanson, Felicia Quon, Arden Hagedorn, Shara Alexa, Cindy Ly, Cayley Pimentel, and Rita Silva at Simon & Schuster Canada.

To Cecilia de la Campa, Torie Doherty-Munro, and Alessandra Birch at Writers House.

To the monks at Glenstal Abbey for their linguistic assistance.

To the publishers around the world who have embraced the Blackthorn Key series.

And finally, most of all, to you, dear reader. It's been a joy to share this world with you. I hope you've loved spending your time with Christopher, Tom, and Sally as much as I have. And I hope they'll continue to live on in your heart, as they do in mine.